You Get What
You Play For

You Get What You Play For

A Novel

JEFF FARLEY

ATRIA PAPERBACK

New York London Toronto Sydney New Delhi

ATRIA PAPERBACK

A Division of Simon & Schuster, Inc.
1230 Avenue of the Americas
New York, NY 10020

First Atria Paperback edition August 2012

ATRIA PAPERBACK and colophon are trademarks of
Simon & Schuster, Inc.

For information about special discounts for bulk purchases,
please contact Simon & Schuster Special Sales at 1-866-506-1949
or business@simonandschuster.com.

The Simon & Schuster Speakers Bureau can bring authors
to your live event. For more information or to book an event,
contact the Simon & Schuster Speakers Bureau at 1-866-248-3049
or visit our website at www.simonspeakers.com.

Designed by Akasha Archer

Manufactured in the United States of America

10 9 8 7 6 5 4 3 2 1

Library of Congress Cataloging-in-Publication Data
Farley, Jeff.
     You get what you play for / Jeff Farley.—1st ed.
        p. cm.
1. Teenage pregnancy—Fiction. 2. African American teenage girls—Fiction.
3. Single mothers—Fiction. 4. Mothers and daughters—Fiction. 5. Inter-
personal relations—Fiction. 6. Brooklyn (New York, N.Y.)—Fiction. I. Title.
     PS3606.A6995Y68 2012
     813'.6—dc23

                                                           2012018258

ISBN 978-1-4516-7428-6
ISBN 978-1-4516-7429-3 (ebook)

"The path we choose, and the path that's been paved for us aren't always the same."

—Jeff Farley

You Get What You Play For

Chapter 1

I couldn't believe that I had to take a day off to come to family court, and I wasn't even sure why the hell I was here. I had gotten served out of the blue with papers from my daughter's father to appear; our daughter, Mariah Butler, was fifteen, so I knew it wasn't a custody issue. What the fuck could he want now . . . blood. I had always hoped that by the time I was thirty-two my life would be in order: not perfect, but certainly not a damn soap opera full of drama. What's that song from the eighties, "Momma Used to Say?" Well, that's some profound shit, I should have recorded the answer record and called it, "My Dumbass Should Have *Listened* to What Momma Used to Say." Obviously I wasn't the only one going through some kind of bullshit. Family court was packed, and who do I see when I look up? Niece, a.k.a. Denise Carter, another one of my baby daddy's baby mommas.

Niece was about my age, early thirties, and while we didn't look alike, we had the same *type* of look. Jamal liked his women light-skinned, shapely, pretty, but not too sweet-looking, and you *had* to have nice feet. If your dogs were barking, keep on walking. He also liked his women a little hood; now I'm not saying I'm hood, but I'm a Brooklyn chick, so yeah, it's in me. Niece and I had reached a point where we were cool with each other. That wasn't always the case, but once we matured and realized Jamal was the salt in our wounds, and he was getting off on that "play one chick against another" shit, we were like, "Girl, fuck that trick-ass clown, just run me my child support." Jamal had an eleven-year-old daughter with Niece named Essence Butler.

"Hey, girl!" she shouted across the room.

I guess it's nice to see a familiar face in places like that, you know: court, prison, death row. It gives you an opportunity to say, "Oh my God, what are you doing here?" No sooner did she get over to where I was standing did she say, "Oh my God, what are you doing here?"

At first, I was going to make up something. I didn't want her to know that it had anything to do with Jamal.

"I don't know why Jamal is taking *me* to court," she said, before I could even utter a word.

"You too. . . . That's why I'm here." I responded in utter confusion.

Niece and I stood there and started catching up on things when this strange look came across her face. I knew that look, but I usually saw it in high school when someone was about to get fucked up. I looked around because I figured Jamal had come strolling in with one of his many bitches, looking like a fake-ass Jay-Z. Instead, I saw Yvonne Davis, another baby momma twice removed. Yvonne was a few years older than Niece and I. She was really attractive with a nice figure, she may have even been mixed. Niece and I rocked them good weaves, but she had that pretty shit that grew right out her scalp. Her face told the story of a hard life. If Niece and I were a little hood, Yvonne was too hood to be true. She came over pushing a stroller with her six-month-old daughter, Brea Butler. Along the way she cursed out three people in the span of thirty feet.

"Damn, they need a fucking traffic cop up in here, stupid-ass people standing in the middle of the floor. Then they look at you crazy if you run over their foot. Get the fuck out the way then . . . excuse my language, you bitches know I don't talk like this," she ranted.

Yvonne and I were cool, not as cool as Niece and I, but it was civil. Those two on the other hand, well, it was like locking Foxy Brown and Lil Kim in a room with one Chanel bag and telling them, "Winner take all." Since they had both been involved with Jackass more recently, I guess the fire was still burning and Jamal was fanning it every chance he could.

"So, what's going on, Charisse?" she asked.

"Not a damn thing. Trying to figure out why I had to take a personal day from work," I responded.

I guess she called herself trying to break the ice. "Hello, Niece. You *can* speak you know," she said as she rolled her light-brown eyes.

Niece just looked at her out the corner of one eye and sucked her teeth.

"Picture that," she responded.

I figured the best way to ease the tension was to take it

to the kids. The last thing I wanted was for two beautiful black women to put on a show in public like the fucking Basketball Wives or the Real Housewives of Atlanta. I always thought the word *wife* meant you were married to somebody. Oh shit, you learn something new everyday.

"Look at Brea. She is getting so big, and she's a little dime piece," I intervened.

Niece obviously wasn't as impressed, or just couldn't admit to it.

"She all right, she looks just like Essence when she was a baby," she responded with attitude.

"I wonder what the fuck Jamal is up to?" asked Yvonne. "We might fuck around and end up in jail knowing his ass . . . that's why I bought the baby. I'll make the judge feel sorry for a bitch."

I was afraid we would all find out soon enough. By the time we got into the courtroom, curiosity and anxiety had been replaced by the feeling a cow gets when he's on his way to the slaughterhouse; he's like, *I don't know where the fuck I'm going, but I bet my leather ass it's not good.*

We sat down and I looked around the courtroom. To me it had that same psychological feeling as hospitals; they were grim, cold places. A few seconds later in the door walks this tall, scruffy-looking dude who needs a haircut, a shave, and an iron for his clothes. Upon closer observation we were all like, "Oh shit, that's Jamal." Jamal Butler, who in his own mind thought the only difference between him and Denzel Washington or LL Cool J was that that they had powerful Hollywood agents, was if nothing else Mr. Stay Fly. This man would not leave the house unless all the tools of his trade were immaculate, and since his trade was fronting and bullshitting, his tools were his wardrobe, jewelry, and a nice car, so to see him walk into court looking like Grady from *Sanford & Son* caught us all off guard. Jamal walked over and kissed his daughter and smirked at the three of us before going to his seat. His attorney was this middle-age Italian man wearing a black Armani suit, slicked back hair, and those fucking shoes I hate with the tassels on the front that went out of style in the eighties.

When the judge walked in I smiled. It was a black woman in her midfifties with salt and pepper hair named Judge April Peterson. She looked like that aunt everybody has in their family. I saw Jamal and his lawyer laughing at her. Her breasts had to be a 44 triple G. "You see that bitch's titties?" Yvonne asked while chuckling.

"How can you miss them," I replied. "And you might not refer to the judge as *that bitch* in her courtroom," I added.

The judge opened the file on her desk and scanned the contents for a moment.

"Okay, I assume you're Mr. Butler," she said, looking at Jamal.

"Yes, Your Honor," he replied humbly.

"And you're here because you want to lower your child support payments due to financial hardship?" she asked.

I looked over at him in disbelief as he stood up with a sad expression on his face.

"Yes, Your Honor," he replied.

Yvonne started flipping right off the bat, and I knew we were going to be in trouble.

"Lower his muthafucking payments!" she yelled. "Judge,

you going to let him get away with that bullshit! I should get my uncle and them to whup your punk ass!" she added.

Then she made matters even worse by talking directly to Jamal and his lawyer.

"She's a black woman, stupid ass, she's on our side! You don't think she's ran across a few trifling niggas in her day."

I put my head down in embarrassment and I heard the judge's gavel slam down on the bench.

"Excuse me! Is that the way you speak at home?" the judge asked sternly. "You will *not* use that type of language in *my* courtroom, is that understood, young lady?" she yelled.

I think Yvonne figured out this woman was not to be fucked with.

"Yes, Miss Judge Lady," she responded.

"And the fact that I'm a black woman will have no bearing on my decision, I'm impartial," she pointed out.

At that point I guess Jamal and his attorney decided it was time for the theatrics. I've seen some great performances in my day, but this bullshit was Academy Award quality. Jamal put his head down on the table as if he wasn't feeling well.

"Mr. Butler, are you feeling all right?" Judge Peterson asked.

Jamal had a boyish charm about him that he used when it suited him. If you had any maternal instincts, you could easily get suckered in.

"I'm all right Your Honor, just a little light-headed," he responded.

His lawyer stood up then, right on cue.

"Your honor, my client *loves* his children, he worships the ground these beautiful, precious girls walk on. He would give his own life without the slightest hesitance for any of them. But as I explained in my court papers, the man is struggling just to survive. He can barely eat, much less pay the mortgage on his modest house or his condominium," he said.

I thought to myself, *What fucking house?* I knew he had a condominium. Yvonne tapped me on my shoulder and asked me.

"What condo? Jamal is such a fucking lying-ass dirty dog," she uttered angrily as the lawyer continued his speech.

"And it is for this reason your honor, and *only* this reason, that we respectfully request that Mr. Butler's child support payments be lowered considerably."

I knew the judge was looking over at us as three nice-looking, gold-digging hos who had kids by this cat who was supposed to take care of us. I always found that women who have achieved a lot academically or in their careers, and who are not as physically attractive, tend to look at women like us judgmentally. I've actually heard family members say behind my back, "Yeah, all that fine shit was good when she was young, but now she's just another single mother with stories about how many dudes used to sweat her." Even still, there was no way the judge would go for this.

"This is some real bullshit," Yvonne uttered loud enough for everyone to hear.

Niece looked at her like she was getting ready to snatch that black silky shit right off her think piece. Jamal's attorney took Yvonne's ghetto shit and ran with it.

"You see, Your Honor, every time my client tries to rationalize with them he fears for his life. In fact, it embarrasses me to admit that I was slightly afraid myself when I first entered this courtroom," he said while glancing fearfully at us.

"All I want is for my client to be able to survive, to be able to have a sandwich if he's hungry, maybe with an occasional luxury such as cheese," he added.

I started looking for Ashton Kutcher to come out and tell us we were being punk'd, or maybe Russell Simmons would walk into the courtroom and say, "God bless and good night": this was pure comedy.

"According to the information I have, Mr. Butler here is a successful businessman and entrepreneur," Judge Peterson said to the slick-talking lawyer.

"Now I know it may have appeared that my client's hair care businesses were thriving, and at one time they were, but my Nubian brothers and sisters just aren't getting haircuts like they used to. Dreadlocks, braids, and those lace front wigs that beautiful woman like yourself are wearing has really taken a bite out of his business," he added.

By the time Jamal stood up and showed the judge the hole in the bottom of his shoes and told her how she reminded him of his mother, she'd actually cut each of our monthly payments by 50 percent. The outcome had Niece and Yvonne on some real temporary peace treaty shit.

"Charisse, you take the kids on home. Me and Niece are going to follow this muthafucka," she said.

"Don't worry, they won't find the body," Niece added.

At first I was like, *Fuck it. Karma's a bitch—he'll get his.*

But when I glanced over at him and his smug ass winked at me, my tune changed quickly. *Yeah, get that son of a bitch, and make it hurt.*

We went outside and cursed Jamal out among ourselves for about ten minutes. When I finally reached the parking lot I see Jamal just as he's about to leave. He didn't see me watching him, and Mariah wasn't going to see him unless he was on the screen of her phone. I watched him go to his black Range Rover, open the back door, and change his jacket, shirt, and shoes. He put on his jewelry and drove off. I was glad Mariah didn't see that, for whatever reason, she still had a high opinion of her father, and she was already miserable enough without me bursting one of the few bubbles she had. I had to admit, though, that Jamal had game, and he didn't even have to sleep with you to fuck you.

Chapter 2

1992

I didn't think there was any other place like Brooklyn in the world. Coney Island with that run-down, noisy ass Cyclone that made you feel like that shit was about to derail, to the run down noisy ass number 3 train that was the true meaning of shake, rattle, and roll. Doorknocker earrings, dirty backpackers, Chubb Rock, Special Ed, and Dana Dane . . . fuck that, Spike Lee was from Brooklyn and he had his office right on DeKalb avenue.

I also knew that Harlem had the reputation for having the fly dudes, and having big-time hustlers and drug dealers. One time me my friends and I went up to the Rucker on 155th and Eighth Avenue, and was like *"Daaamn!"* I had never seen so many Benzes, BMWs, Jaguars, etc., in all my life. This one Dominican cat had some shit that said 850i on the back; it was a BMW, and that muthafucka was green like new money. They even had NBA players out there. This was the big time, and I was soaking it all in. But when niggas stepped to us, I knew we were out of our league.

"Don't write a check your ass can't cash," I told Brenda as she flirted with one dude in a thick gold link chain who looked like Ice-T.

The experience was worth the trip, just to get out and see how people in a different borough got down. I got offers to be driven home from about five different cats who were either balling, or doing a great job of faking moves. I just remembered what my aunt had told me since the time I started wearing tight jeans: "Oil prices are high as shit, so if a man burns his gas, you can rest assured he wants some ass."

When we got back to Brooklyn and got off the train, this fake-ass drug dealer from the neighborhood named Artie, who liked Brenda, rolled up on us in his dull gray Acura Legend and shouted, "Brenda! Why your ass still frontin'? You know I'm going to get that ass sooner or later, know what I'm saying?"

Usually Brenda would have flipped on him and probably threw a brick or a bottle at his car, but hey, we had just come back from Harlem and the Rucker, so we were above that type of shit now.

"Come here for a minute, Artie," she asked nicely.

At first he hesitated; he was probably thinking, *If I go over there this crazy bitch might give me a concussion.* But when he pulled over Brenda calmly walked over to the car and leaned in the window.

"You know when I'll give you some ass, Artie? I'll give you some ass when you get a BMW 850i, and get rid of this played-out piece of shit, that's when," she stated before walking away casually. His feelings were hurt. Artie never said anything to her again except for, "Hey, Brenda, how you doing?"

I always wondered why guys said lame shit they knew would be a turnoff. I remember when I turned fourteen, and had a little freedom to go out beyond the neighborhood. Guys used to ask, "Where you from, shorty?" or my favorite stupid-ass question, "Light skin, where you rest at?" I would always say, "I'm from Jamaica Estates." The rumor was that the prettiest girls were supposedly from Queens. They came from nice suburban families and went to private schools. I remembered seeing this movie with Eddie Murphy back in the day called *Coming to America,* and the girl was pretty and lived in a fat house in Jamaica Estates. Fuck it, sounded like a good lie to me. Bronx chicks had a reputation for being hard and quick to cut a bitch. The Brooklyn rule of thumb was, if you get into a fight with a chick from the BX just stop, drop, and roll, because they like to play with fire up there. They burned down the whole South Bronx one time, just for fun. I didn't really consider Staten Island a borough until Wu Tang and Method Man came on the scene.

Nitra, Brenda, and I were inseparable. The three of us had been friends since the fourth grade. Brenda was a big chick, tall, thick, with a short haircut but real shapely with hips for days. Brenda also had the most beautiful dark skin, a smooth chocolate color. She was naturally smart as hell; she never really applied herself, but still managed a B average. Brenda was what people referred to as a fighter, and like most people who fight on the regular she was good at it. If somebody barked at me a little too much and I felt threatened, I would turn Brenda loose and all the bullshit would cease with the quickness.

Nitra, she was the talker. She had a smart answer and scowl on her face no matter what the situation was. If somebody was too nice to her, she went on the defensive. If somebody wasn't nice enough to her, she went on the defensive. And if somebody ignored her, she would just curse their ass out. Nitra was medium height, thin, with a caramel brown complexion. She wasn't what guys considered pretty. One time in sixth grade this boy in our class named Ricardo told her she looked like ALF and she never got over that shit. Every time she gets a perm and her hair straightened, the first thing she says is, "Yeah, I bet a bitch don't look like Alf now."

Nitra was the only one of us who wasn't still a virgin. Guys used to play on her self-esteem, or lack of it, and as I got older I would go to her house and see how she had men coming in and out. I had a feeling that she had been through some foul shit, and she kept it inside, which is why she was always so fucking mean.

One time we were all spending the night at Brenda's house. Usually we stayed at my house for sleepovers, but whenever we wanted to stay up all night, play music, and basically go unsupervised, we stayed at Brenda's. You just had to make sure you locked her bedroom door so that her pervert-ass stepfather, Walter, didn't come busting in ten times, hoping to catch a peek at me or Nitra getting dressed. So here we are, sitting there on the bed watching *Hangin' with Mr. Cooper* or *Family Matters* and talking shit about everybody in school when the phone rang. Two seconds later Brenda's mother, Gail, bangs on the door like she's locked in a meat freezer and can't get out.

"Brenda, pick up the goddamn phone! And don't be on my shit long—the fucking bill is already ridiculous!" she screamed.

"All right! Damn, I don't want whoever it is knowing my mother is so dumb she don't even know you don't pay for incoming calls!" Brenda yelled back.

If I had talked to my mother like that I would have made sure to write my farewell note first. When Brenda got on the phone we knew it was a guy 'cause her whole expression changed.

"No, I'm not busy. Me and my girls were just trying to figure out where we're going tonight," she said.

I looked at Nitra and said, "I thought we were going to bed, same as every other Friday night."

Brenda then told whoever it was, "My address is 785 Shepherd Avenue. . . . No it's East New York. Brownsville isn't too far away though. Okay, call me when you get on Eastern Parkway." Brenda hung up the phone and jumped up and down excitedly.

"He's coming to get us!" she said.

"Who?" asked Nitra.

"Barry, the cat I met up in Harlem at the Rucker," she said.

"Not that nigger with the four teeth and five grandchildren" asked Nitra.

"He ain't that old, and did you see that gold watch he was wearing?" she replied.

"Bitch, you'll get a gold watch when you retire too."
Nitra snapped back.

It took Barry about an hour to get to Brooklyn, and by
that time we had all gotten ready from our secret stash of
clothes and shoes we kept at Brenda's house. This was the
first time we were actually going to put it to use, though.
Even though Gail wasn't much of a mother in terms of
discipline, we still waited outside. Besides, he was closer
to her age than ours, *much* closer, and she wasn't above
cheating on Walter with a man who had a few dollars. All
of a sudden we hear all this fucking noise coming down the
street and this nasty-looking, big-boat, shit-brown colored
Lexus pulls up blasting "Mr. Loverman" by Shabba Ranks.
Nitra rolled her eyes.

"Oh shit, he aint only old, he's an old Jamaican," she
sneered.

Nitra didn't even let him get out the car before that
mouth started.

"Where's the Benz?" she asked.

"What Benz?" he replied.

"That crispy black shit you was sitting in when we met
you, I know you're old, but you aint senile," she replied.

"Oh, that was my mans car," he said with a mouth full of
metal. It was like I could I hear Slick Rick singing *"Seems
like you have a mouth full of gold teeth"* from "Mona Lisa."

When he got out, he was so short he couldn't even
see over the car's roof. And then we watched his little
leprechaun ass hop around to the sidewalk and he had
the audacity to have one leg shorter the other. Nitra and I
wanted to bust out laughing, so we ran in the house.

"Oh shit! Lucky Charms is a muthafuckin' gimp," she said.

I knew he was disappointed too, we must have looked much older in that Harlem sunlight. "How old are you?" he asked.

"Forty-eight," said Nitra. "Sixteen times three, you do the math, sixteen times three equals forty eight equals five to ten," she added sarcastically.

He was really probably thirty-four or thirty-five, and had a lot more in common with Shabba than the fact that they both loved his music.

When Barry took us out to eat at the diner on Linden Boulevard, I could tell he was embarrassed, like people were looking at this little cat and these three young girls. Then this dude walks over who knows him.

"Barry, what the deal, baby? I thought that looked like your whip outside. How's the family? Which one of these is your daughter? You got a daughter, right?"

If Barry had a gun in his pocket, instead of in his car—where he most likely had it stored—he would have blown this dude's head clean off.

"My daughter's good, she's home, these are, ah . . ." he stuttered.

"We're his nieces," said Brenda. "He came to take us out for my birthday."

When the dude walked away we laughed like hell, Barry was mad cool, 'cause he didn't get upset that we gigged on him all evening.

"You taking us to the movies?" I asked.

"We can use your senior citizens discount, or you want

to go to Rye Playland? I'll lift you up on the merry-go-round," Nitra added.

When she got up to go the bathroom Barry was like, "Your friend got jokes, but check this out. Is it just me, or does she look a little like that furry ting from the TV."

As we were leaving I made eye contact with this guy in the parking lot, he was all right looking, tall, dark brown, short Afro, but he was fly as hell. He had on a black leather jacket, some slacks, and some casual suede shoes. He just looked really nice, not like a thug at all, but still cool. At first glance I gave him twenty-one, which was still too old for me. He got into this white Toyota 4Runner and drove off. Barry took us back to Brenda's house. Gail didn't even know we had left; she had gotten high by the time we got back, and was in a good mood.

"Where you bitches went?" she asked as we walked through door. "If you're out there turning tricks, leave my muthafuckin' cut on the table . . . Nitra, what you go for? In case you find a alien that want to buy some pussy . . . I'm just kidding, baby."

When we were younger, Brenda used to be embarrassed by Gail, but now she didn't care one way or the other.

The next night we stayed at Brenda's again. My mother wasn't thrilled about me staying overnight, much less two nights in a row, but when she needed to make overtime by working the midnight shift, I think she preferred that I wasn't alone in the house. My mother loved Brenda and knew she would protect me.

"It's Saturday night. Brenda, can't you call the old folk's

home and get one of your other men to come take us out?"
Nita asked.

"Let's go to the movies, I want to see *The Bodyguard*," I
said.

"*The Bodyguard?* Bitch please, you always want to see
that sappy love shit, *Ghost* and all that. A bunch of white
people crying over nothing, and the happy-go-lucky nigga
around trying to make them smile . . . fuck that, let's go see
Malcolm X," said Nitra.

Brenda just looked at her and said, "It aint even out yet.
That shit don't come out until like November. And when
the fuck did *you* turn into Angela Davis? Bitch, you made us
sit through *Home Alone.*"

When we finally decided on a movie, we combined all
our money and came up with $3.19, so we took that to the
video store and rented this movie called *Die Hard*. On the
way back Nitra found a blunt in the street; none of us had
ever smoked weed before. "Let's take this back to the house
and smoke it," Brenda said half jokingly.

"All right, fuck it, and let's get a pink Champale. If we're
going to get fucked up, lets get fucked up," I said boldly.
Suddenly the idea was kind of exciting to me. "What if Gail
smells it?" I asked.

"Then we'll have to pass the dutchie to the left hand
side four times, instead of three," Brenda answered.

We went up in her room and locked the door. Gail
and Walter weren't even home, and neither were her little
brother and sister.

"Oh shit, it's on tonight," I said.

"I always wanted to get high and listen to music," said Nitra. "My music teacher told us Miles Davis used to get high as a kite and listen to music," she added.

"That muthafucka used to get high and *write* music. You ever notice Miles Davis and that nigga Eddie King from *The Five Heartbeats* look like twins," I told her.

"Well, Charisse "Know-it-all" Hawkins, I can't write music, so bitch, listening to it'll have to do."

We put on Dr. Dre's album *The Chronic* 'cause that shit seemed like an appropriate selection under the circumstances. My first pull of the blunt was damn near my last. The stuff was so strong that it went all up in my nose and I started choking. My eyes filled with tears and I couldn't breath, but after that shit hit my system, I got the Chinese eyes and it was all good. We smoked the whole blunt until it burned Nitra's fingers.

"I feel like I'm going to pee myself," Brenda said as she lay out on the floor.

"Well, get your big ass up and go to the bathroom," I responded.

"I can't," she responded before a brief pause. "The muthafuckin' floor is spinning."

Nitra was quiet, which was unusual. I looked over at her and she was staring at a poster of Tevin Campbell on the wall.

"I wonder if he's gay. They say Luther is gay, they say Michael is gay, I heard Freddie Jackson likes men," she pondered. Then Nitra started screaming at the top of her lungs "They crawling on me, get them off, get the bugs off me!"

I didn't see any bugs. Brenda and I started panicking.

"What if she OD's?" Brenda said.

"Can you OD from weed?" I asked.

"I don't know. Damn, we need my mother, the marijuana expert," she responded.

Nitra finally stopped screaming and just kind of slumped backward.

"I'm so tired, and I'm hot, and I'm hungry," she said.

"You need to stay your ass away from anything to do with weed, grass, herb . . . all that. If you see somebody mowing their lawn you should haul ass the other way," Brenda said.

We were relieved, though, and whatever high we had was scared right out of us.

The next morning I woke up with a headache. I thought hangovers came when you drank. Add that shit to my list of things I had to learn the hard way. I got myself together and left before Nitra and Brenda woke up. I was waiting for the number 20 bus on Linden Boulevard for a few minutes when this white 4Runner rolls up.

"Hey, remember me?" the guy behind the wheel asked.

I took a step back away from the curb and put a scowl on my face.

"No, am I supposed to?" I asked.

He laughed and and refreshed my memory.

"Linden Diner? The other night I saw you in the parking lot."

"Oh yeah, I remember."

"So where you going this time of morning?" he asked.

I acted like I didn't hear him.

"I said, where you going this time of morning?" he repeated.

"Home to make breakfast for my husband and six kids," I responded sarcastically.

"So what's your name, or should I ask your husband?" he asked as I ignored him. "Well, can I give you a ride?" he had the nerve to ask.

"I don't know you." I was getting very annoyed by this point, and happy to see the bus was coming, so I didn't have to curse him out. I got on the bus and looked out the window. He was just pulling off, almost like he was in shock and thinking, *I can't believe this young bitch played me.*

When I got home, Vivian McNeil was in the kitchen making some coffee. "Hey, Mom!" I said, as cheerfully as I could.

She smiled at me with this strange look on her face, almost like she knew I had been doing something she didn't approve of. She looked into my eyes, or maybe I was just paranoid from the guilt.

"So how was work?" I asked, trying to take her mind off me.

"Work was work. They gave Emma that shift I put in for, but I'm not envious. You know what they say, the *grass* always looks greener on the other side." She then poured her coffee and went upstairs. I just stood there like, *How the fuck did she know?*

Chapter 3

All in all, life was good. I had just started my senior year at Brooklyn Technical High School, and my grades had me in a position to consider the top medical schools like Columbia, NYU, Cornell, and the University of Pennsylvania. Ever since I could remember, I wanted to be a doctor, and my mother worked her ass off, sometimes day and night, to make sure that would be possible one day. I used to have nightmares about my mother dying; I think it was because I was so afraid that if something ever happened to her, I wouldn't be able to make it. She was one of those people who other people drew strength and guidance from. My mother and I didn't look anything alike; she was dark, and thick but very shapely. Everybody used to see her and think she was that lady from *Waiting to Exhale,* Loretta Devine. That's exactly who she looks like. My father was this light-skinned man with curly hair named Mario Hawkins. My mother told me that back in the seventies men like him were at a premium.

"Your father was a pretty-ass negro. He had that good

hair, and back then black women wasn't as big on fine cars, and all that jewelry and shit. But if you had you a light-skinned, curly-haired man, looking like Leon Isaac or Max Julien, all the kinky-headed chicks was jealous."

"Leon who?" I asked.

"Well for your generation it would like Al B. Sure, or that damn boy from that movie *Jumping Jack City*," she said.

"You mean Christopher Williams? And the movie was *New Jack City*," I pointed out.

I hadn't seen Mario Hawkins since I was three and he lived right here in Brooklyn. My mother told me I had eighteen or nineteen brothers and sisters out here. If a light-skinned, curly-haired cat tried to talk to me, I always used to wonder if he could be my brother, so I was never into that type. As a matter of fact I didn't really care about looks—I always liked the cat that wasn't the popular choice. My mother wasn't very receptive toward men now, even though she was hardly old. I could tell that even with all the bullshit, negligence, and lack of support, my mother still had a soft spot for my father. Whenever his name came up, or someone asked about my father she was quick to tell them with pride, "Yeah, her father went to medical school for two years."

I remember thinking, *Well, the muthafucka ain't no doctor. Last you told me he's a building super.* I guess if nothing else I got my book smarts from him, but that didn't make me give a fuck about him any more or any less. As far as I was concerned he was a nice-looking man my mother had had sex with. Thanks for the nut, homeboy; I couldn't have made it here without your help.

The school year started as expected. I was digging my senior status. Nitra and Brenda were struggling to graduate on time, not because they couldn't do the work, they just *wouldn't* do the work. Most of my teachers, and one in particular, felt like my choice of friends was inappropriate for someone with my potential. Mr. Gaines was my favorite teacher; he was a young white guy who was cool as shit. He knew more about hip hop than any of his students, and he had a black girlfriend who worked for *Vogue* magazine, who used to come up to the school and tell us what the latest fashion trends were. "Charisse, your friends are what Italian mobster's call cement shoes. All they can do is drag you down," he used to tell me.

I tried to explain that we had all been friends for years and he would say, "Just cause your old couch looked nice in your apartment in the projects doesn't mean you take it with you to Park Avenue."

Mr. Gaines had a fucking analogy for everything. He also hated that I cursed so much, but if I got my brains from my piece-of-shit father, then I got my mouth from my mother. About the second week of school I started noticing something strange about Brenda, not physically, but in her appearance. Her clothes were wrinkled when she came to school and her hair was undone.

"What's going on with you?" I asked as we were walking down the hallway.

"What's going on with you?" she responded in a sarcastic tone.

"I was just asking cause you been looking downright raggedy lately," I snapped back.

"Mind your fucking business sometimes. Goddamn, if a bitch don't feel like combing her hair she don't have to," she snapped, before rolling her eyes and storming off down the hallway. This boy named Peter had the misfortune of crossing her path and bumping into her. I closed my eyes 'cause I didn't want to see what was coming. "Bam!" When I opened my eyes I saw him laid out, spread-eagled with papers scattered all over the hallway. His glasses were broke and he had a big-ass knot on his head. He got up crying like a bitch. "What am I supposed to tell my mother?" he asked, sobbing.

"Just tell her, right place, wrong time, Mom, shit happens," Nitra said laughingly.

I didn't think it was funny, and I was more concerned about what was bothering Brenda. We didn't speak for about three days; she wasn't even talking to Nitra.

"What the fuck did I do? I'm not the nosy, judgmental one," said Nitra.

I just shot her a dirty look. "Not that you are either, Charisse," she added.

That day when I got home my neighbor, Mrs. Blackmon, was outside. Mrs. Blackmon was what old people referred to as "something else." She was in her mid to late sixties and was from Panama. Her ass was huge; even the young guys couldn't resist looking at it on the low when she was outside working in her yard.

"Mrs. Blackmon, stop bending over like that. They all looking at your ass," I would tell her.

"I know. I can feel the heat from them staring, I still got it, huh?" she would answer with a big smile.

She had three kids, two sons named Ray and Jonah. Ray was locked up for dealing drugs, and Jonah had gotten shot and killed in Flatbush in the late eighties. She also had a daughter named Jewel who had had seven kids by the time she was twenty-six. Jewel had that same hourglass figure as her mother when she was my age.

"She gets off on having a big ass," my aunt Belle would say about Jewel. "Now, if she kept all them men off of it she would stop populating the world with them future purse snatchers and little hos."

I think Mrs. Blackmon was counting on me *almost* as much as my own mother to make it.

"I'm going to fix you a big pot of peas and rice this weekend," she told me when I stopped at her gate. "Soon your ass is going to be as big as mine."

I just laughed and thought to myself, *Aint that many peas and rice in all of Brooklyn.* When I got in the house my mother was making dinner. She was standing in the kitchen in her underwear, with her wig on crooked, and singing, "I'm every woman," while she fried chicken.

"Damn, I hope I don't look like that when I'm your age," I joked.

"Shit, you better hope you look *half* this good," she replied. "Charisse, what's going on with Brenda?" she asked. "I saw her stepfather on the train and he said she moved out," she added.

It all started making sense to me: The wrinkled clothes, the hair, the attitude. Brenda, my best friend since I don't know when, was homeless. I went upstairs and cried for the rest of the day. I couldn't even imagine what she was feeling or going through. The next day I was trying to figure out how to approach her, *without* blowing up her spot, and I wanted to tell her my mother said she could stay with us. But how could I do that when I wasn't even supposed to know? Brenda had a lot of pride, and feeling like a charity case wasn't on her list of favorite things to do. I had finally got myself mentally prepared to approach her; we were best friends and what kind of friend would I be if I knew she was sleeping in the park, or God knows where, and I didn't do shit about it. I was walking down the hall looking for her when somebody taps me on the shoulder from behind. I turned around and there was Brenda. She had on a fly new outfit and some black shoe boots. Her hair and nails were done, and she had a smile that lit up the hallway.

"Charisse, bitch, wait until I tell you what's going on!"

"I already heard," I responded.

"Who told you?" she asked.

"My mother."

"Well, how did she know. Damn, I just moved in yesterday."

"Moved? Moved in where?" I asked in a very "what the fuck are you talking about?" voice.

"I moved in with Dave. I live in the Bronx now."

Time-the-fuck-out. Brenda was sixteen, and while she looked older, she didn't need to be living up in the Bronx, especially not with some muthafucka I never heard of.

"Who the fuck is Dave?" I asked.

"Dave. Dave the train conductor we met last month."

I had to think for a minute.

"The short, light-skinned one."

"Brenda, that cat is like thirty."

"Thirty-three," she said matter-of-factly.

I didn't say a word, but my facial expression said it all.

"You know what, Charisse Hawkins . . . fuck you! Don't stand there with that judgmental look on your face," she snapped.

"I'm not judging you," I responded.

"Yes, you are, you always act like your shit is perfect. 'I wouldn't do this, I wouldn't talk to that guy, this guy's socks don't match, he's too old, he's too young, I'm going to fucking Harvard, or Princeton,' or wherever it is your Ivy League ass is going."

I never knew Brenda felt like that. Other girls I knew used to tell me her and Nitra were jealous of me, but I never gave it much thought. Just as Brenda stormed off, Nitra casually strolled up and looked me up and down with this silly, playful grin.

"Sooooo, what happened, hmm?" she asked.

"Brenda moved in with this cat that's thirty-three in the Bronx and I . . ."

"Uh, let me finish the sentence." She said in her usual condescending way. "And you gave her your 'tsk-tsk-tsk, shame on you, bad Brenda' look, and she cursed you out as opposed to slapping the shit out of you like she wanted to. I'll bet that's it."

Nitra casually strolled away. I was like, *What just happened, these bitches are crazy. I am not the one who's wrong here.* I have always hard a time admitting I was wrong, basically 'cause I hardly ever was. How come I could see what was so obvious while other people just didn't get it?

Nitra later told me that Gail had actually put Brenda out over a fucking piece of chicken, a center breast to be exact. Brenda ate the big piece of chicken that Walter had wanted for himself, and when he got up in her face she gave him a two-piece. From what I was told there were three hits in the fight: Brenda hit Walter, he hit the floor, and then Brenda hit the bricks.

Brenda ended up transferring to DeWitt Clinton High School up in the Bronx. The school year was just starting, and I had lost my best friend. Nitra was also acting different; it turns out she had a new man in her life as well. Nitra had started dealing with this pint-size thug named Nice. He hung out near our school, selling weed and talking shit every time we walked by. God forgive me, but he looked like a piece of crusty shit. "Ugly" isn't an adequate description. This nigga was pose material for Halloween masks. Ugly. Just the thought of him and Nitra reproducing made me want to send them a box of condoms marked "Anonymous." One afternoon after school when Nice didn't have her on lockdown we walked over to the Albee Square Mall.

"So, have you heard from Brenda?" she asked.

"Nope, and I don't have a number for her. I guess she's all right," I replied.

"I spoke to Brenda a few days ago. She asked about you," she said.

I tried to play it off like whatever, but the truth is I was glad to know she was okay. "So, what's up with her?" I asked.

"She said everything is cool now. I guess at first Homeboy thought he was her father, and was on some 'do as I say shit,' but she said she told him, 'Dave, I will separate you from *all* your fronts if you don't sit the fuck down somewhere,' and he chilled out."

I laughed until I cried cause I could picture her ass saying those exact words. When we got in the mall I went and bought the shoe boots I wanted from Nine West. It was still early, so we just wandered around, wish shopping. We went in this jewelry store on the first floor, looking at all the shit we would buy *if* we had the money when I saw this pair of bamboo earrings. Ordinarily I don't try jewelry on in the store, but I had to put these joints on. I was admiring how good I looked in the earrings when I noticed someone standing behind me in the mirror.

"Those look good on you."

I turned around and standing behind me was the guy with the white 4Runner.

"The earrings fit you, boo."

I took the earrings off and rolled my eyes at him.

"Why is your friend's attitude so fucked-up?" he asked Nitra.

"Because obviously, she ain't feeling you," she responded.

I don't know why I just didn't like this dude, he wasn't bad looking, and obviously dressed nice, and even though he was a few years older than me, he wasn't that old. There was just something about him: That fucking fake-ass innocent smile maybe, the fact that he just kept popping up out of the blue. Something told me to just keep it moving. "Come on, Nitra," I said. We walked right past him and left the mall.

"I hate muthafuckas like that, just 'cause you don't want

to talk to him, you got a fucked-up attitude. I could tell he was a bitch-ass nigga."

I didn't even bother to tell her that this was my third time seeing him.

"What makes you think he's a bitch-ass nigga?" I asked.

"I got five brothers, *two* of them are bitch-ass niggas. So I know one when I see one." Suddenly, I felt like somebody was following us, so I turned around, and this cat is coming up behind us with this stupid-ass smile on his face. Nitra started flipping.

"Goddamn homeboy, no means no!" she shouted. "Charisse, you want me to go find Nice and them?"

"All that ain't even necessary, shorty" he said. "I just wanted to apologize to your friend here. I just think she's mad beautiful. I wasn't trying to violate. My name is Jamal," he added.

"It's cool," I said.

He dropped something into my Nine West bag.

"I wrote my number on the back of that card. *If* you decide to call me one day, maybe we can talk," he said.

Then he just walked away and didn't look back.

"I'm not calling that muthafucka," I told Nitra.

"Make sure you don't. Fucking loser."

When we walked over to the train station, Nice and his crew were standing around smoking weed. I saw fear on Nitra's face. As soon as he spotted us he came bopping over. I knew he was about to show off for his crew.

"You don't fucking listen. Didn't I tell you don't be hanging out on Fulton! You so fucking stupid and hard-headed. What was you doing up there? You and your homegirl looking for dudes?" he asked.

"No, we just went to the mall to pick up her shoes," she said.

"Well, next time ask a nigga first, all right . . . all right?"

Nitra just nodded her head yes. I had never seen her so quiet. All I kept thinking was, *She had the nerve to call that other dude a loser.* My aunt Belle has a saying that goes, "Everybody can smell shit, unless it comes out of their own ass, then it don't stink." Nitra and I hopped on the train and went home. She didn't say a word the whole ride.

When I got off the train, I ran into this guy named Jason Tucker, who was getting off the same train, but had been riding in a different car. Jason and I lived on the same block, and had been in the same kindergarten classroom. He used to be a goofy little fat boy, but now he was about six-four, handsome, and one of the top high school basketball players in the city.

"What's up, Jason? Long time no see," I said with a big smile.

"Charisse!" he said as he smiled back. "I was having a rough day, but it just got better!"

"Here we go with the flattery. Yeah, gas my head up," I said.

"Now, Charisse, you know I've been in love with you since Miss Fuchs's class. Remember our mothers wouldn't let us buy candy in the morning, so I would take my little quarter and give it to my cousin so he could buy *you* those penny bubble gums you liked."

"Big Bol's!" I said, remembering fondly. "Oh damn, you remember that."

"I remember everything about you," he said. "I thought you was coming to see me play one day?" he then asked.

"I am, I am. I promise," I responded.

"Don't make promises you don't plan on keeping. I'm a senior, so it has to be this year."

"I know, I'm a senior too, duh. Did you decide on a college yet?" I asked.

"It's between St. John's and Duke," he replied.

"What about you?" he asked.

"I'm leaning toward Cornell. It's far enough away to be considered far, but close enough to be considered close."

We continued to chat until we got my house.

"Well, Charisse, let me know about that game. Don't front on me," he said.

"I won't, Jason, I won't," I replied.

I really wasn't fronting; my intention was to go to a game.

When I got in the house I went straight up to my room so I could try on my new shoe boots with a dozen different outfits. As I pulled the box out of the bag, another small bag fell out onto the bed. I picked it and looked inside. It held one of those little jewelry boxes that looks like gold lamé. When I opened the box I found two pairs of bamboo earrings. One was the pair I had tried on at the store in the Albee Square Mall, and the other was equally as nice, just a different style.

At first I thought.

Oh shit, Nitra is a fucking thief. But then it dawned on me that the earrings were in a box with that cotton-looking shit, and inside a bag. I looked in the Nine West bag again, and all the way on the bottom was a business card from the jewelry store. On the back of the card it read, YOUR EARS WERE MADE FOR THESE, JAMAL BUTLER 718-555-1217.

Chapter 4

*M*y mother had three sisters who all lived in either Brooklyn or Queens, and were all very close. Aunt Belle, who was my favorite, Aunt Della, and Aunt Ruby. I loved them all, but Aunt Belle was funny as hell. I couldn't wait for her to come over and tell us the stories about her and her husband Abadu. He was young enough to be her son, and had only come from Africa a few years ago. My aunt, like my mother, wasn't too strong in the couth department.

"So I told that goddamn jungle bunny to either get a *real* job, or get your real ass another place to live," she told us. "That shit is embarrassing. Here I am coming from work and this greasy muthafucka is standing out there on Fulton Street selling tapes, just grinning. I was so fucking mad, I just went over there and knocked the whole table over, and then he looks at me and asks, 'But why, momma? Why?' I said, 'Speak English muthafucka. You're in America now.'"

Abadu was used to her abuse. He was tall and not a bad looking man, so my mother and I knew that when he was grinning at her, he was really thinking, *You old bitch, just*

keep buying my nice clothes so I can keep saving money until I get
enough to leave your dusty ass.

I still laugh about the time she told us she hid all his
shoes so he wouldn't go out and party, and when she went
to bed he put on his clothes and sneaked out barefoot.

"I should have known that wouldn't stop him," she said.
"The muthafucka didn't know what shoes were up until
recently."

None of the sisters had much luck with men. Aunt
Della's husband had left her and their two kids about ten
years ago. He didn't even have the decency to lie about
leaving, you know, just gave the old "I'm going out for a loaf
of bread" line. He finished his dinner one night, took a shit,
and when he came out of the bathroom, he calmly looked
at her and the kids and said, "I can't stand you or these
fucking stupid kids. I'm leaving and for Christ's sake, please
don't look for me."

My aunt Ruby and her husband, Mr. Woodrow, didn't
have any children. They had been married for fifteen years
until she came home one night and found him giving a lap
dance to the UPS deliveryman, wearing one of her wigs
and a pair of her pink silk panties. "Why, you fat faggot!" she
yelled.

He spun around and told her, "If *your* ass wasn't so fat,
maybe I wouldn't be a faggot. Now, do you mind? I have
company."

When my mother went to bail Aunt Ruby out later that
night for throwing hot water on them, she said my aunt was
sitting in a cell reading the Bible.

"I found Jesus!" she screamed when my mother walked in. "They're trying to institutionalize me." She got off because they said the sight of him in her drawers caused temporary insanity. Mr. Woodrow ended up getting married again, to a woman. That really drove her over the edge, and now she walks around with a Bible 24/7. She's one of those people that if you fuck around and sit next to her on the train or bus, you'll be like, "I *knew* I should have sat in that other seat."

While I loved my mother, and all my aunts, I vowed I would *never* be like them. I understood about the lack of education; that's not something that was a priority for them growing up. It was about getting a job to help out as soon as you were old enough to work. I was talking about the bad decisions, the bad choices in men, the not being able to envision anything better in your life than what you had. Your life's dream shouldn't be "I hope I hit the number today!" That's another thing that set my mother apart from her sisters: She was determined that I was going to get an education and have a career, and not just a job.

"I'm not struggling, so you have to do the same shit one day," she would say. She wanted the cycle to end with her.

A few weeks later I was sitting in my room, bored as hell. I couldn't call Brenda anymore, and Nitra was fucking sprung, both obsessed and scared of Nice all at once. She barely came to school anymore, and if she did it was, "Hi and bye." Nice must have told her I was cut off, so she cut me off.

I wanted to ask her though, "Why would you take a

chance on not graduating when you were barely skating by as it is?" But I didn't need to get cursed out and told to mind my business again.

I was digging through my dresser looking for something and I came across the small gold box with the earrings. I hadn't worn them, but I hadn't called Jamal to give them back yet either. It was like in the cartoon when you see an angel sitting on one shoulder. *Return the gift because it's the right thing to do.* And then there's a devil on the other shoulder, *Bitch, if you don't put them earrings in your ear I will stick this pitchfork right in your ass.*

Something kept pushing me to call him, and at the very least say, "Thank you," if I was going to listen to the devil. I dialed the number he gave me and nobody answered, so I tried it again. This time a man answered, but he was all out of breath and sounded annoyed. "Hello."

"Hello, may I speak to Jamal?" I asked softly.

"Who this?" the man asked.

"It's Charrisse."

"Who?"

"Charisse, from Albee Square Mall. I'm looking for Jamal."

Then he said something that should have set off the alarm right then and there.

"Oh shit! What's up, my nigga, you know you played me right," he said.

There was a slight tinge of laughter in his voice so I just figured he was joking around.

"I wanted to call and say thank you for buying me the earrings," I said.

"Word. Come on now, you know I got you. But check this out, call me tomorrow, all right." After we hung up, I remember thinking, *He must be at the gym working out or something.* The next day I forgot to call him back.

Aunt Belle came over with the latest stories on Abadu. It always killed me how whenever she would tell us what he said, she had to do it with an African dialect, or her version of one anyway. It was like having *Def Comedy Jam* in your living room.

"So this idiot calls me at work yelling and screaming, 'Honey, honey, I have found a great job, they say I will be make millions!'"

"'If you're selling dope, pack your shit, put out all that incense so you don't burn my house down, and hop the first elephant back to Zimbabwe, 'cause I'm calling the cops,'" she told him.

"'No, momma, no! This is good. Wait, I must come to your job and show you. I am so happy, you will be happy,'" he screamed enthusiastically.

"About an hour later I'm sitting at my desk and I hear somebody spraying some shit, then I hear Abadu's voice," she said. "So I get up and walk over, and here he is, dressed in a red suit, explaining to my coworker how this Amway air freshener works.

"'It not only smells good, but it attacks every molecule of bacteria in the air,'" he explained.

"I was so goddamn mad that I couldn't even talk right," she said as we laughed hysterically.

"'Abadu, take your black ass home before you get fucked up,'" I whispered in my yelling voice.

"'But why, momma? This is my new job. I am going to make so much money for us!'" he responded.

"'And where the fuck did you get this clown suit?'" she asked.

"'I bought it for only two hundred dollar, they said you must dress for success.'

"'And where did you get the money to dress for success?'" she asked.

He took two steps back and answered, "'I took it from the rent, but listen, Momma . . .'" Before he could get another word out she had snatched the tape dispenser off her coworker's desk and knocked him clean out.

After Aunt Belle left I asked my mother what was wrong; she hadn't been herself the whole evening.

"Nothing, just a little tired is all, I need to hit the lotto so I can quit working," she said.

"Well, when I start my practice, you'll be living on easy street, and I'm going to get you a car," I told her.

"I don't need all that, trust me. When I see you graduate, every drop of sweat will have been *more* than worth it."

The following day, I ran into Jason again when I was coming home from school. He was just leaving for one of his games as I was going in the house.

"Okay, so what's your excuse today?" he asked.

"My excuse for what?"

"For not going to my game. Come on, you can go with me right now," he said.

"I can't go, I'm not dressed, I've got homework, I . . ."

"Your full of it," he said with a big smile. "You look

incredible, and as for your homework, we'll be back by seven thirty," he said.

"All right, I did promise."

"Yes, you did," he responded with a big smile.

"Let me go inside and tell my mother," I said.

I went inside and Mom was cooking. I told her I was going to watch Jason play.

"Have fun, and be careful," she said.

She didn't ask where, what time, nothing. That was because Jason was the kind of guy my mother had hoped I would date, *when* I started dating. She knew his family, and he was just a nice young man, and while I was never big on that light-skinned, curly-haired type, Jason was a real looker. Besides, I knew his father, so I knew he wasn't my brother, but while every chick in the neighborhood was hoping to be his girl, I just saw him as my friend Jason, who always had something to say that made me feel good.

The game turned out to be a lot of fun. Jason scored, like, forty points and people were treating him like a celebrity. All throughout the game, every time he scored or made a good pass, he would look over and wink at me. I heard one of the guys on his team ask him, "Yo, Jason, is that your girl?"

He said, "No, we been friends forever." The guy then asked if it was okay for him to try and talk to me. "Hell no! I said she's not my girl, but I didn't say she's not *going* to be." After the game, Jason and I stopped at McDonald's before getting on the subway to go home. I was one of those people who would never eat or drink on the train, but we ate, talked, and laughed all the way back to Brooklyn.

"So when is our second date?" he asked.

"We might want to try a first date, first," I responded.

"We just had our first date."

"Going to your game was fun, but that's not what I call a date."

"I'm not talking about the game, I'm talking about the picnic on the train. The only thing missing was some grass and a few ants, but we did see a few rats on the tracks."

Once we got in front of my door I got a little scared because I thought it would be awkward. I wasn't sure if he was going to try and kiss me, and I wasn't sure if I wanted him to or not. One thing was for certain though, I had a great time, and I was going to go out with him on a real date.

"So, when is our date?" I asked.

Jason was smiling so hard he could hardly get the words out.

"What about Saturday? We could catch a movie, or go to Red Lobster," he said.

"I can only pick one?" I asked jokingly.

"On my budget, only one of us might be able to see the movie or eat as it is. I'll just wait outside the theatre until you finish watching the movie."

"What happened to all the money I heard colleges pay guys like you, the free cars, all the naked white girls?" I said sarcastically.

"That's not my style, I'll get my own car and a white wife when I graduate from law school." He then looked at my earrings. "You're the one with all the money. Those earrings must have set you back a grip," he said.

"They were a gift," I responded.

"Somebody must really love you," he said.

Later that night I was thinking about Jason when I realized that I had never called Jamal back. When I dialed his number this time he answered right away.

"Hello."

"Is this Jamal?" I asked.

He was ready for me this time.

"Charisse, what's up, beautiful? You know how long I been waiting for you to call?"

"Please, I'm sure you've hardly been waiting for my call," I told him.

"What? I've called the phone company to check the lines. I took a hearing test just to make sure I could hear when the phone rang. Shit, I even called New Edition to get Mr. Telephone Man's number."

I just busted out laughing.

"Damn, I wish I was there to see that smile," he added.

"Jamal, do you know how old I am?" I asked.

"I don't know, no older than thirty-five, thirty-six." He said it with a dead serious voice and again I burst out laughing. "For real, I guess about sixteen or seventeen."

To be honest I was impressed that he was honest about knowing my age. I hated when older guys would tell me, "My bad momma, I thought you was like nineteen or twenty."

My ninth grade teacher, Mrs. Trotman, had already explained the psychology behind an older guy's reason for doing that.

"When an older guy approaches a well-developed younger girl, he's counting on the fact that she looks at herself as too mature for the boys in her age group. So by him flattering her with his false assumption that she's older, consciously or unconsciously it makes her feel like she's ready for things she may not be ready for," she explained. "Plus, your average fifteen-year-old boy doesn't have a car," she added.

"I'm sixteen, Jamal. Don't you think I'm a little young for you?" I asked.

"That depends, boo. If I was asking you to go out and vote, or run to the liquor store for me, yeah. But since I just wanted to talk to you, and get to know you, no."

"How old are you?" I asked.

"I'm twenty-three, but I don't see why that should make any difference," he said.

"Of course you don't. You're the one that's twenty-three."

Jamal got real quiet for a second. I could tell he was getting frustrated, especially after he'd spent two hundred dollars on some earrings.

"So you want your earrings back?" I asked.

"Nah! Fuck that, I gave them to you because I wanted you to have them," he answered sharply.

"So you go around buying earrings for strange girls all the time?" I asked.

"Hell no! That's the first time I *ever* did some shit like that! You know what, Charisse? You think I'm some kind of trick-ass nigga? All I was trying to do was show a beautiful young woman how special I thought she was. Why don't you call me when you grow up."

All I heard was a dial tone. My first instinct was to call

him back and say, "Fuck you. Take these earrings and shove them up your ass."

Getting hung up on was one of my pet peeves; I hated that shit with a passion. Part of that was my ego; the other part was that it meant I didn't get the last word in. I called Jason instead, and we talked on the phone for three hours before my mother burst in my room and started yelling.

"Charisse Hawkins, I *know* your goddamn ass ain't still on my phone!"

"Mom, it's Jason," I answered, thinking that would make it okay.

"Jason? I don't give a damn if it's Jason, Freddie Krueger, or Michael Myers. Get off the goddamn phone now!"

"Stop taking the Lord's name in vain," I said jokingly.

"I'll take your ass in vain if you don't hang that phone up," she said in all seriousness.

All I could hear was Jason cracking up on the other end. When I got back on the line he was laughing so hard he could hardly speak.

"I didn't know your mom had a mouth like Richard Pryor," he said.

"That's nothing. All you heard were a few 'goddamns' and 'asses.' If I stay on this phone the 'muthafuckas' and the 'bullshits' will start flowing," I said.

"All right, so hang up and I'll call you right back on my phone," he replied. I hung up the phone and within three seconds it rang back. I barely got the receiver up to my ear when my mother burst in again.

"And tell Jason his folks aint related to goddamn AT and T either," she said.

Jason and I just laughed and decided we would talk again the next evening after he got home from basketball practice.

The next day on the way to school all I could think about was Jason and it totally bugged me out. Chubby little bubble-gum-having Jason was getting ready to be my man. As much as I was thinking about and feeling Jason, I still couldn't get over the fact that Jamal had hung up on me. Something about that was kind of a turn on. I mean, I really fucking hated getting hung up on, but I somehow respected him for hanging up on me. When I got to the school there was a crowd of people standing outside, there were two police cars, and I saw a few teachers standing around looking. My first thought was that someone had gotten shot and robbed. As I got closer I could see someone lying on the ground and what looked like blood. A girl named Latisha came running toward me, crying.

"That's Nitra! Nice beat her up real bad."

The tears started running down my face and I ran over. Nitra was lying there unconscious, with her mouth and nose bleeding. The police had Nice in handcuffs. He had this sneer on his face like he was some kind of tough guy. I was so fucking mad, I just lost it.

"You little punk bitch! I got somebody for your ass, nigga! I'm going to get Knowledge and Giovanni from Red Hook! You little fucking faggot. Let him go, let his ass go. He know them *real* thug niggas will get his little bitch ass."

Nice was scared as hell. He knew the dudes I was talking about, and he knew they would kill his punk ass if I put the word out. They all treated me like their little sister, once they realized I wasn't giving them no ass. One of the police officers came up to me and told me to calm down.

"I know you're upset, young lady, but don't threaten anybody. We'll deal with him," he said.

"Yeah, all right, I said what I had to say," I responded defiantly.

I really felt like snatching the officer's gun and shooting Nice, not in the head or anything to kill him, but right in his little punk ass. I guess some of the teachers in my school were just as worried about the outburst as they were about Nitra's health, because when I got home that day, someone from the school had called my mother and told her what happened.

"Anything you want to tell me?" she asked as soon as I walked in the kitchen.

"Nitra's boyfriend beat her up outside the school. They had to take her to the hospital," I replied.

"And you threatened to have him killed? Who the fuck are you supposed to be, John Gotti?" she asked.

"I was just upset. I saw my friend bleeding on the ground because of this little bastard."

"Charisse, since when did you start associating with gangs and hoodlums?"

"I don't, but I know people," I said with a smart attitude.

"Oh, you know people, your bad ass knows bad-ass people, huh?" she snapped back. "I know that's your friend, and it hurt you to see her lying there, but you're not her protector, and you're not some street girl. I'm not telling you to stop being her friend, but I *am* telling you to mind your goddamn business."

Later that night Nitra called me from the hospital. She said that other than a swollen lip and a mild concussion, she was fine. They were keeping her overnight for observation, and she planned to be back in school on Monday.

"I heard about what you said to Nice," she said.

"Nitra, why you fuck with that little piece of shit? You could be dead right now."

"Charisse, I fucking love him. He made a mistake. He said he was sorry," she said.

"And you believe him?" I asked.

"I'm not pressing charges—the cops can kiss my ass. And I don't need you to get nobody to go after Nice either . . . understand? He loves me so much. It was my fault this morning. He fucking told me not to do something and I didn't listen."

"He's not your father!" I said angrily.

"My father! I don't even know who the fuck my father is. And you're not my mother! I don't have to explain myself or my man to you," she said before hanging up the phone. This getting hung up on shit was getting to be a bad habit with people. I was like, *Fuck it, let him keep Mike Tyson–ing her dumbass*. Now was the time I really missed Brenda and being able to talk to her. I tried to call Jason, but his ass was dribbling a ball somewhere. My mother was pissed off, so I couldn't go in her room and talk. So I called Jamal.

"Hello, who's this?" he asked.

"It's Charisse."

"Who?" he asked again, fronting like he didn't know who it was.

"Charisse," I repeated.

"Oh, what's up? You sure you got the right number?"

"Yeah I got the right number. I just wanted you to know I didn't appreciate you hanging up on me. That's rude," I said.

"Knock it off. You liked that shit, that's why you're calling back," he said with an arrogant, cocky tone. "So, Charisse, on the real, you got a man? Wait, let me rephrase that. Do you have a boyfriend?"

"You got jokes, huh. I'm talking to somebody right now," I answered.

"He goes to your school, or is he still in preschool? That's about the age you like them, right?" he said sarcastically.

"You too obviously," I said, returning the sarcasm.

"So who is this cat you talking to?"

"Why? I'm sure you got a stable of bitches. You got a nice car, you dress fly, please, you don't need to talk to me." I said.

"How do you know what I have?" he asked. "And how do you know what I need?"

I didn't have an answer for that question. I just knew he didn't need Charisse Hawkins, and he *damn* sure couldn't have her.

Chapter 5

*T*he next month or so was supposed to be that "brand-new" relationship period with Jason that I had always been told would happen when you started dating someone. The stage where you stay on the phone 21/7, and that's because the other three hours you spend smiling in each other's damn face. Jason never *officially* asked me out, but I didn't think people did that anymore. He just started referring to me as his girl, and when guys asked me if I had a man now, I told them, "Yes." The only problem was, I didn't have a man, a boyfriend, a buddy, or even a pen pal 99.9 percent of the time. I could only imagine what women who dated, or were married to, NBA players went through. I was just dating a high school star and between the games, practices, recruiters, interviews, and campus visits, I barely spoke to Jason, much less saw him. When Jason did manage to fit me into his schedule, his beeper would go off every five minutes.

Jamal, on the other hand, was Mr. Persistence. I could count on getting two *I'm just checking to see how you're doing* phone calls a week, and at least one *No disrespect to your man, but I saw these flowers and thought of you* appearances at my school. At first I was like, *Whatever.* I wish Jason would show me a little of this attention, but after a while I started looking forward to Jamal's calls and after school visits. Jamal played the friend role to a tee. He was so attentive and seemed interested in what I was thinking, what I was feeling, and no matter how much I vented about my frustration with Jason, he *never* tried to put him down. We actually got into an argument about it one night on the phone.

"Damn, Charisse, that dude is just trying to do big things. You need to be more supportive of your man," he said.

"I am fucking supportive! The world doesn't revolve around his basketball career. If you want to be with somebody you find time for that person," I replied with an attitude.

"I hear you. I don't want to argue, and I'm on your side," Jamal responded.

I didn't even realize he was setting me up, pretending to defend Jason, but really he was just using that to hit a fucking nerve and use my own insecurities against me. He was taking everything I told him as a *friend* and giving that shit right back to me in a pretty box, just like the earrings. He transformed himself into everything I told him Jason wasn't.

I started getting addicted to the attention from Jamal. That shit was like a drug to feed my ego. I was the center of someone's universe, and I wouldn't have to share the spotlight with a team, a basket, or a bitch named Spalding.

That Friday night Jason and I had made plans to go to

the movies to see *What's Love Got to Do with It,* and he had promised me no matter what came up, nothing would interfere. I knew when I answered the phone at four-thirty that day and Jason was on the other end that he was about to break another promise.

"Charisse, you'll never guess what came up, baby," he said excitedly.

I didn't even ask what, I just kept quiet to avoid cursing him the fuck out.

"One of the reps from the Adidas basketball camp got me tickets to the St John's game tonight at the Garden," he added.

"Jason, I *really* wanted to go to the movies, but if we have to go to this game . . . all right," I said in an attempt to be supportive.

He got really quiet, I knew he wanted to say something, but he knew I wasn't trying to hear what he had to say.

"*We* are going to the game, right?" I asked.

"Charisse, tomorrow night it's me, you, the movies, and BBQ's . . . I promise," he replied.

For some reason the anger that was ready to explode a moment ago went away. I didn't even stress it.

"That cool, Jason. Enjoy the game," I said before hanging up the phone.

About five minutes the phone rang again, but I didn't answer it.

"Charisse! Telephone!" My mother yelled from downstairs. "Any other time you answer it before the damn thing rings."

I figured it was Jason calling back to tell me he was taking me to the game. He knew I was upset with him.

"Yes, Jason?" I said as I picked up the receiver.

"Survey says . . . wrong answer," Jamal said jokingly. "I figured I would catch you before you went out, tell you to be safe and have a good time," he added.

"You can't be much safer than in your own muthafucking house," I responded sarcastically.

"I thought you were going to the movies," he said.

"So did I, but St John's is playing somebody at Madison Square Garden, and your man can't miss it."

"So why aren't you going?" he asked.

"That's a good goddamn question, but Jason can kiss my ass," I replied.

Jason and I weren't having sex yet. I knew he wanted to and we had discussed it, but I wanted to wait. He said he was cool with it, but I started wondering if he didn't make time for me because *we* weren't fucking, or because *he* was fucking somebody else.

"So let's go to the movies," Jamal came out and said.

"No, I don't think that's cool," I replied, before thinking about it for a second. "You know what, fuck it. What time are you picking me up?" I asked.

I wanted to get back at Jason and this seemed like the best way to do it. I also didn't want to sit in the house on a Friday night. I knew if I told my mother I wasn't going out with Jason I would have been on lock down, especially if she found out it was a twenty-three-year-old, so I didn't say shit . . . don't ask, don't tell.

Jamal took me to the Metropolitan movie theatre on

Fulton Street to see *What's Love Got to Do with It,* and then he took me to Junior's for a piece of cheesecake before driving me home.

"I had a really good time, Charisse," he said as we drove down Flatbush Avenue.

"Me too. Thanks for taking me," I replied.

Jamal started laughing to himself.

"What's so funny?" I asked.

"I was just curious as to how you're going to tell Jason you went out with me," he said.

"How do you know I'm going to tell him?"

"Wasn't that the whole point of going? I mean, don't get me wrong, I'm glad I got to spend some time with you, but give a nigga a little credit. This was about getting back at Jason."

I felt really bad because he was right, and the fact that he was so cool about it made it even worse. When we got back into my neighborhood I looked out the car window when we stopped at a red light right near the bus stop. There were a group of girls about my age or a little older waiting for the bus. I saw how they all stopped talking and tried to see who was in the car as Jamal turned up the music just loud enough to grab their attention. I liked the feeling of these chicks sweating me, and Jamal knew it. He looked at me and smiled as he did his "gangster lean" in his seat.

I couldn't really describe Jamal in one sentence. I mean if you asked me to describe Jason I would tell you, "He's a good dude who's into sports and school," or if you asked me about my friend Giovanni I would say, "That nigga is a thug to the core. His future will definitely include changing his government name to a number." Jamal seemed to be a little bit of everything; it was like he didn't know whether he was a street cat, a scholar, a playboy, or a hustler. When we were in the theater he was acting regular, but I noticed when we left that whenever he saw a guy who looked hard, or like a hood, his whole shit would change up, his walk, his talk, and even the look on his face. I thought that shit was funny, like I was walking down Fulton Street with Dark Kent and he kept turning into Super Thug.

When we got to my block I told him to drop me off on the corner. The last thing I needed was my mother or Ms. Blackmon seeing me get out of his car. I just wished Jason could see me. Jamal kissed me on the cheek and said good night. He watched me make it home before pulling away from the corner. When I got inside my mother was sitting in the living room watching *The Tonight Show*.

"This Jay Leno guy is pretty damn funny . . . they never should have cancelled Arsenio Hall, though. He was the black people's Johnny Carson," she said.

"Yeah, who's on the show tonight?" I asked, trying to make small talk.

"Julia Roberts, I think, and Patti LaBelle. That's who I'm waiting for," she replied. "So how was the movie?" she asked.

"Good . . . I'm tired though. I'll see you in the morning," I said as I started walking upstairs.

"Jason called. . . . He said he was sorry he didn't take you to the movies, but it was important for him to go to this game. He said he's decided to go to St. John's to play ball, so he could be closer to you."

I thought she was about to start yelling and screaming, but she didn't raise her voice or move from her spot.

"I was sixteen once, Charisse," she said calmly. "I remember thinking I was grown. Back then the big thing was smoking cigarettes. You were afraid to smoke in front of your parents. And even though you knew smoking was bad for you, and you heard all the stories about lung cancer and emphysema, you did it anyway, and you felt like it was *your* choice. I've always tried to teach you to make good choices, Charisse. That's all a mother can do," she went on to say.

The next day was Saturday. It was a really beautiful day outside, the fall chill was in the air, the sun was shining bright. This was my favorite time of year. I called it "Fly sweater and leather weather." I spent the majority of it doing homework and laundry. Jason had called me about one o'clock and apologized about the night before; he also told me about his plans to attend St. John's.

"I had a chance to talk to Coach Mahoney, and he really wants me there," he said. "And obviously St. John's is one of the best academic institutions in the country."

"My mother told me," I responded. "But isn't your dream to play in the NBA? The other schools are better for basketball, right?"

"The NBA is a long shot. I mean, I'd love to make it, but I can major in political science at St. John's, then go to law school after my career if I'm lucky enough to get drafted. And just so you know, Mark Jackson, Chris Mullin, Jayson Williams, and Malik Sealy all came out of St John's," he stated.

Part of me wanted to go out with Jason that night. But I

was also hoping that Jamal would call, now that I knew my mother trusted my judgment and I wasn't restricted. And since *technically* Jason never asked me out, *technically* I wasn't his girlfriend. Jamal was just my friend. Later on that day I was sitting in my room watching television and waiting for him to call, not Jason, but Jamal. I started to wonder, *Did he really have a good time last night? Maybe he's not feeling me. I wonder what it is about me he doesn't like?* All these things were running through my mind. Jason called me three more times to see what was up for the night, but I kept telling him I wasn't sure if my cousins were coming over. I was really trying to see if I was going to get a better offer, or at least the offer I was hoping for.

About six o'clock I took matters into my own hands and called Jamal, he answered on the second ring. I could tell someone was in the car with him, a female someone.

"Are you busy?" I asked with a slight attitude.

"Nah, I'm just heading out to the city with a friend," he replied.

"A friend like who?" I asked.

"A friend friend," he responded. "You better save that third-degree shit for Jason," he added.

I was so fucking mad I didn't know what to do. I felt like he was cheating on me and he wasn't even my man. All I knew was he was giving *my* attention to some other bitch and I wanted him sweating me, and *only* me.

Later on Jason and I walked over to Kentucky Fried Chicken to get something to eat. Every word that came out of his mouth was about basketball, the St. John's Redmen,

Alumni Hall, how Lou Carnesecca used to be the coach. I wanted to tell him, "Shut the fuck up! Please!"

"You sure went to bed early last night," he said as we stood in line at KFC.

"What's that supposed to mean?" I asked.

"Nothing, I'm just saying you went to bed early, that's all."

"Don't accuse me of anything," I said sharply. "If you want to ask me something, come out and ask me."

"Charisse, what the hell are you talking about?" he asked with a confused look on his face.

"Maybe if you didn't take your ass to the game last night, I wouldn't have had to go out with somebody else," I blurted out.

Jason took a second to process what I said before responding.

"You went out with somebody else?" he asked, almost in disbelief.

"Yeah, you didn't have no time for me." I said. "*And* he's twenty-three with his own whip."

"So that's how you get down?" he asked. "I'm at the Garden checking out a game to see if I want to play for St. John's so I can be closer to you, and you're out with the next man," he added.

"I didn't ask you to go to St. John's. All I asked you to do was take me to the movies," I responded.

"So is that where you went? You know what, I don't even want to know. What difference does it make? He has a car, right? Now I know why you wanted to come here, it's only right that a chicken head would love chicken."

"Fuck you! Go talk to some of those dumbass cheerleaders who think you're a big fucking deal," I said before walking away and leaving him standing there in line.

I should have been honest with Jason and just told him that I wasn't sure how I felt at that point. He deserved that much, especially after I found out he was only considering St. John's because of me in the first place. Instead I chose to alienate a person I really did like and ruin a friendship because I felt like I wasn't getting the attention I needed. Jamal had got me hooked on that shit, and the only way he would continue to give me that attention was if I made myself available to him, and I couldn't do that if I had a *boyfriend*.

When I got back to the house I called Jamal's car phone again but it was off. He had the kind of phone that was actually hooked up to his car and sat in between the driver and the passenger. I remember being impressed when I saw it. I didn't know too many people who had a mobile phone. Finally Jamal answered his phone about nine-thirty that night.

"Damn, you and your friend must be having a good time," I said with a major attitude.

"Shouldn't you be out with Michael muthafucking Jordan?" he replied.

"We broke up, or should I say I broke it off."

Jamal got really quiet for moment, like he was thinking.

"What happened?" he asked curiously.

"Look, you call me when you're not with your *friend*."

"I dropped her off a while ago. She really is just a friend. I took her to the city to pick up something," he replied.

"I know you got girls. Don't play yourself," I said.

"I got friends, some of them are female, but I don't have a girl," he responded. "Let me call you when I get to the crib, this phone is mad fucking expensive," he added.

Jamal called me back about an hour later. I wasn't stressed for time, or looking over my shoulder because my mother was working a double overnight shift. We stayed on the phone for almost three hours, until damn two a.m. talking about everything, music, clothes, school . . . and sex. I didn't tell him I was a virgin but I think he knew. I found out that he was an only child and went to Queens College, and lived with his parents in Jamaica Estates. The more we talked, the more I liked him. The night we went to the movies he didn't really say much, but I felt like I was really getting to know him now.

After two weeks of seeing him everyday after school I felt like I was falling in love. He would pick me up, take me to get something to eat, or to buy something if I wanted it and drop me off before heading to night classes. The goodbye kisses were getting longer and longer, and while I was little afraid, I started wanting to take it a little further.

Jason and I hadn't spoken since the day I left him at Kentucky Fried Chicken. I wanted to call him to apologize, but I also felt like he should apologize for calling me a chicken head. I told my mother we had broken up; she didn't really say anything one way or the other.

"At your age you shouldn't be dating one person exclusively," she said. "Same goes for Jason. If it's meant to be it will be. Right now school should be your damn boyfriend or girlfriend."

I didn't want to hear that bullshit. What I wanted to do was tell my mother about Jamal, but I already knew the speech she was going to give me about *staying in my lane* and *all a twenty-three-year-old could want from a sixteen-year-old is sex 'cause you don't have shit else to offer at your age.* It's like she hadn't been in love in so long that she forgot what it felt like, and I think my father destroyed her faith in love and men in general.

Jamal picked me up after school on Friday and for the first time took me to his house in Queens. He lived in a really big house on Hoverdon Road that looked like a small mansion. It was ironic because I always used to tell people I was from Jamaica Estates, even though I had never even been there.

"You didn't tell me you came from a rich family," I said as I looked at the shiny black BMW 740 in the driveway.

"We're not rich. My pops is a superintendent for the transit authority and my mother is the head nurse at Elmhurst hospital. They do all right, but if they were rich I'd be driving a Porsche and not a 4Runner," he said modestly.

The inside of his house was fly as hell. The basement was furnished. They had a pool table, a bar, and a real Pac-Man game. The house had five bedrooms and three and a half bathrooms. I was open, and it looked like the house I envisioned myself living in one day. Jamal took me up to his room, which was the first time I had been alone with a guy in his bedroom.

"Sit down, make yourself comfortable," he said as he handed me a newspaper. "So your ex changed his mind, huh?" he asked.

"What are you talking about?"

"Oh my bad, you didn't know? Read the article," he said.

I sat down on the edge of the large wood queen-size bed and looked at the paper. The headline read, JASON TUCKER HAS A CHANGE OF HEART and went on to say that Jason had decided not to go to St. John's, and had committed to UCLA in Los Angeles.

"Jay going out there with them Cali chicks, mulatto dimes, Asian dimes, Sunset Boulevard . . . and he's going to get the star treatment . . . wow," Jamal said, as though rubbing it in.

Jamal came and sat down next to me after he turned on the stereo, he didn't waste any time getting started. He put his arm around me and started kissing me.

"Fuck Jason," he said in my ear. "He didn't know what to do with a *woman* like you."

I still had my jacket on and was clutching my purse against my chest. Jamal was trying his best to get my jacket off, but I didn't want his parents to come in and think I was some little ho disrespecting their house.

"Stop," I said without really wanting him to. "What if your parents come home?"

"They went away for the weekend," he replied.

Jamal suddenly stopped and moved a few inches away on the bed and put his hand over his face.

"This is crazy, Charisse. I haven't even known you all long, but, but . . . I love you. I'm *always* going to be here for you and I'll never do anything to hurt you," he said, while his eyes welled up with tears.

I gave my most prized possession away to Jamal Butler on Friday, November 12, 1993. It was painful pleasure, but this wasn't how I envisioned losing my virginity. It was supposed to be on my wedding night, or at very least in the college dorm room of my future husband. I put my underwear back on and curled up in his bed that now smelled like sex and Cool Water cologne.

"Jamal . . ."

"What's up, princess?" he asked as he rolled over and put his arms around me.

"I love you, too."

Chapter 6

The next two weeks were crazy. I was never the type to cut school, but I stayed out three days over that time to go to Jamal's house and have sex all day. He had me in there watching porno movies and drinking wine, while he made all these promises about how he was going to take care of me, buy me a house, a car, jewelry, and I believed it and kept giving my body to him willingly. At the age of sixteen I had done something that most black women have a hard time doing in their whole lifetime. I found the love of my life, the man who would never cheat on me, lie to me, or hurt me, and basically give me any and everything I wanted. That day when I got home, my mother was already there. I didn't expect to see her.

"Mom." I said as I walked through the door with my hair slightly out of sorts. "What are you doing home early?" I asked.

"I wasn't feeling good, so I came home to lie down," she responded as she looked at me up and down.

"Can I get you something?" I asked as I stood there

holding my jacket closed. I hadn't put my bra back on, and when you're a C cup, it's not like she wouldn't be able to tell.

"No . . . so, how was school today?" she asked suspiciously.

"You know, just another day," I answered.

My mother stood up and walked over to me. She snatched my jacket open, looked at my breasts, then closed it and looked in my bag and pulled out the black lace see-through Victoria's Secret's bra that Jamal had bought for me.

"I hope your stupid ass had enough sense to get some birth control pills from somewhere, or at least to tell whatever man you're fucking to wear a condom," she said in disgust.

I didn't know what to say, I knew she was hurt, and it also dawned on me that I wasn't on any form of birth control, and Jamal wasn't wearing shit except his socks when we had sex.

"Mom, I'm sorry. I wanted to tell you, but I didn't think you'd understand," I said.

"Understand what?" She said with anger in her voice. "I told you I was sixteen once, *and* I'm your mother. I had you—you think I couldn't see that there was something going on with my own daughter? Your whole attitude has changed, Charisse. I told your aunt on the phone the other day, I think your niece is *fucking;* I just hope she knows what the *fuck* she's doing."

"I'm not *fucking* anybody!" I said defiantly, while stepping back to avoid the slap I anticipated coming. "I make *love* to him."

"Love? You make love!" She laughed. "Is that what he

tells your dumb ass when you're taking your clothes off?" she asked while shaking her head.

"You don't even know what love is, child. It's more than screwing, or somebody who barely even knows you buying a few gifts and telling you he loves you," she added.

"You don't even know him." I said defensively.

"Charisse, I don't have to know *him* to know him. I've been there, done that."

"Just because my piece-of-shit father walked all over you don't mean it's going to happen to me," I yelled. "And if he walked in that door right now, you'd still take his sorry ass back."

My mother slapped me so hard I got dizzy. The sting from her hand shot all the way down my legs. She hadn't hit me since I was six or seven years old. She began to cry. I wasn't by any means a perfect child, but I had never disrespected her before, and at that moment I knew our relationship would never be exactly the same again.

"Just make sure your ass graduates, you can't live here if you're not going to school," she said as walked upstairs.

I called Jamal and told him what happened between my mother and me.

"I want you to come over and meet her," I told him.

"Yo, I'm not trying to get in the middle of you and your mom beefing. Besides, I got mad shit to do the rest of the week."

"It'll only take a few minutes. I just want her to meet you, that's all."

I spent the next few minutes pleading with Jamal to drop by; his excuse was he didn't have time. I found it strange that he could always find the time to come get me and take me to his house, but all of a sudden he was just too busy. Finally I got tired of asking.

"All right, maybe next time," I said.

"Cool," he replied, before hanging up.

I turned around and my mother was standing at the door. She scared the shit out of me.

"Charisse, he's not coming over here. He's not busy, he's afraid," she said with a smirk on her face. "What's the boy's name?"

"His name is Jamal, and he's twenty-three. He's a man, not a boy."

"I don't care if he's thirty goddamn three, he's still a boy to me. A *man* wouldn't be afraid to come over here. A real *man* wouldn't be convincing a child to cut school to have sex, but you wouldn't know what the fuck a man does, because you're not a woman yet. You just think you are because when you look in the mirror you see a woman's tits and ass."

When I met Jamal's parents he introduced me as his *friend* Charisse. I didn't think anything of it, I figured guys felt corny saying, "This is my girlfriend Charisse," or "Mom, Dad, this is my woman Charisse." I also overheard him telling them that we went to school together; I guess he didn't want them to know I was sixteen. Jamal's father was cool as hell. I had dinner over there one night and he went out of his way to make me feel comfortable, more so than even Jamal. His mother, Regina Butler, was a bitch. She didn't like me and I didn't fucking like her little, short, ugly ass. Jamal's father was a really handsome man, and I was trying to figure out why he married this troll with a bad perm; *Maybe she was better-looking when she was younger.* I thought to myself until I saw their wedding picture in the living room. Whoever said, "All brides are beautiful," was a muthafucking liar, or had just never seen this real-life Wanda from *In Living Color* in a wedding dress.

As time went on and the weeks passed, I noticed that the phone calls died down a little, and he was always busy on certain nights. It didn't really bother me though. I knew that the only way I could maintain my relationship with him was to keep it low key and out of my mother's face. Her main concern was school, so if my grades had started to slip, or I cut school one more time, all hell would have broken loose.

By Christmas Day I had started feeling sick almost every morning. On the days when my mother cooked breakfast, the same aroma of sausage or bacon frying in the kitchen that used to get my ass up and downstairs in two seconds flat made me nauseous and feel like throwing up. *I hope I'm not dying,* I said to myself.

I had planned on spending the early part of the day at home with my mother, and then going over to Jamal's in the evening. His father had told me that they were having a big family Christmas party at the house. I guess Jamal forgot to mention it, but I assumed he would come and get me.

"Merry Christmas, old lady!" I said to my mother as I ran over and kissed her.

"Merry Christmas, Reecie!" she responded with a big smile.

Christmas was her favorite holiday. The sound of Nat King Cole and Johnny Mathis singing Christmas songs filled the house, and she and my aunts always prepared certain dishes that they didn't make at any other time during the year, not even at Thanksgiving.

"Do you want me to fix you a plate?" she asked.

"No, I'm not hungry," I responded.

"What's going on with your appetite? I usually can't keep your ass out of the kitchen."

"Maybe I'm anorexic," I responded jokingly.

"Black women don't do that shit, and your ass looks like you put on a few pounds. You better leave that junk food alone before you and Mrs. Blackmon are sharing bloomers."

We went into the living room and exchanged gifts. She had already given me money to shop, but she always had one or two things under the tree just so I would have something to open. This year she got me a bottle of perfume and a pair of Guess jeans. I gave her a green sweater and the same exact bottle of Jean-Paul Gaultier perfume that she got for me.

"Charisse, let me see the clothes you bought for Christmas," she asked.

"Um, I took the money and put a shearling jacket on layaway," I replied.

"The whole three hundred dollars? How much was the jacket?"

"Like five hundred."

"Well, damn, when are you going to get it out . . . next Christmas?" she remarked.

If my mother found out that I had spent my Christmas

money on a Panasonic cellular phone for Jamal she would
have killed me. I wasn't sweating it though; I knew he had
probably got me something off the hook.

That afternoon the doorbell rang. My mother answered.
I was in the kitchen; I had finally gotten hungry and
decided to eat something. I heard my mother talking and
then I heard a man's voice. I thought Jamal had popped
up without calling so I jumped up from the table and
practically killed myself running into the living room. When
I walked in Jason was standing there with a gift in his hand.

"Merry Christmas, Charisse," he said as he handed me
the box.

"I wanted to apologize to you and your mother for
calling you a chicken head. That's not what you are, and
that's not what you raised her to be, Miss Vivian."

"It's all right," I said. "I didn't you get you anything
though. Sorry."

"I wasn't looking for a gift, I'm just glad were cool," he
said before giving me a hug and kissing me on the cheek.
"I love you, Charisse, always have and always will," he
whispered in my ear.

Jason gave my mother a kiss on the cheek and left. My
mother locked the door behind him and stood there for a
second with a confused look on her face. She then looked
over at me.

"What the fuck is a chicken head?"

Jamal didn't call me until two o'clock that afternoon. He
said he had just woken up because he was up late playing
video games.

"So what are you doing today?" he asked.

"I thought I was seeing you," I responded. "Your father told me about the Christmas party."

"He did?" Jamal seemed surprised for a second. "My mother decided not to have it," he added.

"So why don't you come over here and get me, you can finally meet my mother, then we can hang out at your house for a while," I suggested.

"My car is acting up, I don't know what's wrong with that shit."

"So I'll take the train out to Queens and catch a cab to your house before it gets too late. I want to give you your gift."

"Uh, I tell you what, let me put some oil in my car and then I'll come get you, cool?"

Something seemed strange; at first I thought maybe his mother told him, "Don't bring that little bitch to my house on Jesus' birthday," but even if that was the case, he still didn't seem excited about seeing me or exchanging gifts.

I took a shower and got dressed before going downstairs to wait for Jamal. I sat there on the sofa from three-thirty to eight p.m., fully dressed, waiting for Jamal. Every few minutes I would get up and look out of the window, and after five, I started trying to call his phone, but there was no answer. I began to get so worried that I couldn't sit still.

"Mom, what if he got into an accident?" I asked frantically.

She didn't move from her position on the bed, she just cut her eyes at me as if to say, *you fucking dummy. Go sit your stupid-ass down by the window and wait for him . . . just like you used to do for Santa.* That's exactly what I did. I put the folding chair right by the front window and thought that every set of headlights coming down my street were his. Finally, about nine-thirty my phone rang, I picked it up on the first ring.

"Hey, baby," he said. "Yo, this car shit has got me so stressed out."

"What happened?" I asked, more relieved than upset.

"I been trying to get my shit fixed all day so I could come get you. I am fucking pissed," he said.

"Don't worry about it. I'm just glad you're all right." I said.

"Baby, I'm so tired, I'm just going to bed early. I'll call you in the morning . . . Merry Christmas."

"Okay, I lo . . ."

I didn't even get a chance to tell him how much I loved him before he hung up.

Jamal came by the day after Christmas, but only after I told him my mother had left for work. As soon as he walked in the door I threw my arms around him and kissed him, but for some reason he seemed indifferent and annoyed.

"So you got your car fixed?" I asked.

"What?" he asked, as though he didn't know what I was talking about.

"The car . . . you got it fixed?"

"Oh yeah, no doubt," he said as he kept glancing at his watch.

I went under the tree and got his present. I couldn't wait for his reaction.

"Merry Christmas," I said excitedly.

Jamal handed me a plastic bag from a store on Jamaica Avenue. I looked inside and it was the *ugliest,* fucking cheap-looking sweater I had ever seen. It was purple and he didn't even bother to wrap it. The price tag had been torn off, but I had seen this same sweater in downtown Brooklyn for $9.99. I knew it was some bullshit he had just stopped and picked up on his way over here.

"Thanks, baby! I needed a sweater this color," I said while trying to hide my disappointment.

"Yeah, I looked around like a muthafucka for the right gift, but that sweater looked like you," he said.

Damn, if this sweater is what I look like, I'm fucked up in the game, I thought to myself.

Jamal unwrapped his gift and seemed surprised.

"You bought me a phone. . . . Why?" he asked.

"The man in the store said it was the latest model. I thought it was fly. Look how small it is," I responded.

"I got a phone in my car already, Charisse, and that fucking bill is off the hook. I don't have paper to be paying two muthafucking phone bills," he said ungratefully. "You got the receipt? I'll take it back and get something I want . . . thanks though."

My feelings were hurt, I had taken every penny my mother gave me and spent it on that phone and he didn't seem to give a fuck. But all I could think about was how I didn't want him to be upset with me. After about thirty minutes of sitting on my sofa switching channels with a sour look on his face, he stood up.

"Hey, boo, I have to go." he said.

"Damn, you just got here. I miss you," I said as I walked over and put my arms around him.

"I miss you too, but I got mad shit to do, you understand?" he replied as he gently pushed me away. "Could you go find that receipt for me?"

When Jamal left I went upstairs to lie down. I had started feeling sick again, more so than any other day. I ran into the bathroom and threw up in the toilet. I felt like I wanted to die right there on the bathroom floor. I got up to look in the medicine cabinet; I was praying that we had some Alka Seltzer, Tums, Maalox, or a fucking gun so I could shoot myself. I found some milk of magnesia, but I also noticed that on the shelf below was a brand-new box of Kotex. The box was unopened, and it wasn't until that moment it even occurred to me.

"I haven't gotten my period in a while," I said out loud. "Oh fucking no, I couldn't be."

I immediately thought about what my mother said about birth control. Jamal and I had been having sex at least twice a week with no protection. He kept telling me, "Don't worry, I'll pull out," but he never did and I never said shit. I wasn't sure if I was pregnant or not, so I didn't want to panic. I got dressed and ran to the neighborhood drug store to get an EPT. I must have walked down that aisle twenty times waiting for people to get the fuck out so I wouldn't be ashamed to pick it up. Finally the coast was clear and I snatched one up with the quickness and hid it under a roll of paper towels. I saw the way the woman behind the counter looked at me as she put the test inside the bag. It was the same way I looked at girls in my school who were pregnant.

Blue had always been one of my favorite colors, but I was praying with all my soul that I didn't see that color when the results of the test showed up. The shit came back as blue as the ocean, which is exactly what the fuck I felt like jumping in, preferably with a brick boulder attached to my red Reebok 5411s.

I spent the rest of the day crying and calling Jamal over and over again. He told me that I should only use his pager in case of emergency. Well, this was a fucking *emergency*. I blew that shit up—911—911—911—and he still never called back.

When my mother got home that evening I was in the bed lying down. I had started feeling a little better but was still pale and flushed from all that vomiting earlier.

"What's wrong with you?" She asked when she came to my bedroom door.

"I felt sick earlier. I was throwing up. The milk in my cereal must have been bad," I replied.

"I just bought that milk yesterday, and I had it in my cereal and my coffee this morning. It was fine," she said with a strange tone as she walked over to my bed and then stared at me in silence. I had to stand up. I felt like she was examining with her eyes.

"Mom, why are you looking at me like that?" I asked.

Out of nowhere my mother slapped me in the face so hard it knocked me to the ground. I grabbed my face more in shock than pain.

"Mom!" I yelled.

"No! No! No!" she yelled back as tears streamed down her face. "I didn't work all these years for you to throw it all away! Why, Charisse, why? In God's name, why?" she screamed.

"What are you talking about?" I asked as innocently as I could.

"You're pregnant! I see it in your face!"

"Ma, I ain't pregnant!" I declared.

"Put your clothes on . . . now!" she demanded, before looking at the clock and realizing what time it was. "We'll deal with this in the morning. Take your stupid ass to bed."

Jamal never did call me back.

The next morning my mother got me up at seven a.m. to get dressed.

"Hurry up, the cab will be here in ten minutes," she barked at me.

Vivian Lorraine McNeil did not believe in taxicabs. She had been taking trains and buses all her life and actually preferred it, so when she said the cab was on the way, I knew it was going to be a long-ass day.

Thirty minutes later I found myself sitting in the waiting room of a clinic surrounded by a bunch of teenage girls, all black or Hispanic, some of whom looked no older than twelve or thirteen, some with baby bumps and some without. The only thing we all had in common was *nobody* had a smile on their face, and there wasn't one dude with anybody in the room. I guess they figured they had done enough by bringing us all together for the SYB, a.k.a. Stupid Young Bitches, summit.

"Charisse Hawkins," the woman with clipboard called out from behind her desk.

My mother and I got up and walked into the back area. I was never so scared in all my life. I had prayed all night that the EPT was wrong, and that by some miracle I had a stomach virus, or in a worst-case scenario, something you could fix with a shot. The worst part of the whole experience was seeing the look on my mother's face. The way she looked at me had changed forever. I wasn't her baby anymore.

Chapter 7

*D*uring the train ride home from the clinic my mother was speechless. I guess staying calm was the only way she could keep from choking the life out of me. As we were walking home from the train station it started to snow; they were the biggest most beautiful flakes I had ever seen. I watched as my mother sighed with each deliberate step she took, and the white flakes landed softly on her uncovered head in such a way that it looked gray, like a grandmother's.

When we got in the house I went up to my room and picked up the phone to call Jamal.

"After we get this little situation taken care of we're going to get you some birth control pills," my mother said as she came to my door.

"What do you mean 'get it taken care of?'" I asked.

"Oh, you didn't know? Well, let me enlighten you. You're getting an abortion. You weren't planning on keeping it, were you?" she asked with a "you can't be fucking serious" smirk on her face.

"I don't know what I'm going to do," I uttered. "I haven't even told Jamal yet."

"I don't give a flying fuck if you told Jamal, Jamaica, Jabbar, or Jesus! I already made the decision for you!" she announced before slamming my bedroom door.

I dialed Jamal's number again, this time he answered. I was crying so hard that he could barely understand what I was saying.

"I need you to come over here . . . now!" I cried.

"What the fuck happened?" he asked.

"I just need you to come over here . . . please, Jamal." I said through the tears and sobbing.

Jamal paused for a moment and sucked his teeth like I was really inconveniencing him.

"Yo, is this shit really important?" he asked with an attitude.

"Yes."

He paused again before answering.

"Goddamn. All right, Charisse, I'll be over there in a few hours. I'm out in NJ right now."

Nitra and I hadn't really spoken since the whole incident with Nice, but I needed someone other than my mother to talk to, so I called her.

"Charisse! Oh my God, I have been thinking about calling you. I'm so tired of avoiding you in school. Got a bitch creeping around the hallways like fucking Secret Squirrel or some shit," she joked.

"You're the one who stopped fucking with me. I thought Nice told you to cut me off."

"He did . . . little short bastard, but I still love him," she stated. "I got something to tell you, but I don't know how to say it," she added.

"Well, I've got some shit to tell you too. You're not going to be believe it," I said.

"You go first."

"No you go . . ." I replied.

We got both quiet for a second as if mustering the strength to blurt it out.

"I'm pregnant!" we both said at the same exact time.

"You're what?" we both asked each other at the same exact time.

"Oh my God, Charisse, I can't believe *you* are pregnant! Bitch, I can't even believe you gave somebody some pussy with your tight, conceited ass," she joked.

"What did your mother say?" I asked.

"She don't really give a fuck one way or the other. She's like, 'Just make sure you get food stamps and WIC so the little bastard can have some milk 'cause I'm not helping one bit.'"

"My mother and I both just found out today. If she thought the food in jail was a little better I'd be dead already. And I think she's still considering murdering my ass."

"So who's the father?" she asked.

"Jamal."

"Jamal who?"

"Do you remember the guy from the jewelry store in the Albee Square Mall," I said.

"Please, *please* tell me you're not talking about that bitch-ass nigga that kept grinning in your mug piece."

Before when she referred to Jamal as a "bitch-ass nigga,"

didn't bother me one way or the other. But now I didn't like that shit.

"Can you please not refer to my man as a 'bitch-ass nigga?'" I asked nicely.

"No doubt," she laughed. "But say what you want about Nice, that little nigga is who he is, what you see is what the fuck you get. But that Jamal muthafucka, I got to keep it real. I don't like his frontin' ass."

"Have you heard from Brenda?" I asked while trying to change the subject before I got mad.

"Wait, bust this, that bitch is pregnant too!" she yelled.

"You lying!" I responded.

"Word to mother."

Suddenly I didn't feel so bad. My two best friends since I can remember were in the same boat as I was, and whether you're on a cruise on the *Queen Mary,* or the SS *Poseidon,* its always feels better when you're not alone. Nitra and I talked for about an hour and she gave me Brenda's number in the Bronx.

"Charisse!" my mother yelled from downstairs.

"Let me go before she comes up here flipping," I told Nitra. "I'll call you before we go back to school."

I went downstairs and found all my aunts sitting in the living room, looking mad as hell. The first thing I thought was *I hope Jamal don't show up now.* My aunts would have *no* reservations or qualms about fucking his ass up until he was in a deep coma.

"Should I bust her upside her head first, or do you want to take your best shot, Della," Aunt Belle said as I entered the room.

"Calm down, calm down. We're here for talking, not busting," Aunt Della replied calmly.

"Vengeance is his said the lord," stated Aunt Ruby as she held up her Bible. "Romans 12:19," she added.

"Well, me and Jesus are just like this," Aunt Belle said as she intertwined her two fingers. "So I'm just doing his work."

"Charisse, baby, how did this happen? I mean I know *how* it happened, but how did it happen?" Aunt Della asked.

"Go on and tell, Charisse," my mother said. "Tell her how you're in love and got you a real live, genuine Mayan, he's twenty-three. He obviously likes them young . . . and dumb."

"Twenty-three! He's a grown man," Aunt Della said angrily.

"And she's still a minor. So I say we beat his ass for twenty-three hours straight, and then we call the cops," Aunt Belle snapped.

"And wait, you ain't heard the best part. This child here, who's sixteen and didn't even graduate yet but has been accepted to the top colleges, doesn't have a job, and can barely take care of her own self . . . isn't sure what she wants to do."

"Vivian, please, she a *child*. She don't have no goddamn say, and she don't have no goddamn choice . . . please," said Aunt Belle.

"Don't take the Lord's name in vain."

"Ruby, didn't I just tell you, me, and the Lord are here," she stated while taking her two fingers and pointing to her eyes.

"Well, I know nobody in this room wants to hear this, but the Lord doesn't make mistakes. A child coming into the world is a blessing," Aunt Ruby said.

I felt like I didn't even need to be standing there. They were discussing my life like I didn't have any say-so in it. This was my body and I didn't care what the fuck they were saying.

"Y'all all sitting here talking like you led you these perfect lives, like you know what's best for everybody. *Nobody* in this room got a man, except Aunt Belle, if that's what you want call him, but you all got kids. This is *my* life and Jamal is *my* man. If I decide to keep *my* baby, that's what I'm going to do," I said with conviction.

Every eye in the room was wide open and every jaw dropped. They weren't expecting me to do anything but stand there and cry and plead, "You don't understand, you don't understand." It was them who didn't understand. Jamal wasn't a loser like the men they had chosen. I stormed back upstairs without saying another word.

By the time Jamal got to my house my aunts had already left. I guess they felt disrespected and had taken the stance that "a hard head makes a soft ass." At first he called me from his car phone.

"I'm here. Come on outside," he said.

"No, you need to come inside," I replied.

"You there alone?"

I could see him sitting in the car, talking to me and looking at the house, as I peeked out of my bedroom window.

"My mother's here."

"Damn, Charisse, you know I'm not trying to hear all that shit. I'm breaking out," he said.

"I'm pregnant," I said clearly. "We went to the doctor today."

Within ten seconds my doorbell rang. When I answered it Jamal was standing there looking stressed-out. He came in without saying a word and went directly over to the couch and sat down. My mother heard the bell and came downstairs to see who it was.

"Mom, this is Jamal."

"Hello, Miss Hawkins, nice to meet you," he said while removing his hat.

"It's Miss McNeil, and is it? I really can't say it's very nice to meet you, Jamal. We have a problem here."

"I know," he replied meekly. "Charisse, I'll come by first thing in the morning to pick you and your mother up, and I'll pay for everything. Don't worry, we'll get this taken care of immediately."

"'Taken care of.' You sound like her," I replied.

"Charisse, I'm not ready to be a father, and you're not ready to be a mother. I'm a senior in college and you're a senior in high school. That don't sound like parent material to me."

"Jamal, I don't appreciate you having sex with my daughter when you knew how old she was, and both of you should have known that if you weren't using any kind of protection this was bound to happen. But I do appreciate you having enough sense to know that this is the only way to handle this situation," my mother said.

I was so upset that I just started crying uncontrollably. I

couldn't believe that he was on some *Fuck it, just get rid of it, no biggie, here's the money* bullshit. I also knew that if I got rid of that child I would be aborting more than a baby; I'd be ending my relationship with Jamal. I wasn't willing to lose either.

"I'm keeping my baby!" I yelled before running upstairs and getting under the covers. I heard the door downstairs close about five minutes later and the stairs creaking as my mother made her way up. I thought for sure she would come into my room and do that "supportive mother" thing and hug me while saying, "Everything's going to be fine." Instead I heard her bedroom door close and the volume from her television go up. Whatever she was doing in there she didn't want me to hear, but I knew already. I wasn't the only one who went to bed and cried that night.

Chapter 8

Five Months Later
1993

Getting up to go to school had become the hardest thing for me to do. Thank God it was spring; at least the weather was nice now. The flip side was the cold weather had allowed me to hide my stomach under big sweaters and coats. I kept telling myself I wasn't embarrassed, but I kept asking my mother if we could move to another neighborhood where I didn't know anybody. I had managed to avoid running into Jason and Ms. Blackmon for the most part. She rang the doorbell one day to bring me a pot of peas and rice and I opened the door, thinking it was my mother; she was always forgetting her keys.

"Good lord, Charisse, your face got so fat, girl," she said with her accent.

"I put on a little weight. You know people stay in the house all winter and eat," I replied jokingly.

"Yeah," she said with a curious look on her face. "Them do a lot of ting in the house in the winter," she responded.

I had a feeling that Ms. Blackmon knew, we lived right next door and she was used to me dropping by to talk and eat on a regular basis. The funny thing is I think she wanted to avoid me as much as I did her. I guess sometimes not knowing for sure is better than seeing it and having to deal with it.

My mother had basically given up on me going to medical school, no matter how much I told her I was still going. I still planned to attend, just not right after high school, and obviously I wouldn't be going away to school. I honestly thought she was going to put up a bigger fight about me keeping the baby. One night we got into an argument, and I said some things I probably shouldn't have. After that, it was like she had washed her hands of the situation.

"Charisse, maybe you should call your father and talk to a man."

"Please, that man is not my father, he's your baby daddy," I snapped. "He can't tell me a damn thing,"

"Seems like nobody can, not even Jamal. I mean, the boy told you straight out that he didn't want you to keep the baby," she said with a slight chuckle in her voice.

That shit cut like a knife. She hit the nerve that was the most sensitive. Deep down I knew what the future was going to be like, and the fact that everybody was right made me angry. When I looked in my mother's face it was like she couldn't wait to see me fall on my face and say, "I told you so."

"When the baby gets here he'll feel differently," I said.

"Is that what you think?" she asked. "You think that's going to keep him? That's what already drove him away."

I just stood there looking at her. I didn't even know who to be mad at, but I took it out on her.

"Like you drove my father away? I guess you would know what it takes to drive a man away."

"That was a totally different situation. We were adults; I was thirty-years-old and living on my own when I had you. If I had known he had sixty other kids . . ."

"What . . . you wouldn't have had me. Please, you were so proud of having that pretty man that you would have done whatever to keep him . . . even having a baby."

From that point on she didn't tell me anything except an occasional reminder that she had a full-time job, and she wasn't in the market for a second part-time job as a babysitter.

Jamal's parents were just as opposed to me having the baby, and when my mother called them and pointed out that their son had gotten a minor pregnant, he told them that I lied and that I told him I was nineteen.

"Your daughter is just trying to trap my son. He told me you live over there in that goddamn ghetto," his mother said. "My son thought she was older. If she's sixteen and out there seducing grown men, well . . . I wonder where she learned that? We live in Jamaica Estates in a five bedroom colonial with a two-car garage and a carport. I don't blame her for trying to get away from that war zone in Brooklyn, but not at my son's expense."

"'Your son's expense?' My daughter was going to medical school," My mother argued back.

"Yeah right . . . she was going to medical school and she gave it up to have a baby by a guy who doesn't want her or the baby? She thought she had any kind of future like that, and *this* is the choice she made? Excuse me for saying this, but if that's. true then she's too dumb for beauty school, much less medical school," his mother said sarcastically.

My mother slammed the phone down in her ear. "Arrogant snobby bitch," she said. "If I saw her on the street I'd slap the taste out of her mouth."

Vivian McNeil wasn't going to let anybody put me down, no matter how disappointed she was in me.

"I hope I can be half the mother you are," I said to her during one of our infrequent mother-daughter moments.

"So do I, because if you're half the mother I am it means you're not doing it by your damn self."

My relationship with Jamal was a whole other story. No matter how much he ignored me, or talked down to me, I still held on to the hope that once the baby was born he would see her or him and we would just be one big happy family. As much as I told myself that bullshit, this was the same guy who made it his business to pick me up from school everyday when he wanted some ass, but wouldn't come get me when it was freezing outside and my pregnant ass was taking the subway home. I had never actually caught him cheating, but we weren't having sex anymore, so everybody I talked to including my mother, my aunts, Nitra, and even Brenda, whom I had reconnected with, said the same exact thing. "If he aint getting it from you, he's getting it from somebody else, quite a few somebody's probably."

I remember being at Jamal's house one day and looking at some pictures. He was in a few of the pictures, hugging all over this real pretty light-skinned chick who he said was his "cousin." I didn't question him because in some of the pictures his mother's ugly, insect-looking ass, his father, and other family members were also included. Still, something about the photos was fucking with me.

"You have a real nice-looking family," I said to his mother when he went upstairs and she came down. "I was just looking at the pictures on the table."

"Yeah, those were from the Christmas party last year. I had them out so I can put them in my holiday album. Did you see Jamal's friend. My God, that child is gorgeous, and her figure! I'd kill for a body like that," she said spitefully.

I sat there so mad I could have gone Amy Fisher on Jamal and his mother, but instead I held it until we got in the car.

"I thought your family didn't have a Christmas party, you fucking liar," I snapped.

"What are you talking about?" he asked.

"You know what I'm talking about. Your mother said those pictures were from the Christmas party. The party your lying ass said had been cancelled."

I could always tell when Jamal was busted in a lie. He would try to laugh it off with that *You're bugging* smirk.

"You're bugging," he said true to form, with that stupid-ass half laugh.

"And that girl ain't your cousin. Your mother said that was *your* friend. Who the fuck is she, Jamal?"

"You're bugging," he said again with a stupid-ass scowl on his face now.

"What the fuck? Is your needle stuck?"

"She aint my *real* cousin, but you know how when you been friends with somebody for mad years you call them your cousin," he explained. "You let my mother gas you up if you want. You know she likes fucking with you," he added.

It was my seventeenth birthday on this particular Friday night. As usual I was home alone, watching television and stuffing my face with Pepperidge Farm Goldfish crackers, Hostess cupcakes, and Pepsi, waiting for Jamal to stand me up yet again. The phone rang.

"Hello."

"Yeah, bitch, you know what it is!" the person said.

"Brenda?"

"What's up girl!" she screamed into the phone. "It's Friday night and I just got paid," she added before breaking into Johnny Kemp's song: "'Just got paid, Friday night, party hunting, feeling right,'" she sang.

"Where are you?" I asked.

"Look out the window," she replied.

When I looked out the window I saw Brenda outside waving up at my window. She was standing in front of a shiny new black Lexus SC400 coupe.

"Come on, bitch, get your shit on and let's roll," she said.

I threw my clothes on and went outside. Brenda and I had talked on the phone quite a few times and kept saying we were going to hook up, but what with school, being tired constantly, and her living all the way in the Boogie Down, it hadn't happened.

"Happy birthday!" she yelled as we waddled toward each other and embraced.

"Look at your fat ass!" I laughed.

"I *know* you ain't talking shit. I bet your big ass was upstairs eating when I called."

"You know it was," I replied. "Whose car is this? This shit is butter."

"This is Dave's car. He just got it," she replied as we got in and melted into the supple, gray leather interior.

"And he let you drive it? You don't even have your license."

"Dave is down in Florida visiting his kids and fucking his ex-wife. He left the keys to the car, and his bank card in his "secret" hiding place, and you know what they say, finders keepers."

"I didn't know Dave had kids and a wife—I mean ex-wife."

"Neither did I until his daughter called the house one day, looking for her father. I asked her who's your father? She said David Farmer."

"Damn, men are some fucking liars. Eighty percent of what comes out of their mouth is bullshit," I said.

"Ninety," she clarified.

"I still think he's going to flip when he finds out you drove his car."

"Your man is a puuuuunnnkkkk. David ain't going to do shit but say, 'That's not right, Brenda. The cops could have pulled you over and taken my car.'"

"You got Dave shook, Brenda?" I asked while laughing.

"*What!* Charisse, I was, like, three months pregnant, and I guess he felt like it was safe to test me. He came in the door one night, barking at me big dog–style, and then, bust this, he mushed me right in my face," she said, still in disbelief. "I tapped that punk nigga's jaw with a two piece and sent his ass to see the sandman. Then he going to come to me the next day with his muthafuckin' lip looking like an inner tube and ask me if I'm okay. I said, nigga, are you okay?!"

I laughed so hard I could hardly catch my breath. This was just like old times, except we were both pregnant, and we were joy riding in a fifty-thousand-dollar Lexus.

"So who is that cat that knocked your prissy ass up?" she asked. "I asked Nitra where he was from and she said straight out of Suckersville U.S.A.," she added.

"She's having a fucking baby with Jiminy Cricket and talking shit about my man." I replied. "His name is Jamal Butler, he's in college, and his family lives in Jamaica Estates."

"Phat crib?" she asked.

"Hell yeah." I boasted as though it were mine, or as though I was even welcome there.

"Is he excited about the baby?" she asked. "That's one good thing about Dave. He waits on me hand and foot, and if that muthafucka brings one more toy in that house I'll scream," she boasted.

I just looked at her with a forced smile.

"Yeah, Jamal is driving me crazy too. He's so anxious for the baby to get here he don't know what to do with himself," I lied.

I hated liars, but I couldn't bring myself to admit that he didn't want me to have the baby. And the only one waiting on someone was me, waiting on him to call, to show up, but most of all waiting on him to be the Jamal I met in the beginning.

"We should go by and pick up Nitra," I said as I changed the subject.

"You know she's on lockdown. I called her on my way out here and she was like, 'Oh, I'm not really feeling all that good.'"

"That's 'cause Mighty Mouse told her she wasn't feeling that good."

We didn't have any particular destination in mind, so we just drove around, eventually into Manhattan. Brenda was a great driver, and she was so calm and relaxed behind the wheel. Even when we saw the police, they never looked at us twice, other than admiring the car.

"How's Gail doing?" I asked, referring to her mother.

"She's all right. She's in rehab right now trying to get her shit together," she replied.

"And what about Walter and his crazy ass?"

"Walter got crushed by a garbage truck in Brownsville. I always told Gail he was going to leave her flat, and that's exactly how he left her . . . flat as a pancake. Perverted bastard," she said with no remorse.

We drove all the way from Harlem down to the Village before getting on the Brooklyn Bridge to head back.

"I'm going to stop at Junior's and get you a cheesecake for your birthday," Brenda said.

"The last thing I need is a cheesecake," I replied.

"So you don't want it?" she asked.

"Hell yeah, I want it. My fat ass said I didn't *need* it. Don't get it twisted."

"So how come you're not spending your birthday with Jamal?" she finally came out and asked.

"He's home studying for some kind of exam. He's a senior, so my man is glued to those books," I said halfheartedly.

Brenda and I were lucky to find a parking space right on Flatbush Avenue in front of the restaurant. I didn't really want to go inside. I had become paranoid about people staring at me.

"So what are you going to do when you have the baby, carry it around in a Macy's shopping bag?" she asked. "You ain't the first teenager to have a baby. You're a funny-ass chick though," she added while shaking her head and smiling.

"Funny how?" I asked defensively.

"You're not embarrassed about being pregnant. Your problem is you still think you're better than the rest of these bitches out here that're in the same muthafucking boat as us. We used to talk mad shit and ask how chicks could be so stupid when we saw them pregnant or pushing a stroller. Now *you* are that chick and you know people are saying the same thing about you," she said straight out before getting out to go inside Junior's.

This was the part about Brenda I didn't miss. She kept

that shit 100 percent real whether you liked it or not. I was sitting there in the car, changing the stations on the radio and thinking about how I was going to bust that cheesecake down to the plate with a cold glass of milk when I got home. I looked up for a second to see if Brenda was coming, and as I glanced at the traffic driving by, I saw a white Toyota 4Runner that looked exactly like Jamal's. There was a girl with long hair sitting in the front seat, but the car drove by so fast I didn't see the driver. I watched the 4Runner make a left on Fulton Street and then disappear around the corner. I knew in my heart that was Jamal I saw, but I immediately started convincing myself otherwise. *That 4Runner had different rims. That truck was actually beige. I think the driver was a middle-aged white man,* I said in my head. In a manner of seconds I had gone from being sure I saw my boyfriend driving down Flatbush with a new chick to seeing the an old white man in a 4Runner with rims blasting his music.

Brenda came out of Junior's carrying two bags; she had bought me a medium cheesecake and a pastrami sandwich. My appetite was gone though.

"What the fuck is wrong with you?" Brenda asked. "It's crowded in that piece. I know how impatient your ass is," she said jokingly.

"Whatever," I replied stoically.

"You feeling sick?" She asked. "You look like you saw a ghost or some shit," Brenda said as she pressed a button and changed the station to Hot 97 Funk Flex was the DJ that night, playing "One to Grow On" by the UMC's before cutting in "My Mind Is Playing Tricks on Me."

When Brenda dropped me off I went into the house. I
didn't even try to call Jamal to see where he was, to see if he
was home in Jamaica Estates studying. One of my teachers
used to have a saying: "Most of the time when people lie,
they're lying to themselves, the rest of us just happen to be
in the path of that lie." That night, there was nobody else in
my path; I just wanted to be able to sleep in peace.

Chapter 9

*B*y the beginning of June I was gearing up for graduation. Shopping was the one thing that I looked forward to no matter what was going on, but when you're seven months pregnant who the fuck wants to go look for a dress and shoes for graduation. This time shopping became a reality check. The simple fact was that I was still counting on my mother to buy my graduation clothes. That's the shit you don't think about when you're proclaiming, "I'm keeping my baby." And when people who love you are telling you, "You're not ready. What the fuck is your rush?"

It was a bright, sunny Saturday afternoon. We were on 35th Street and Sixth Avenue by Macy's when I noticed this white girl about my age, staring at me. I thought she was looking at me and thinking, *This is where my father's taxpayer money goes, to the welfare and food stamps this bitch will be collecting in a few months.* In retrospect, maybe that's what I was thinking about myself. When I turned around, ready to curse her out, she smiled wide and waved at me. *Who the fuck is this crazy-ass Blossom-looking bitch waving at me all stupid,* I thought.

"I'm going inside Conway's for a minute," my mother said as she walked away, leaving me standing there about to confront either the friendliest white person in New York, or a lesbian teen with a fetish for pretty, pregnant black girls.

"Hey, remember me?" the girl asked with a huge smile as she walked over.

I looked at her carefully, and while I'm no racist, she looked like every other white girl I had seen in my life.

"No . . . from where?" I asked with a little Brooklyn edge to my tone.

"Your name is Charisse, right?"

"Yeah."

"We met last year . . . at Columbia University, the academic fair? We hung out all morning," she explained.

"Oh my God. Paige, right?" I asked as it all came back to me.

"Yeah," she replied happily.

We hugged and I thought to myself, *It's nice to see her again, but this bitch is acting like she found her long-lost best friend.* I also found it strange that she didn't acknowledge the fact that I was pregnant.

"So what have you been up to?" she asked.

"Just trying to graduate, and get this baby out of me," I replied.

"Less than three weeks to graduation," she said as she gave me a high five. "We made it!"

"Have you decided on a school?" she asked.

"No, I've had a slight change of plans. I'm going to take

a semester or two off and then try to get into Brooklyn College, or maybe NYU," I replied. "What about you? Columbia right?"

"No. I'm going to Pepperdine," she answered. "My parents' idea," she explained.

At that moment a silver Mercedes sedan turned the corner from 36th Street and pulled over.

"There's my mom. I have to go. Is your house number still the same?" she asked almost in a whisper while walking away.

"Yeah."

Paige was acting like she didn't want her mother to know she was talking to me. When she got in the car I was only a few feet away on the sidewalk.

"Who is that," I heard her mother ask clearly.

"She was just asking which way to Lexington Avenue," Paige responded as they pulled off.

My mother came out of Conway two minutes later, and after getting a hot dog, a knish, and a soda, we got on the subway headed back to Brooklyn. When we got off the train at our stop, I asked, "Can we take a cab home? I'm exhausted."

My mother started to laugh as she looked over at me.

"Charisse, way before you were born this fighter named Ronnie—no, wait it was Sonny. Anyway, Sonny Liston told Muhammad Ali, when he was still Cassius Clay, 'You can run, but you can't hide,' she quoted as we walked right by the Natacha livery cab base.

"My feet are swollen," I pleaded.

"Mine too, they'll go down," she responded.

We made it to the house without having direct contact with any of the people on my *Goddamn, there they are* list. But instead of taking my ass straight into the house, I became entranced at the sound of the ice cream truck coming down the street. In Brooklyn where I lived, Mr. Softee was the black people's Pied Piper. The white truck with blue trim at the bottom would come down the block nice and slow, playing that fucking annoying song over and over, and people would come flying out of their houses, waving money at him to stop. I stood there debating for a moment before greed got the better of me, then I bum-rushed the truck for a double cone, half vanilla and half chocolate, with rainbow sprinkles. He handed me the cone and I was just about to pay him.

"The least I can do is pay for your ice cream," someone said as he reached over my shoulder and placed a five-dollar bill on the counter of the truck. My worst nightmare was about to come true: Jason was standing right behind me. I froze for a second with my eyes closed. I know the ice cream man was like, *What the fuck is wrong with this crazy-ass heifer?*

"I know you got a man and all, but I was hoping you'd keep a promise you made to me when we were kids," he said while still standing behind me. "You plan on standing there all day?"

"I'm trying to remember what my mother wanted," I replied nervously. "What promise?"

"To go with me to my senior prom."

I turned around slow. The ice cream was already starting to melt in the warm sun and run down my hand. Jason had the biggest smile on his face, until he looked at my stomach. I literally saw a lump in his throat as he looked for the right words.

"Wow . . . uh, wow," he said. I could see the pain on his face and his eyes begin to well up. Jason took a deep breath and tried to smile through whatever he was feeling. He hugged me, but even the hug felt distant.

"Congratulations," he forced out before looking at his watch. "Hey, take care of yourself, okay? I have to go. I got a game with my AAU team—you know, basketball-basketball-basketball . . ."

Jason kissed me on my forehead and walked away. His usually upright strong shoulders were slumped and he was walking with his head down. I tossed the ice cream cone in the garbage can.

"You want another cone, miss?" the ice cream man asked. "Your friend left his change."

"No . . . I think I took enough from him already," I answered.

The rest of the day I sat in my room, thinking about the look on Jason's face. It wasn't too different from the look on my mother's face, as well as those of my aunt and several of my teachers.

That night I got a call about eight-forty-five p.m. from Paige. I wasn't expecting her to actually call me.

"I hope you don't mind me calling you," she said. "I just needed somebody to talk to, somebody who could understand how I feel."

"I'm not sure what you're talking about, but sure, I'm happy to listen."

"How did you do it?" she asked.

"Do what?"

"Talk your parents into letting you keep the baby," she said. "I was pregnant a few months ago by my boyfriend, who's from Harlem. My mother and father made me get an abortion and stop seeing him," she said.

"You boyfriend was black?" I asked in a surprised tone.

"Puerto Rican. But it wouldn't have mattered if he was black, white, Asian, or from Mars. Once I told them I was pregnant, I became like a prisoner in my own house. Today when you saw me, that was probably the longest they'd left me by myself in the last three months," she said.

"Well it's just me and my mother. I don't see my father. She didn't want me to have this baby either, but I was having this baby no matter what."

"Carlos really wanted the baby too. He tried to talk to my father man to man, and when they found out he was twenty-one, they had him arrested," she said as the anger in her voice became apparent. "I fucking hate them. It's my life. I was all set to go to Columbia in the fall, but now they're sending me out to California to live with my aunt and uncle, who just retired from the military, so I can go to Pepperdine."

For the next hour she cried, she vented, and she reflected on having an abortion against her will at five months.

"It was a boy, his name was . . . is Carlos Jr.," she cried.

I knew Paige came from money. I remember her telling me at Columbia that her father was the president of some big investment firm and that she lived in Trump Tower.

I guess I was really naïve. I thought only young black and Spanish girls became teenage mothers. Paige had the whole world at her fingertips. She was intelligent, pretty, and money was no object, but she kept talking about "not wanting to be here" if she couldn't be with Carlos. I told her she could call me whenever she felt like talking. I had made an unexpected new friend.

The next morning my mother came into my room and woke me up.

"You've got some mail," she said as she placed an envelope on my nightstand. "I'm going to church. I'll see you when I get back."

It was Sunday, and as far as I had always known the mailman didn't deliver mail on Sundays. I reached over and picked up the envelope. It was a blank, but there was a letter inside. When you're seven months pregnant the first place you go in the morning is the bathroom. I took the envelope with me. When I opened it, inside was a letter from Jason.

Dear Charisse,

I don't even now what to say except yesterday was a day I'll never forget. I know things didn't work out with us, and we haven't talked in a while, but you are never too far from my mind, and never ever out of my heart. I love you, Charisse Hawkins, always have and always will. I know it might be selfish to write this letter; if you're having a baby you must be in love, and if you're in love, he must be treating you really good. I just wanted you to know you're still the most beautiful girl I've ever seen, and I wish you the best in life. Take care and good luck in becoming a doctor—that's what you're meant to do.

> *Your friend,*
> *Jason*

P.S. I'm not taking anyone to my senior prom. I still remember sitting on your stoop and asking you, we couldn't have been any older than 8 or 9. I still don't want to go with anyone else.

That was the first time that I realized that I wasn't just a girl he had a crush on. I was someone he really loved.

Jamal had actually started calling and coming around more frequently. He always wanted to fool around, but I wasn't feeling sexual at all, so his visits usually ended in an argument.

"Damn, you can't give a brother no head or nothing," he would say.

"The only thing I'm putting in my mouth is food," I would reply.

"If it wasn't for me your ass and tits wouldn't be looking like that, and you can't hook a nigga up."

I was still young, but I had gotten hip to his bullshit. I figured whoever he was fucking must have been all tricked out and cut his corny ass off. I still loved him though, so I dealt with whatever he dished out. I could be feeling like death, but if he called and said he was coming, I'd hop up off my deathbed and get ready.

Jamal had told me that he wasn't going to be able to go to my graduation because he had other plans that couldn't be changed, but that he would take me out the Saturday before. We ended up going to Great Adventure on a 90-degree day in June. To this day I have no idea why anybody with common sense would take a pregnant woman to an amusement park where she can't get on any rides, and there's nothing to do but walk a million miles in the hot-ass sun watching parents chase their badass, stupid kids and think to yourself, *Is this what I have to look forward to?* or, *If that was my son I'd kick him square up his ass.*

Jamal was nice to me at the park. He bought me anything I wanted, *but* I noticed that he didn't want me playing him too close. I tried to hold his hand a few times. He wasn't having any of that.

"Charisse, it's too goddamn hot to be out here touching and holding hands and all that bullshit."

I looked at him out of the corner of my eye. I guess that was payback for not giving him head, or maybe because there were 10,000 dimes out there in every color, shape, and age. He was trying his best to watch every one of them on the low. I had to catch myself a few times; I was looking at these chicks like, *That bitch does not look better than me.* Or *I'm way prettier than she is,* and then I realized that I was twenty-five pounds heavier, my feet were swollen, my nose was spreading like Skippy, and my usually fly hair was pulled back in a pony tail. As if my insecurities weren't on full blast already, I looked straight to my left and saw Jason. He was standing by the basketball game where you shoot to win a teddy bear, surrounded by five or six girls.

"Come on, Jason, win me the big Bugs Bunny," I heard one white girl say.

"No, I want the giant Scooby-Doo," said a black girl who was trying to sound white. "Come on, Jason, please," she added as she grabbed his arm playfully.

"That must be some college player. Look at all them hos on his dick. My nigga," said Jamal.

Jamal knew who Jason was, but he had never actually seen him.

"That's Jason," I informed him.

"That's Jason?" he responded in a surprised tone. "Is he mixed?"

"No, now come on and let's go," I replied.

I looked into Jamal's face and I could see that he was about to go into that stupid-ass "thug" transformation. Once he actually saw Jason, and how good-looking, tall, and nicely built he was I could the see insecurity coming out on his face.

"Yo, we can't leave without saying what's up. Know what I'm saying," he said in his J-Money voice.

Jamal walked over to Jason and tapped him on his shoulder.

"Jason, what's up? Nice to meet you. I'm Jamal . . . Charisse's man," He said.

Jason looked at me standing there a few feet away; he knew I was embarrassed, so he tried to make an awkward situation less awkward. He extended his hand to Jamal.

"Nice to meet you, man," he said. "Hey, Charisse, today must be Brooklyn day."

"All right, my nigga. I'm going to let you get back to the ladies. It's your world, pimp."

Jason just chuckled at him. "These are the cheerleaders from my school. The whole team is out here. It's a school trip," he said. "Enjoy your day and get home safe," he added before turning back around and making the basket to win a giant teddy bear. Jason walked over to me and handed it to me.

"That's the baby's first stuffed animal," he said.

Jamal was so heated he didn't know what to do. He stormed past me.

"Come on let's go," he said angrily.

Jamal was ready to go home now. He didn't say another word to me all the way to the car. I felt like fucking with him, so I sat the big teddy bear in the seat right behind him and put the safety belt on it so every time he looked in the rearview mirror, it would be looking back at him. We were almost back in New York, going over the Verrazano Bridge, when he finally said something.

"You ain't grown out of that light-skinned, curly-haired, pretty-boy shit yet, huh?" he said sarcastically.

"That's not even the *type* I like . . . obviously," I replied as I looked at his nappy-headed ass. "I told you Jason and I have been friends since kindergarten."

"He's going to UCLA right?" he asked.

"You know that where he's going. You were the one who showed me the article in the paper, remember."

"That muthafucka is going to be turning pussy away out there," he said. "I heard his game ain't all that though."

"I know. That's why, like, sixty colleges were recruiting him, cause he ain't all that," I responded sarcastically.

"You sound like your still on his shit," he snapped. "And I'm telling you now, I don't want none of them niggas around my kid."

"What niggas?" I asked. "What are you talking about?"

"Nothing, I'm just saying."

I had started getting a real bad headache and I didn't have the strength or desire to ask him what he was talking about. Besides I'm pretty sure he didn't know his damn self.

That night when I got home I really felt sick. I was light-headed and nauseous and went right to bed. My mother wasn't home, so I didn't want to take a chance on passing out or falling since I was by myself.

The next morning I tried to get up to go to the bathroom but I was so dizzy I couldn't stand up. My head was throbbing and my hands were trembling.

"Mom," I called out as I struggled to make it to her bedroom door. "Mom, I don't feel so good."

My mother looked in my face and helped me to sit on her bed. She called a cab and told the dispatcher we were going to St. Mary's Hospital before helping me get some clothes on and getting herself dressed. I remember hearing the cab's horn outside and walking out the door. The sunlight was unbearable. I had to close my eyes and let my mother guide to me to the cab. I was just praying to God that he didn't let anything happen to the baby, or to me. I asked Him to forgive me for anything I had ever done wrong. Here it was Sunday morning and I was praying to God; I couldn't help but wonder if I shouldn't have spent a few more Sundays that way, but in his house instead of mine.

When we arrived at St. Mary's, we went straight to the emergency room. They took me in immediately once they saw that I was pregnant. The doctor who examined me told us that my blood pressure was up so high I was in danger of having a massive stroke. I told her I had been out in the hot sun at Great Adventure all day, walking around.

"That's why children shouldn't have children," she said with an attitude. "Whatever hydration and fluids you have in your body are already being divided between you and the baby, and you think walking around in the heat is a good idea? How old are you?"

"Seventeen." I replied.

"You got it half right," she said. "You were exactly where you were supposed to be yesterday, just not the way you were supposed to be there."

Within twenty minutes I had a room. They had to keep it dark because they were afraid that even the light might trigger my blood pressure. My mother remained calm even though I know she was upset and wanted to write, *I told you so* across my forehead in permanent marker.

"Can you go try and call Jamal?" I asked my mother as she sat in my dark, quiet room.

I could almost hear her say in her mind, *Fuck Jamal, excuse me, Lord, I know it's Sunday, but I also know You know the muthafucka I'm talking about.* But she was being cooperative for my sake.

"Okay, I'll go call him now," she replied as she stood up and walked to the door. "I'll be right back."

"Mom."

"Yes, Charisse."

"Don't you need his phone number?"

My mother couldn't reach Jamal, or so she said. I couldn't do anything but lie there and try to sleep. Every so often I would hear my mother snoring, I didn't say anything, though; when I looked over at her I saw the face of a woman who was tired, very tired. She had spent the last seventeen years raising and supporting a child all by herself, scared to death that the cycle was going to continue.

That night when she left she kissed me goodbye and told me she would be back in the morning.

"Charisse, Ms. Blackmon knows you're pregnant. I think when you come home you should go talk to her. She's like family. How many times did she make it possible for me to go to work by keeping you, and she still looks out for you." she said.

"As soon as I get home. I love you, Mommy."

"I love you too, Reecie," she responded, almost in tears. She hadn't called me that in a long time. I can only imagine how she felt, knowing what kind of mother she was, having to leave her only child lying in a dark hospital room. She deserved better than this.

Later that night I started feeling really sick again. I rang the bell for the nurse to come in, and she took my blood pressure.

"All right, baby, just relax and close your eyes. Everything is going to be okay," she said, trying to sound calm. I knew something was really wrong. I wasn't in pain, but I was moving my mouth and no sound was coming out.

I remember looking around for my mother before feeling a pinch in my arm and blacking out. The next thing I knew I was waking up with a terrible taste in my dry mouth. I tried to sit up, but I was so sore I could hardly move.

"Don't try to get up, your stitches are still fresh," the nurse said with a deep West Indian accent as she walked in the now dimly lit room carrying a pitcher of water and a plastic cup. "You're still heavily sedated, but the baby is doing fine and your mother's on her way."

I knew I was drugged-up, but when she said, "The baby is doing fine," I was like, *I ain't the only one who's high*. She gave me a painkiller and a cup of water.

"What baby?"

"You had a girl, tree pounds and one ounce. She a feisty little ting." She added, "But relax, we'll take care of her. Your pressure is coming down nice."

Mariah Elise Butler was born on Monday, June 24, 1994, by cesarean section at 6:24 a.m. She was named after my new favorite singer, Mariah Carey, and my grandmother Elise McNeil, who died when I was ten. She was small, but she was a fighter. I always thought it was a sign from God that I wasn't due until August, but I ended up giving birth on the day of my high school graduation. Instead of walking across a stage at Brooklyn College getting my diploma, I was lying on my back getting a C-section.

I heard my mother almost fainted when she got to the hospital later that morning to discover she was a grandmother almost two months earlier than expected. But she fell in love with Mariah immediately. Whenever she talked about her she would refer to her as "my baby." I wouldn't actually get to see Mariah until later on that day when the doctors felt comfortable that my pressure had stabilized. The next day the nurse told me about the drama I missed when Jamal finally got to the hospital.

"Girl, it was the funniest ting I ever seen," she said. "The woman with the red hair . . ."

"That's my aunt Belle," I said.

"Girl, she was ready to whup some ass, me tought your little girl was gon' only have one parent."

"Huh?" I said, trying to decipher her words.

"She look like she gone kill him," she laughed. "But the big one with the Bible try and make her calm down."

"That's my aunt Ruby," I said.

"There was another one there too, I think her name was Della?"

"That's my other aunt. They're all my mother's sisters."

"Boy, she mess around and ask the man where was his folks, and how come they wasn't there," the nurse said with a hearty laugh. "He told her, 'cause they're home minding their business. You should try it."

I looked at her as if to say, "Please tell me you're joking, that fool didn't say that, to *that* crew."

"Girl, the Christian one with the Bible jumped up and said, oh no you didn't. Then the crazy one strike right in the back of the head . . . Bop! And them all jump on his ass. Tank God she a Christian, them could have beat him to the ground." She added, "Your mother sat right and watched the show and didn't say a word."

She went on to tell me that once he regained consciousness,

she took Jamal to the nursery to see Mariah. She was in an incubator, but he stood there for a long time watching her.

"That man really love his daughter, I can feel it," she said as she touched my hand. "That's one ting you're never going to have to worry about, me see it in his face."

When she said that I thought, *Maybe my mother was wrong, maybe everybody was wrong. The baby might bring Jamal and I closer together.*

The craziest feelings and emotions came over me when I saw Mariah for the first time. The walk from my room to the nursery seemed to take hours, everything around me was happening in slow motion. When I saw her lying in that incubator I burst into tears. She looked so small, frail, and helpless. The doctor and nurses kept reassuring me that she was only so small because she was premature and in no time at all she would put on the two pounds necessary to go home. They let me hold her and feed her for a few moments, but I couldn't wait to give her back to the nurse. I loved her to death, I kept thinking, *Oh shit, I'm responsible for a life, forever. I can't just do whatever I want, whenever I want anymore . . . and here I am just reaching the age when I would be able to do what I want, when I want.*

I went back to my room and sank into a depression. I wanted to close my eyes and when I opened them it would be a year earlier. I would be lying across my mother's bed watching *Martin* with her and laughing at him play Otis the old security guard, or Dragonfly Jones. But no matter how I tried, the antiseptic smell of the hospital and the soreness I felt kept bringing me right back into reality.

During the afternoon visiting hours all my aunts came

up to see me. They bought me magazines and candy. Aunt Della even smuggled in a Whopper with cheese and fries. When they left, Brenda surprised me with a visit, which really cheered me up.

"Damn, bitch, you always have to be first, don't you," she said as soon as she walked through the door.

"Don't make me laugh, girl, it hurts too much. You stole Dave's car again?" I asked.

"No, he's outside with an attitude," she replied.

"What did your ass do now?"

"I didn't do shit. His ex-wife found out he was living with a teenage girl who was pregnant, so she's taking him to court for child support," she said.

"I thought he was paying child support."

"No, he was paying *let me send what I have to spare* support. Some months that shit was three hundred, some months it was one hundred."

"Well, how did she find out?" I asked.

"I told her," she said straight out. "See, your man Dave decided it was time to start fucking with the next chick on the train with a fat ass and a school pass. I found a phone number in his pants . . ."

"*You* were doing the laundry?" I asked in shock.

"Hell fucking no, I was going through his pants," she stated. "Anyway, I called the number and this chick answered the phone. I played it like I was Dave's sister and found the number on the floor. She told me she met him on the train on her way to school," she explained.

"I know you cursed her out."

"Not at all. It's not her fault he's a lying muthafucka. He caught me out there the same way. I'm way too tired to be busting his punk ass, so I went through his shit . . . again, found the number, and dropped a dime on your man. His ex-wife is cool. She said the second you have that baby, go from the delivery room to the courtroom and get whatever's left after she gets finished."

"You really taking him to court?" I asked.

Brenda held up her hands like a surgeon.

"Ain't no ring on these fingers. Damn right I'm taking him to court. If you got any sense at all you'll do the same thing when you get out of here."

"Have you spoken to Nitra?" I asked.

"Yeah, I can't fuck with her too much. That bitch is just stupid for no reason. You know she's living with Cockroach in his uncle's basement. And I'm not talking about the one from *The Cosby Show*. . . . I heard she got a job at ShopRite and is giving her little paycheck to Runt-DMC."

"I hope she's all right," I said.

"Me too, but we got our own fucking problems," she said before walking over and kissing me on the forehead. "I'll see you soon. Let me walk down over and see my niece before I leave."

Brenda left, and for that brief period she was there I wasn't thinking about what my life had just become. I just couldn't believe it, Charisse Hawkins, queen of the fly chicks, smartest of the smart, coolest of the cool, and the bitch most likely to be the finest resident at St. Luke's Hospital one day . . . was a single parent at *seventeen*.

That night my mother came by the hospital. She had picked up my diploma from school and already had it framed.

"You'll be back home tomorrow," she said. "And my baby will be home soon too—she put on two ounces today," she added excitedly.

"I can't wait to go home and get in my bed," I replied.

I wasn't in any rush for Mariah to come home. At the hospital I knew she was being well taken care of and I was not looking forward to getting up in the middle of the night for feedings, shitty diapers, and crying, and I sensed that my mother couldn't wait for me to be knee-deep in Similac and baby poop.

Jamal came by to visit after my mother left. When he walked in the room he didn't even look the same to me. I turned up my lip and sneered at him. I swear on everything in this world he looked just like my vision of Satan.

"Hey, how you feeling?" he asked. "I just saw Mariah. She's a dime like her mother."

The nicer he tried to be to me, the more I wanted to throw up in his face. I was just praying that he didn't try to hug, kiss, or touch me in any way, so I didn't have to stab him in the Adam's apple with an IV needle.

"My mother and father are coming to see the baby tomorrow," he said.

"Great, her first Halloween," I replied, referring to his mother's mug piece.

"Halloween?"

"Nothing, a private joke," I said.

At that moment the nurse came in carrying a bouquet

of flowers. She handed them to me and smiled, before cutting her eyes at Jamal and leaving.

"Who the fuck are those from," he asked as his attitude changed.

"They ain't from you, are they . . . don't worry about it."

Jamal snatched the card that was attached and read it.

"I knew it was muthafuckin pretty Ricky," he said as he tossed the card on the bed.

The flowers were from Jason. The card said CONGRATULA-TIONS AND GOD BLESS.

"Let me find out I'm going to need a blood test," he said half jokingly.

"Jamal, go see *your* daughter and take your stupid ass home," I said before turning over and closing my eyes. Jamal Butler was the reason I was in this hospital, in this position. It was his fault. I made *love* to him, but he *screwed* me.

When Mariah finally came home a about a week later I wasn't prepared for the amount of time and effort it took to care for a newborn. I didn't know what to do when she started crying, and changing diapers is 100 percent uncut *bullshit*. If you can't go to the bathroom for yourself, then you might want to hold it until you can.

When she saw me getting frustrated my mother would always say, "Somebody had to change your shitty ass."

When I turned fourteen my mother trusted me to go outside by myself when she went to work. That year I couldn't wait for summertime. But this year, I spent the

Fourth of July in the house with Mariah's colicky little ass while my mother went to work and Jamal went to a cookout in Mount Vernon thrown by Heavy D. Mariah cried for two hours straight until she finally went to sleep. Then I cried for two hours straight until she woke up and picked up where she left off. I held her in my arms as I sat in the living room chair by the window and we both cried . . . just the two of us.

Chapter 10

June 1997

*B*y the summer of 1997 a lot of things had changed in the world. My two favorite rappers Tupac Shakur and the Notorious B.I.G. had gotten killed, and you couldn't turn on the radio without hearing a song from a Bad Boy artist. I also had a new favorite rapper named Jay-Z, who was from Brooklyn of course. My only two must-see TV shows, *Martin* and *Married with Children,* had been cancelled, but you couldn't turn on the TV without seeing *Seinfeld* or *Frasier,* and if you didn't own a pair of $125 DKNY sneakers and something by Versace and Christian Dior or Fendi, you obviously lived under a rock or your ass was dead broke, which really seemed strange because it was us broke people running out to buy that shit so we could out "floss" each other. The new hip-hop culture was taking over. In the mid eighties and early nineties it was all good to be *fresh*, but now you had to be *flossing* if you wanted to get noticed, especially if you were a guy. When I was nine or ten I distinctly remember my cousin coming over with his new Trans Am and all the young guys on my block breaking their necks to see that shit. It was black with a big-ass gold eagle on the hood. Now a guy wouldn't be caught dead driving that bullshit. Everything now was BMW, Lexus, Range Rover, or Mercedes. With the new rap music, whether you worked for UPS or the IRS, or your video was on BET, you had to dress and drive like a drug dealer to fit in. By 1997 *everybody* also had a "cellular" phone . . . whether they needed it or not. It was a fashion accessory for men and women, vital to flossing, but unlike your jewelry the smaller your phone was, the more money it probably cost.

Aunt Belle used to say, "You always know when *we* have a few dollars, because we're wearing it *or* driving it." Or she'd repeat her favorite joke about the white man who puts his dollar bill on a bar next to a black man's. "Hey, you look familiar. Have we before met before?" the black man's dollar asks. "Maybe—you look familiar too." The white man's dollars responds. "Where are you from?" The black man's dollar asks curiously. "Well, up until recently I was living in a savings account at the bank," the dollar replied. "No, we never would have met, I was renting a little drawer at the check cashing place and then he bought me here," the black dollar responded.

Three years passed in the blink of an eye. I began working as a teller at Chase Manhattan Bank in downtown Brooklyn when I turned eighteen. The pay was bullshit, but the hours were cool and I liked the people I worked with . . . most of them. Mariah was now three years old, and despite all the things my mother said about not babysitting when I was pregnant, she was a big help. Because she was born prematurely, Mariah was very small for her age. I would get pissed off when people would say, "Aw, she's a doll baby." and then ask "What is she, a year and a half, two?"

"Thank you, and she's three," I would reply with varying degree of attitude depending on which way the wind was blowing. I loved my daughter with everything I had. I provided for her, but my mother wanted me to be one of those have your child attached at the hip kind of mothers and that wasn't me.

Jamal and I had spent the last three years as an on again, off again couple. There were no real feelings left in the relationship on both of our part. But we were going through the typical young ghetto routine, where I was comfortable with his bullshit and the fact that he took care of his daughter. He didn't want me. He just didn't want me with anyone else. I guess I felt the same way too. But for me it was more out of fear. I was afraid if he really got into another chick it would affect his relationship with Mariah and potentially have an affect on my finances. I knew he had bitches on the side, but that's where he kept them. I even dated occasionally; the difference was I wasn't fucking nobody, no matter how fine they were or how they were balling. No, I was still giving the ass to him whenever I felt the itch that needed to be scratched. Meanwhile he was banging everything that moved and some shit that wasn't.

I guess I was afraid of the unknown, until one Friday Jamal showed me just how much respect he didn't have for me.

"Hey, woman!" I shouted to my mother when I walked through the door from work. "My dinner better be on the table!" I added jokingly.

Actually I had planned on taking my mother out to dinner at Red Lobster. Jamal was supposed to pick up Mariah that afternoon so that his mother could keep her overnight for the first time . . . ever. When I went in the kitchen Vivian McNeil was sitting at the table feeding Mariah in her high chair.

"I thought Jamal was picking her up by four o'clock?" I asked.

My mother just rolled her eyes at me.

"He called at about three-thirty and said his mother wasn't feeling good," she replied.

For the most part Jamal was a good father. I mean, every now and then he would be a little late with our agreed-upon child support, and at least once a month he was good for an "I'm on my way" and never show up, but overall I didn't have any real reason to beef about him as a dad. He did a great job of separating his relationship with Mariah from whatever we had between us. Ordinarily I would have just waited until he called then cursed him out, but I was feeling unusually confrontational. Once Mariah started to cry and scream, "I want my daddy, I want my daddy," that was it. I was so fucking heated that I couldn't wait to get in my 1993 Toyota Celica and drive out to Queens.

I hugged and kissed Mariah before going upstairs to change my clothes.

"Where are you going?" my mother asked when I came downstairs in my sweat suit and sneakers.

"I just have to run out for a second . . . I'll be back in an hour," I replied.

My mother stood in the kitchen doorway, holding Mariah, who was on her way to sleep.

"You can't change him, Charisse," she said as she looked at me with both compassion and sorrow. "Jamal is going to be Jamal, just like Jamal has always been Jamal. He's never going to be the way you want him to be, or the way you thought he would be, just like his mother isn't ever going to embrace this baby the way you want. You're angry with yourself because this story is playing out *just* like everybody said it would, and just like you had seen in this neighborhood a thousand times. You've always been special, Charisse. I knew when I held you as a little girl just like I'm holding her. I said to myself, *This child is destined for great things. . . .* Don't keep lowering yourself to his level. Let it go."

"All right, I just need to cool off for a few minutes. I'll be right back," I replied, before walking out the door.

I got in my car and decided I would surprise my mother by going to get food from Red Lobster on Queens Boulevard, a few blocks away from the Queens Center mall. It was payday, so maybe I would detour and make a stop there to treat myself, and the baby to a few things. The only thing I loved more than shopping for me was shopping for her. She was the best-dressed three-year-old in Brooklyn, and I had the receipts and credit card statements to prove it.

• • •

I don't know what possessed me to bypass the Queens Boulevard exit on the Jackie Robinson and take my ass out to the 188th Street exit on Grand Central Parkway, but I did. I pulled up in front of Jamal's house. His new 1998 Mitsubishi Diamante was in the driveway. I got out and rang the doorbell; Jamal came to the door with no shirt on.

"I thought you said you've been working out, you need to cover that up . . . for real," I said half jokingly.

That's was Jamal's cue to say something slick like, "You still want it," or to invite me to come in so we could fuck real quick before anybody got home. I knew from the fact that his car was the only one in the driveway that he was alone at home.

"Charisse . . . what are you doing here?" he asked with a strange look on his face. "Where's my daughter?"

"She's home with my mother. You know where she is 'cause you didn't go get her," I responded, sensing something was wrong.

"You can't just roll up over here without calling and shit . . . I'm about to get in the shower and head out," he said, trying to rush me away. "I'll get my daughter tomorrow."

I knew he had a bitch upstairs and I was heated.

"Well. I need to go upstairs and get my leather jacket out of your closet," I said.

"You mean the black one?" he asked.

"Yeah."

"The one I brought to your house a year and a half ago in the fall when muthafuckas actually wear leather," he said sarcastically. "Go home, Charisse."

I snatched Jamal's cell phone off his belt clip and threw it into the street. It broke into several pieces.

"What the hell is wrong with you, girl!" he shouted. "You lost your fucking mind?"

"Fuck you, Jamal!"

"You know what, whatever . . . I'll get another phone tomorrow," he said arrogantly. "You can stand out here all night with the muthafucking mosquitoes if you want," he added before going inside and closing the door.

I thought about busting his car windows, but I didn't want to end up at the local police precinct. Instead I just started yelling up at his window. Jamal and his family thought they were bourgeois niggas who thought they were above such behavior. He's the kind of cat who tosses garbage on the street on your block in the hood, but didn't want you dropping a gum wrapper on his.

"I hope you're fucking her good, Jamal! Or at least bought her some better earrings than them hollow pieces of shit you bought me, you little dick muthafucka!" I shouted. "Yeah, bitch, don't get gassed up by the nice house. That nigga is twenty-seven and still living in a room!" Jamal didn't even bother to respond. I started to feel really stupid standing there by myself. As I was getting into my car his mother pulled up into the driveway. She got out and looked directly at me with a smile on her face, and a second later another person got out the passenger's side. It was a Spanish-looking chick with long black hair who looked about my age in the face. My heart dropped. As much as I didn't want Jamal, as much as he annoyed me like nobody else could, and as much as I talked shit, when I saw her, I was really hurt. The fact that she was gorgeous didn't help either. I sat there for a moment watching them pull the bags out of the backseat. Jamal's mother looked over at me again and this time she added a wave with the smile. We hated each other so I didn't know what the fuck this bitch was cheesing about. Actually I did. Her fake-ass smile was her way of saying, look at my son's new woman, bitch. She's lighter, prettier, and that shit on her head that she keeps whipping around is actually coming out of *her* scalp.

I went home that night with a serious reality check. My ego had taken a big *L*. I always felt like, *Yeah, if I really wanted Jamal, I could have him, because I'm the baddest chick he's going to get*. And when you see your ex, or in my case your part-time ex, with a chick just as pretty, or prettier than you, that's some real shit to deal with as a woman.

"Did you clear your head?" my mother asked when I got back home.

"No, my stupid ass went to Queens and got my feelings hurt," I replied.

"What did she look like?" she asked.

"How did you know another chick was involved?"

"Because 99 percent of the time that's the cause of hurt feelings," she answered. "I told you to let it go. The only one who ultimately suffers in the type of foolishness you and Jamal are doing with each other is that baby sleeping upstairs. Trust me, I know."

"And to answer your other question, she looked like the girl from that *Money Train* movie, Jennifer Lopez," I said in disgust.

"Well, give him credit. If nothing else he's always had

good taste. Charisse, when is the last time you talked to Brenda? She's been on my mind lately."

"About two or three months ago. She was doing real good. She told me Tiana was big and getting into everything in the house."

"Was she working?"

"No, she's still in school . . . she goes to Manhattan College in the Bronx," I replied.

"Well, does she go to college in Manhattan or the Bronx?" she asked as though I had told her wrong.

"The school's name is Manhattan College, but it's in the Bronx."

"I thought you were going back to school . . . your job pays for part of it, right?"

"Soon," I answered.

"When is soon?" she persisted.

"Soon is later than right this second, but before never," I snapped. "Look, can you not start that tonight. I really am not in the mood," I said as I stormed upstairs. Mariah was lying in my mother's bed sleeping; I curled up next to her and kissed her on the forehead before turning on the television and falling asleep myself.

The next day Jamal called me early in the morning to say he was coming to pick up Mariah for the rest of the weekend.

"Don't have a whole bunch of bitches around my daughter," I said while thinking, *And that includes your mother.*

"Whatever, I'll be there in about an hour," he replied.

"What are you guys doing today?" I asked.

"Why?"

"So I know how to dress her . . . goddamn, just answer the question, stupid ass."

"Just put anything on her. We're taking her to the mall shopping before we go out anyway," he said.

I hung up the phone and put Mariah in the tub. It didn't really dawn on me that he had said, *"we're* taking her to the mall," until he called back. He said he would be there in fifteen minutes and I heard a female talking in the background.

"Who's that?" I asked.

"Niece," he replied without hesitation. "I'll see you in a few."

There was no fucking way I was letting Jamal come by here with some chick and catch me looking raggedy; I didn't give a fuck what time of day it was. I threw on a tight pair of jeans and a nice top that covered up the big ass CHARISSE tattoo on my breast. That shit was numero uno on my list of things I regretted doing. Actually it was like cuatro. Either way I'm sure his mother had told this bitch Jamal's baby mama was some ghetto chick and I didn't want to fit the stereotype. By the time Jamal honked the horn I was Puff Daddy video girl ready. When I bought Mariah out to the car I was shocked. The woman sitting in the front seat wasn't the same one I had seen at his house the day before. This chick was also light-skinned, but she was black, maybe from one of the Islands. She had long hair that I knew was at least partially a weave, and was even prettier than the other girl.

"Hey, Princess!" Jamal said as he took Mariah and hugged her. "Charisse, this is Niece. Niece, this is Charisse."

We exchanged cordial Hellos and kept it moving. Jamal placed Mariah in her car seat.

"I'll bring her back tomorrow evening . . . not too late," he said.

"Oh shit, I forgot her medicine in the refrigerator . . . hold on one second," I said before running in the house.

When Jamal walked over to the steps to get it from me I couldn't resist saying something smart.

"A different flavor for every day huh, playboy. You better not *ever* ask me for sex again," I said.

Jamal put his hands straight out in front of me as if to say, "I don't have no rings on."

"Charisse, no matter who you get with, no matter who you fuck, I was the first. I was the Little Richard, the Jack Johnson, the Jackie Robinson of that ass. The originator. Your man, your boyfriend, your muthafucking husband, will always think about that shit when they see me . . . understand."

"You trick-ass clown, go ahead with yourself, *Mr. Tramp.*"

I waved goodbye to Mariah and whatever her name was before going in the house and putting my nightgown back on. A few moments later the phone rang. It was Jamal calling.

"What time does she get her medicine again?" he asked.

"Two o'clock," I replied.

"No doubt. Do me a favor—can you call me and remind me, please?"

"Jamal, I'm going out. Tell your friend to remind you," I said.

He chuckled slightly.

"Please, you went in the house and took them clothes right back off, your ass ain't going no place. Call me at two."

"Kiss my ass, Jamal . . . for real."

I called Jamal at two and reminded him to give Mariah her medicine.

Chapter 11

*T*hat Monday when I went back to work I decided, *Two can play that game*. On an average day I would get at least five marriage proposals, three weekend trip offers, and one married man who wanted to pay all my bills and take me away from this life of deposit slips and ATM machines. I made a strict habit of ignoring the cornballs that came into the bank, muthafuckas standing at your window and grinning at you, trying to flash their fake-ass Rolexes or their car keys so you can see the Mercedes Benz logo.

Over the next week I decided that if a guy asked me out and he didn't look like a serial killer, I was more than happy to accept. The first guy I went out with was Jessie, a manager at Petland Discounts. He was tall and thin and always fucking smiling. This old-school throwback nigga would come in rocking a gold Mercedes piece on a rope chain. My nickname for him was Marty McFly because he was *Back to the Future* when it came to dressing. He had been asking me out to dinner for almost a year, but he wasn't pushy, so finally I said yes. The day before our date my coworker Erica and I had seen Jessie on Fulton Street going in to Jimmy Jazz trying to find something to wear.

"You got that nigga out here spending his whole check on an outfit to take you out, and he probably took out a loan from his credit union to pay for dinner," she said. "And you know your man ain't got a snowball's chance in hell to get past first base," she added.

"Whatever. When he was coming in there and I wouldn't give him the time of day you was screaming, "He's a nice guy—give him a chance," I responded. "Well . . ."

"You're not giving him a chance, you're giving him the business. He's about to pay for the sins of the father . . . your daughter's father that is."

The next day after work I waited outside the bank for Jessie to pick me up. I wanted the date to be over before it even started. I just needed an excuse. About ten minutes later a royal blue Mercedes 190E pulled up; this shit had to be twelve years old.

"Charisse, I apologize, I had to run into the city, and coming back traffic on the bridge was terrible," he said.

"You're eight minutes late. Just take me home okay," I responded with a nasty attitude.

This was what I called the Cosmetic Dating Stage. That's when you sabotage the date before it starts, but you still get to say you're dating.

The next guy I went out with was Lenny. Lenny was an EMS worker who was pushy as hell. He had that Napoleon syndrome shit hard, but he was nice. Every time he came in he would ask, "What you want me to bring you, Ma. I'll go to the store and get it." Erica used to say, "When he asks you what you want tell him a bag of M&M's, and when he ask you what kind, tell him the plain kind, the plain." Lenny's nickname was Ferris Bueller because he *never* took a day off.

Lenny took me to a baseball game. I was sitting there eating a hot dog when this really pretty white chick bumped into him.

"Excuse me, I am so sorry," she said to him with a big smile.

"No problem, love," he replied with an even bigger smile.

When she walked away I caught him looking at her ass out the corner of his eye.

"You want to give her my seat?" I asked.

"Who?" he asked.

"Just take me home," I replied.

"What! I paid a yard each for these seats. You must be out of your damn mind. I don't care if this is our first *and* last date, but I ain't taking you home now," he said.

"That's cool. Well, can I least have another hot dog and soda?" I asked nicely while caressing his bicep gently. "Damn, you work out?" I asked.

This midget's head swelled the fuck up like a helium balloon. He reached into her pants pocket and gave me a fifty-dollar bill.

"Can I bring you anything?" I asked.

"A beer and a pretzel," he answered like he always had it like that. I literally had to hold my breath not to laugh.

I walked right out of Shea Stadium and caught a cab back to Brooklyn. When Lenny came in the bank on Monday, I had his change from the cab in a white envelope.

I passed it to him through the glass at the teller window. He flipped me the bird and stormed out.

The last guy from the bank crew I went out with was named Preston, a.k.a. Steven Spielberg. Preston looked like a professional athlete, dressed great, spoke articulately, and was the kind of guy who held the door for women, and complimented everybody. I was really looking forward to this date.

Preston picked me up in a brand-new green Chevy Blazer that he told me he had just bought a few weeks ago. At the time, I didn't put much into the fact that his key chain said AVIS and that the shit had Florida plates. Maybe he had it registered there for insurance reasons and he had a friend who worked at Avis and had the mad keychain hookup.

"So, Preston, tell me about yourself?" I asked as we sat down to dinner at the Redeye Grill.

"Well, I graduated from Princeton with my BA in Social Sciences, I'm a Christian, and I'm a one-woman man," he said.

"Sounds like you have a lot going for yourself," I responded just before he earned the name Steven Spielberg.

"Thanks. Did I mention that I used to play in the NFL? Yeah I was a quarterback, but I quit to fight Evander Holyfield for the heavyweight title. A few weeks ago I had to change my cell phone number 'cause Oprah was blowing my shit up. Don't worry Charisse, what she and I had is over as far as I'm concerned. I bet you didn't know Oprah's Dominican, don't tell her I told you." This certifiably crazy, pathological, delusional, lying-ass muthafucka said. What was really scary was that I think he believed what was coming out of his mouth.

"Preston, what's your last name?" I asked.

"Cosby . . . Preston William Cosby."

That was my cue to get the fuck out of there. I excused myself to go to the ladies' room, and for the second time in three dates I found myself hailing a cab home.

There was one guy whom Brenda introduced me to named Nigel, who was cool. He was a nice-looking, light brown brother, husky, with a dark caesar and waves; he wore a goatee and drove a nice black Ford Explorer. He was just the right combination of street and book smart. I was sure he had his bullshit about him too, but on the surface he was the opposite of Jamal. Brenda had met him at a temp job and wanted to get with him, so she tried to hook us up because she knew he would like me, but wouldn't get but only so far, and by the time he got sick of my bullshit, she would have figured out how to get Dave's ass out of the picture so *she* could be with him.

Nigel and I had hung out a few times—nothing too serious though. He probably didn't notice it, but whenever I was with him I would find an excuse to call Jamal just to make sure he knew I was with another dude. I could go a week or two of being home every night with nothing to do, not even a phone call to Nigel, but the minute I was in the car with Jamal to take Mariah shopping or go to the doctor, I was dialing Nigel's house or cell number and wanted to know every detail of what was going on in his day.

One time I called Nigel without the "Jamal" angle and he invited me over to his house for dinner.

"I would take you out to dinner, but tonight is the draft, Princess," he said.

Nigel picked me up and took me back to his place in Bedford Stuyvesant. He had a really nice two-bedroom apartment, definitely a bachelor pad with all kinds of sports memorabilia, movie posters all over the place, big-screen TVs, and leather furniture. The house was immaculately clean. The kind of place that made you want to take your shoes off. I guess he figured if the shoes come off, the bra and panties wouldn't be too far behind.

"I already seasoned the meat and made the salad. You want to cook the steaks and bake the potatoes?" he asked in all seriousness.

"You didn't get the memo . . . me and the kitchen don't rock like that," I replied.

"I was just bullshitting with you . . . I could look at you and tell your ass don't cook nothing that don't say, 'Please allow to sit in the microwave two minutes before removing,'" he said.

"And proud of it," I stated.

Nigel threw down on that food, I really felt comfortable around this dude, and that made me *uncomfortable*.

"So what's the big deal about this draft? Who's getting drafted? What are they getting drafted for?" I asked as I sat down in front of the thirty-six-inch television in his living room.

"It's the NBA draft. . . . The Knicks got the seventh overall pick, and I'm trying to see where this one kid from Brooklyn gets picked," he explained.

I actually enjoyed watching the draft. It was fun watching

young black men become millionaires. I was just wondering who picked out the loud-ass suits they were wearing.

"Every time a player gets picked he gets up and hugs his mother," I said observantly. "Where are all the fathers at?" I asked.

"You're a single mother, you tell me," Nigel responded with the slightest tone of disdain in his voice.

The next five minutes were surreal. I was sitting there watching the draft when I saw it with my own eyes. The short white man in the conservative suit, who Nigel explained was the league commissioner, walked up to the podium like a presenter at the *Soul Train* awards.

"And with the ninth pick in the 2007 NBA draft, the New Jersey Nets select . . . Jason Tucker from UCLA."

Jason was sitting at a table with his mother, father, brother, and cousin. He stood up and embraced his parents. I could see his mother crying as he put on a NJ Nets basketball cap and walked up to the podium to shake the commissioner's hand. I couldn't believe it: There was *my* Jason, about to realize his dream. I saw myself sitting at that table and being the one he hugged when they called his name.

"Damn! The Nets took my dude at nine . . . cha ching! That's like a guaranteed three years at $1.5 million per, and that don't include the shoe deal, and other supplemental income and perks . . . I'm happy for that cat," he said.

"So what happens to him now?" I asked.

"My guess is he's going to party hard tonight, and tomorrow wake up and pinch himself, probably start looking for a condo in NJ, and a house for his people. I don't know him personally, but everybody always talks about what a good dude he is."

I didn't bother to mention that I had known Jason just about all my life, or that he had been in love with me just about all my life, but I had seen enough of the NBA draft for that night.

"Can we turn? Ain't there anything else on?" I asked with a sudden attitude.

"I thought you said it was cool," he replied.

"Yeah for thirty minutes, but I don't want to sit here for three hours watching it."

Nigel just looked at me with a sour expression.

"All right, put on what you want to see," he said as he handed me the remote. "I'll go in the bedroom and watch the draft."

"I didn't come over here to watch television in here by myself. I can do that at home," I barked.

Nigel came and sat back down on the sofa next to me while I flicked through channels. I stopped at HBO. *Ghost* had just come on.

"Oh for the love of Jesus, not this sappy bullshit!" Nigel said as he buried his face in the palms of his hand. "The muthafucka is dead. Whether he tries to contact the bitch or not, he's out, gone, see you later, not coming back, so what the fuck is the point?"

"You don't have any sensitivity . . . just like a man," I said.

"Shit, I got more sensitivity than Ralph Tresvant," he replied as he slid a little closer to me and gently squeezed my thigh.

"Well, you and your sensitivity can keep your hands to yourself," I replied as I took his hand and placed it on his thigh.

"Oh, here we go, playing that hard-to-get shit . . . all right, I'll go along with the game."

"Nigel, your chances of getting some ass tonight are the same as Patrick Swayze in that movie: dead and stinking," I responded before pretending to be Teddy Pendergrass and singing in a deep voice, "I think I'd better let it go, looks like another love T.K.O."

After a couple of hours of sitting there watching TV while he cleaned up the kitchen, paid his bills, and ironed his clothes for work, Nigel decided it was time to take me home. When we got in his car he was in a surprisingly good mood.

"Thanks for dinner," I said.

"No doubt, my pleasure, thanks for coming," he replied. "Can you do me a favor though?" he asked.

"What?"

"Can you not call me anymore until you get all that bullshit out your system," he requested calmly.

"What bullshit?" I asked defensively. " 'Cause you didn't get no sex, I'm on some bullshit . . . yeah, all right, whatever."

"It doesn't have anything to do with sex. You think everybody is stupid but you," he stated. "Come on, Charisse. Now you're disrespecting me and practically calling me a herb. You think I didn't notice that whenever you called me you were with your daughter's father, talking all that I miss you, and how was work today nonsense, but when I call you back later to see what's up, you either don't answer the phone, or you're going bowling with your coworkers," he said, almost laughing. "You might not be sexing Homeboy anymore, but mentally that nigga got you fucked up in the head. I *promise* you he's fucking and having real relationships with chicks, but your ass is on some 'I'm not letting anybody in shit.' You don't even know why you're not, you're just not." He added, "And one more thing, the same way I know your little calls are a stunt, that nigga knows it too . . . and when he's sitting there he might not say shit, but he's thinking, *I got her mentally institutionalized, she's scared to let go 'cause she don't know what the world outside of that bullshit relationship we had is like.*"

I looked out the window and remained that way until he pulled up in front of my house. I couldn't look Nigel in his face. I felt like he had undressed me and I was naked. It was like he could see my thoughts with nothing to hide them behind. I didn't even say, "Good night." I got out. He pulled out.

When I got to the top of my steps I looked down the block and saw all the commotion in front of Jason's house. I thought for a moment about walking down there to tell him congratulations and wish him my best, but I was worried that he would look at me like some kind of groupie or as if I was there to say, "Hey, Jason, I'm available now . . . call me." I kept hearing Nigel's words in my head. I looked in the bathroom mirror. Tears started to run down my face. Charisse Hawkins had really made some fucked-up decisions in her life that were becoming harder and harder to accept, or excuse as being "young and dumb."

Chapter 12

My mother called me at work one day to tell that Mariah wasn't feeling well, that she was listless and didn't have much of an appetite. I wasn't overly concerned, Mariah was always small and a little frail because she was premature, but she didn't have any apparent health problems. When I got home she was lying down on the sofa. There were two things I could count on in my day: At least one customer would make me go back on my *I'm not cursing anymore* resolution, and my daughter would lose her mind with excitement when I walked through the door. But this day only one of those things happened.

I called Jamal's mother to ask her what she thought I could give her; she didn't seem to have a fever or a cold.

"Take that baby to the emergency room," she said. "That don't even sound like my granddaughter."

The more time Mariah had spent with her father, the more attached her other grandparents became to her. They were *great* to her. I guess once his mother saw that her son and I weren't going to be together, she felt like it was okay to be nice to me.

My mother and I took Mariah to Kings County Hospital for what we figured was an ear infection or something like that. I even told Jamal it wasn't necessary for him to meet us there when he called me.

One hour turned to three, then four.

"Ma, something just doesn't feel right," I said nervously.

"Everything is going to be fine, Charisse," she replied as she took my hand. I could tell she was just as worried as I was. "That baby is fine."

The doctor came out and sat next to us. Her face was expressionless, so I didn't have any idea what she was going to say, but I felt something was definitely wrong.

"There seems to be something irregular with Mariah's heartbeat. Now, before you get frantic, let me just say that it could be something as simple as atrial fibrillation, or an arrhythmia of the heart."

"Oh my God!" my mother shouted. "She got that bullshit from her father's side of the family. We'll take credit for the thin hair, but we don't have bad tickers," she explained.

"Doctor, is my baby going to be all right?" I asked nervously.

"We're going to run some tests. I'm already arranging for her to get a room," she said. "Mommy, there'll be a bed in there for you of course."

I felt sick to my stomach, and as much as the doctor was trying to be nonchalant and play it like they were just being precautionary, my mother and me weren't buying it. The first thing I did was to call Jamal. He broke down on the phone. I think it's human nature for people to react that way when you hear the words "heart" and "something's wrong" in the same sentence, and that shit is multiplied by ten when it's about a loved one.

Jamal got to the hospital about an hour later with Niece. By that time they had put us in a holding room with Mariah, waiting until her actual room was ready. I was like, *What the fuck did he bring this bitch for?* This was *our* daughter in the hospital. This was a time for the two of us to deal with things. I was already in a bad mood and edgy because of the uncertainty of Mariah's situation, and this was the spark I needed to let out some frustration.

"Jamal, can I talk to you for a second . . . alone," I said with a scowl on my face.

I walked outside the small room past Niece without speaking. Jamal had that look on his face like, *Here we go, Doctor muthafucking Attitude is about to give me a private consultation.*

"Jamal, what the fuck is she doing here?" I asked as soon as we were out of earshot.

"Niece's here because she was with me when you called, and because she's concerned about my daughter," he replied.

"We don't need her concern. Let her be concerned for her own fucking daughter when she has one."

"Charisse, is this really the time for this bullshit? I just want to know what's wrong with Mariah," he said.

"Don't tell me shit!" I snapped as my voice began to get louder. "I wouldn't be standing here wondering what the fuck is wrong with my child. I'd be about to graduate and get a job working in this bitch."

"Oh, now it's my fault, is it?" he barked. "I told you not to have a baby in the first place, stupid ass!"

Without thinking I slapped the shit out of Jamal. I know he wanted to deck me. I could see the anger in his eyes, but he just shook his head and walked away. My mother came flying around the corner.

"What the hell is going on? Everybody in the goddamn hospital heard you!"

"Nothing is going on!"

"I heard you, Charisse. I told you before to let it go. *You* made your own bed, so don't be mad at Jamal, that woman he's with, or me if the sheets don't feel good," she added.

My mother went back to Mariah's room. I stood there for a moment, too embarrassed to go into my own daughter's room. It turns out Niece had asked Jamal to stop on Austin Street so that she could buy Mariah a stuffed Minnie Mouse. That toy was the only thing that kept her calm as the nurses continued to draw blood from her and try and examine a frightened three-year-old.

I found it damn near impossible to sleep that night. I kept getting up to check on Mariah and making sure she was okay. When I finally managed to get comfortable on the stretcher with a pillow they gave me, Mariah was just waking up and Jamal was already sitting in the room, reading the newspaper.

"Damn, you ain't no Halle Berry when you wake up in the morning, that's for damn sure," Jamal said.

"And you ain't no Wayans brother no matter what time of the day it is," I replied with a smile.

Jamal laughed. "Can I at least be a Jackson?" he asked

jokingly. "Anyone but Jermaine—that nigga's haircut is fucked-up, and he *can* take that personal."

It felt good to laugh with Jamal. I can't remember the last time we did that. It also lightened the mood and Mariah appeared to wake up in a great mood. It was going to be a great day.

A few seconds later another doctor came into the room. It was an young Asian doctor who was unusually tall, with dark hair and horn-rimmed glasses. I know it's a stereotype that all Asian people are short, like all black people are criminals and all Jewish people are cheap, but this man was like six-five. A nurse came in a few seconds later,

"Good morning. My name is Doctor Chang. I'm the chief cardiologist here at the hospital, Mr. and Mrs. Butler."

"Whoa, Doc . . . I'm Jamal Butler, Mariah's dad, and this is Charisse Hawkins, Mariah's mom. We're more of a Mister and Miss, feel me?"

The doctor gave Jamal a slight smirk and nodded his head.

"And you must be Mariah. Aren't you a beautiful little princess," He said. "How would you like to go get some balloons with the nice nurse."

The nurse picked up Mariah and carried her out of the room. Jamal and I sat down.

"The results of the MRI came back. Your daughter has a congenital heart defect, and it's something she was born with . . ." he said.

"What the fuck is that?" I asked hysterically.

"Are you saying my . . . our daughter has a hole in her heart," Jamal said as the doctor looked at him in surprise.

"My mother is the head nurse at Queens Hospital," he added.

"That's exactly what it is," the doctor replied. "It makes things much easier for the parents when they have some understanding of the problem, and ultimately about the surgery."

"Surgery!" we both shouted at the same time.

"Yes, the hole is large enough where we feel it needs to be closed."

I'm sure it wasn't intentional and he was just being himself, but the doctor was so blunt, direct, and emotionless. I couldn't stop crying and my first thought was, *Is God punishing me for making a choice I knew I probably shouldn't have?* Praying was something my mother had always encouraged me to do everyday. "And praying should include giving thanks, not just asking for things," she would say.

"God, please make everything all right with Mariah," I cried.

Jamal just sat there. Where my emotions revealed themselves in tears, his began to show as anger.

"What the fuck! Goddamn!" he yelled as he pounded his fist into the palm of his hand.

"This is not something that has to be done today, or even next week. I know this is a lot to digest. Just so you know, while no open-heart surgery is minor, I assure you this surgery certainly isn't uncommon."

We sat in that room crying for fifteen minutes until the nurse came back with Mariah. When she walked through that door Jamal grabbed her up and held her tight before handing her to me, and I hugged her hard.

Jamal and I decided to take Mariah to Queens Hospital for a second opinion, where his mother basically ran the place. We were sure she would get the best treatment no matter what the circumstances were. The diagnosis was exactly the same as Dr. Chang's, and they referred to us New York Presbyterian, the number one cardiology hospital in the city. The specialist there told us that the operation could wait until the new year. They wanted her to enjoy the holidays. Even though I never said a word because I didn't want to put it out to the universe, I couldn't help but wonder if what he was trying to tell us was, *Let her enjoy this Christmas because there may not be a next one for her.*

After Mariah's condition briefly brought us together, things between Jamal and I went from bad to worse. There was so much underlying tension and stress between us that one day it all came to a head at my house. Jamal was coming over to see Mariah, and I asked him if he didn't mind picking up some Kentucky Fried Chicken.

"I don't have any extra money," he complained.

"I'll give it back to you when you get here . . . damn," I snapped back.

When Jamal got to my house he had a big ass bucket of *Kansas* Fried Chicken. The shit we called "Dirty Chicken." Not because the food wasn't clean, but the restaurants were always located on a dirty block in the hood.

"Jamal, I asked you to pick up *Kentucky* Fried Chicken . . ." I said.

"Kentucky, Kansas, Texas. What the fuck, it's all fried chicken, right?" he replied. "I hope you don't feed this greasy shit to my daughter every day. This ain't nothing but fried cholesterol. Your ass needs to learn how to cook healthy. Every time I come in this house it smells like pig feet and cornbread."

"Why don't you stop talking in riddles, Jamal? Be a man and say what you really want to say, bitch."

"All right . . . all right. . . . You know, maybe if you and your country kitchen chef mother wasn't always in here eating muthafucking salt loafs, stroke salads, and fried butter my daughter wouldn't have that problem. I'm surprised she doesn't have hypertension."

"So now it's my mother's fault?" I asked angrily.

"I didn't say it was all her fault, but Aunt Jemima sure didn't help."

When he called my mother Aunt Jemima I wanted to laugh. She damn sure was a pancake-making ass, and was quick to tie a scarf around her head.

"Oh, and it couldn't have come from your little shriveled-up, sickly-looking, always-wheezing-and-huffing-ass mother, huh? How the fuck are you in your fifties and weigh sixty-four pounds? Looking all drawn up like a knot . . . she ain't no head nurse because she loves medicine. That bitch ain't trying to be too far from that IV and oxygen in case her scrawny ass passes out," I said.

"My mother's not sickly . . . she's anemic," he defended angrily.

"You mean anorexic . . . fucking skeleton."

"Well, you know, not everybody is blessed to be a size 28 wide like that quartet of Weather Girls in your family," he shot back.

I don't how we got from chicken to insulting each

other's mother, but we did. I handed him a twenty-dollar bill.

"Take the money, take yourself upstairs to see your daughter, then take your ass home."

As if things weren't stressful enough dealing with issues at home, my manager at work was getting on my fucking nerves. This lazy muthafucka didn't want to do shit but just delegated his responsibilities to everybody else. Mohammad Shahiri was the next person to realize that fucking with me wasn't a good look.

"Charisse, the ATM machines need refilling," he said as soon as I walked in the door. "I thought you were coming in at ten-thirty?"

"It's ten-thirty-five, Mohammad . . . I'll deduct five minutes from my lunch," I replied.

"Charisse, between you and I . . ." he said as he looked around like a rat looking for cheese. "Some of your coworkers have been complaining about the number of personal phone calls you've been getting. Now we all know and understand the situation with your daughter, but we all have problems," he said.

I tried to my best to ignore him all day, but he kept picking at me.

"Charisse, can you help Olivia with the signature cards? Charisse, I need you back on the windows, the lines are getting long."

Basically, the deal was that Mohammad was an Egyptian black man whose biggest wish was to be white. In his mind, because his college diploma said Cornell, he wasn't really black; he was just a white man with a permanent tan. He treated the black and Hispanic employees a little differently than white employees. We were the "tellers," the high-school-diploma-having single mothers still living at home with their single mothers, Jimmy Jazz shopping, front line employees of the banking business. The "bankers, managers, and salespeople" were primarily white; they had set lunch hours, bonuses, desks, and their own phone lines.

Some weeks prior to this I had applied for a position as a sales and service associate, which is the next step up from teller. It would mean added responsibility, but it would also mean making more money, and it would put me in a position to apply for a job as assistant branch manager down the line. Mohammad called me into his office. The district manager, Brooks Josephs, and another woman named Sharon Levin from HR were already inside sitting down.

"Sit down Charisse . . . take a load off," he said, trying to sound magnanimous. "Let me just start by saying Charisse is in perpetual motion around here. Sometimes we look at each other and let out a deep breath because *we* are working so hard," he said with a straight face.

I looked at this shiftless muthafucka in disbelief.

"Charisse, Brooks, and Sharon are here today about your application for the SSA position," he explained.

"You've been with us for more than two years now Charisse," Brooks said. "You're a great teller, you know your job, and you're hardworking . . . we appreciate that, and we don't take you for granted . . . and I'm very sorry to hear that your daughter is ill."

"Brooks and I were ready to approve your promotion,

but Mohammad here has some concerns about your attendance, punctuality, and phone use lately," Sharon said.

I wanted to cut this muthafucka's throat. I really thought about getting some of the goons I still spoke to in my neighborhood to beat the shit out of this stick-head bastard.

"Charisse, I'm not trying to punish you. I just know you're capable of much better, and it's not fair to Jose, who is here every day on time."

"Jose . . . he's been here less than a year, and the only reason I've been late or out lately was because of the situation with Mariah," I said.

I was so angry on the inside I wanted to cry, but I would *never* give him that satisfaction.

"We understand that, but as the manager I've got to do what's best for the branch. I'm sure when another opportunity becomes available, you'll be ready," he said.

I walked out of the room without saying a word to anybody. It was on now. If he wanted to act like a bitch and get down and dirty, I was more than willing to participate.

Ninety-nine percent of the people who worked in the branch suspected that even though Mohammad was married and had a beautiful wife named Teresa, that he was playing hide and go seek my johnson in your butt cheeks with Jose. I represented the 1 percent who didn't suspect it, but knew it for a fact. See, Jose had a big mouth and would get insanely jealous when Mohammad's wife called the bank. One night I stayed late with Jose because he had a huge difference in his cash box, which meant his receipts were all fucked-up. After I helped him find the problem we went for drinks at a bar on South Oxford and Fulton. Three Long Island iced teas later, Jose let his hair down and became "Miss Thing."

"So Miss Thing, what's up with your boy?" I asked coyly. "Mohammad sure has a nice body," I added as I threw up in the back of my throat.

"I know you are not even thinking about fucking him," he responded. "He is already fucking one bitch, his wife, and if it was up to me, she'd get the boot too."

"Why, you get trying to get you a little piece?" I said in an attempt to get an admission.

"Trying . . . please. Me and his dick *been* on a first-name basis for a while now, girl."

"Yeah, right," I replied. "Stop lying."

"You think I'm lying?" he slurred before reaching into his pocket. "Feast your eyes, bitch." Jose pulled out some compromising photos of Mohammad and him in a hotel room. He was so drunk I slid two of them in my pocket. I didn't have any plans to use them for blackmail or anything like that; I just wanted to show them to my mother so we would have something to talk about.

I was going to give Mohammad one more chance to be minimally fair, or at least make me feel like it wasn't personal.

"Mohammad, I haven't had a scheduled Saturday off in more than two months," I said.

"Well, that hasn't stopped you from taking one," he replied half jokingly, but laced with sarcasm.

"Well, I'd like this Saturday off please . . . it's important," I asked humbly.

"Hmmm. I would love to give you this Saturday off, Charisse . . ."

"But . . ."

"But I won't have enough tellers if I give you the day off."

"You're sure," I replied with a cryptic smile on my face.

"I'm sorry," he said as he nodded his head yes.

I walked away on some real cutthroat shit. He was going to have to pay for everybody I had a problem with.

The following Wednesday started out like any other day. The bank was full of customers and Mohammad was flirting with Jose on the down low. All of a sudden we heard someone yelling. Everyone in the bank turned around.

"I'll kill, you Muthafucka!" the attractive woman was yelling. "Where the fuck is that faggot! I'll kill him!"

It was Teresa. She was standing in the middle of the lobby, waving the two photos of Mohammad and Jose in the air with her arms flailing. Mohammad came out to the teller area.

"There you go! Bring your ass out here . . . you want to be kissing and hugging men, then coming home and fucking me, you nasty bastard? Oh hell no!"

I was standing at my window, wishing I had a tub of hot buttered popcorn so I could watch the show. All transactions ceased and every eye in Chase was on Mohammad and Teresa. Jose surfaced from downstairs in the basement, I guess, because he must have heard all the commotion. Teresa really went off.

"This is a fucking office affair! You two homos work together!" she ranted. "Bring your ass out here from behind that glass."

Teresa reached into her purse and pulled out the pair of biggest scissors I ever saw. Mohammad and Jose were shitting twenty-dollar bricks.

"You're not man enough to come out here," she said to her husband before turning to the customers on line. "That is the man who manages the bank where you keep your hard-earned money. A fucking, lying, cheating, dick-sucking pathetic excuse for man . . . and to the men in here, I'd think twice about shaking his hand. You *know* exactly where it's been."

Teresa walked out the door, leaving everybody in shock. You'd thought a robbery had just taken place. In a way I guess it did, because Teresa walked in and left with her husband's manhood and pride. The next day HR and Brooks Joseph took his job away. I felt kind of bad for Jose. He was so drunk that night he didn't even remember showing me the photos. Fuck it, in any war there are bound to be a few casualties. It was ironic though, after all that talk about his degree from Cornell and traveling abroad, by the time his wife put him out and filed for divorce, Mohammad was living back at home with his parents, just like us tellers . . . ain't that a bitch? That night when I got home I didn't feel any sense of joy or victory. I didn't even look at myself in the mirror. I asked God to forgive me for being so devious and mean.

Within the next two weeks we had a new branch manager named Carlos. Cool as all hell. Within three weeks I also had my promotion to SSA.

• • •

By the time the Christmas Holidays rolled around I had started to get nervous, Mariah's surgery was scheduled for January 5, and that shit was coming too fast for my taste.

On Christmas Eve I ran out on my lunch break to pick up a few remaining items on my list. Against my better judgment I bought Jamal a nice shirt and a pair of leather gloves from his daughter, a gesture I was sure would not be reciprocated. I was lucky if I got a "Ho, ho, ho, merry Christmas, bitch" from Jamal at this point. Christmas always had a way of making me happy, so when I got back to the branch I was in a great mood; even the customers were cool, and the $400 in tips I got from customers didn't hurt.

I had just finished up a transaction with someone, when a black woman approached my window. She was wearing dark shades and a wig; she was ashy-looking, like a drug addict, judging from her thin and frail body. There was something familiar about her. The woman passed me a check for $9,000 made out to an Edith Goldberg with a Park Avenue address. I was like, *Damn, it's Christmas Eve, and here she comes with a stolen check that she probably murdered some old Jewish lady for, and I'm going to spend the evening at One Police Plaza filling out reports after I call the cops.*

"Miss Goldberg," I said as she continued looking straight down, "Miss Goldberg," I repeated a little louder before tapping on the Plexiglas window to get her attention.

"May I see your ID, please?" I asked.

"Uh, I think I left it home," she mumbled.

"May I have your address?"

"Just give me my check back," she replied.

When she lifted her head slightly and opened her mouth I noticed a gold tooth in the front of her mouth. *I know that mouth,* I thought to myself.

"Nitra."

She looked up and removed her sunglasses. Her eyes were glazed and she was in shock. I hadn't seen or spoken to her in years.

"Charisse . . . is that you?" she asked. "Oh my God."

She turned around and ran out of the bank. I grabbed my jacket and followed her. Fortunately there were no others customers in line at the time. When I got outside and looked around, I saw her leaning against a building, hunched over. Nitra couldn't make it ten feet without nearly collapsing. I walked over to her and she began to cry.

"Charisse, go away, please . . . I don't want you to see me like this," she said as people walked by and watched us curiously. It was freezing outside, and all she had on was a paper-thin, filthy beige trench coat that was too small.

"Nitra, what the fuck happened? What happened to you?" I asked.

"I got on that shit. Nice got a bitch strung out on that smack. I'm all right though," she said through the tears.

"No, you're not, out here on Christmas Eve trying to cash bad checks. Your ass will end up in jail," I said.

"I've been locked up twice in the past two years," she informed me. "Muthafuckas at child welfare put my son in foster care, but I'm going to get him back when I get my shit together."

"Where's Nice?" I asked, hoping she would reply, "Dead." God forgive me for wishing that on anyone.

"He lives with this Spanish bitch out in Linden Plaza. I saw him one day and asked him for five dollars and he spit on me. He won't even fuck with his own son."

"Look, I have to get back inside, but here's twenty dollars. You remember where I live, right?"

"Yeah, bitch, I'm a drug addict, not a fucking amnesiac."

"Well, you come spend Christmas with us, take a cab, take the train, my moms is cooking so you know what time it is."

"Okay . . . I'll be there," she replied as her eyes lit up when she touched the money.

Nitra clutched that bill like it was gold. Her limp, energy-less body suddenly straightened up. She hugged me and kissed me goodbye.

"It was great seeing you, Charisse," she said before walking away.

I knew from the way she said goodbye that Nitra wasn't going to show up at my house later. I stood there and watched her as she blended into the crowd. It was like she just faded away. I had shed a lot of tears for myself and for my daughter in recent times, but now I was shedding tears for my friend.

Chapter 13

$\mathcal{M}$ariah had open-heart surgery on the morning of January 5, 1998. Six hours of pure hell. My family and I sat in the waiting room with Jamal and his parents for the entire time, mainly in tense silence, with an occasional prayer or the reading of an appropriate scripture by Aunt Ruby. The operation went well, but it was torture to watch Mariah with all the tubes and machines hooked up to her little body. The stress and uncertainty of the operation seemed to galvanize Jamal and I; he was really strong during everything, and was there for Mariah and I 24/7. I'm not sure if it was the vulnerability or helplessness I was feeling, but I started feeling like maybe we could make things work, especially for Mariah's sake. The problem was Jamal wasn't single, he and Niece were together.

"So, how are things with you and Niece?" I asked him out of the blue as we sat in Mariah's room the day after the surgery.

"Good. She held a brother down through this whole shit. Niece is good people," he replied.

That didn't sound like a man who was madly in love with a woman. It was more like he was describing a good friend, or maybe that's just what I wanted to hear.

"When people are there for you when you need them, you have to respect that," he added.

This was a different Jamal than I had come to know over the last few years. He seemed humble and sincere. He was also working two jobs and back in night school taking classes toward his master's degree.

"So what about you? I know dudes are knocking on your door all day every day," he said.

"Yeah, well, they must be disguising themselves as mailmen and Jehovah's Witnesses," I answered.

"Oh yeah, I see your friend Jason is doing his thing with the Nets. He might mess around and win rookie of the year . . . I'm happy for that cat."

"I wouldn't know. I don't watch basketball and I haven't spoken to him in a while," I said.

Jamal just nodded his head to acknowledge my response; he didn't seem to be gloating or trying to rub anything in. I was really like, *Who the fuck is this cool-ass dude and what did he do with my daughter's father?*

My mother sensed that I was allowing myself to develop feeling for Jason again from the way I started speaking about him, or defending him whenever anyone in my family said something negative about him.

"Charisse, I don't know what's going on between you and Jamal, if anything is happening, but all I'm going to say is, 'First time shame on him, second time shame on you.'"

After we got Mariah home and situated, my mother

watched her while Jamal and I went out shopping for all the things Mariah needed at that time. It was freezing that day, maybe 15 degrees, but the sun was shining bright as we drove down Eastern Parkway. The sense of relief we both felt was evident. Mariah wasn't totally out of the woods, but she had come through a difficult surgery with flying colors, and the prognosis was excellent. Jamal placed his hand on top of mine as I looked out the window at the beautiful brick building along the leafless tree lined streets. We went into the city and took care of everything for Mariah. I felt good knowing that my mother would be home with her during the day while I was at work, but I needed to get everything she needed because obviously she wouldn't be able to go outside for quite a while.

"You're a trooper, Charisse. Thanks for taking good care of my daughter, and I'm sorry for everything I put you through," he said sincerely.

"Jamal, I have to give you props. I couldn't have made it through this shit alone. I mean, my mother is incredible, but I really appreciate you," I replied.

"I know you're probably going to tell me to mind my fucking business, but now might be a good time to reach out to your father. Life's too short to stay mad; even if you see him and curse his ass out, at least you made peace with all that shit you're suppressing."

"All right, Frasier . . . my father is not a subject I want to get into today," I replied.

"Is it just me, or does Mariah seem a little different?"

"Different how?"

"I know she just had a big operation and it takes time

to recover, but she just be staring off into space on some real *Twilight Zone* shit . . . what fucking part of post-op is that?"

I had noticed it as well but didn't want to say anything. Prior to this whole thing Mariah was an alert, sharp, attentive little girl. Now, just as Jamal said, she would just zone the fuck out when you're talking to her. You could almost see the lights go off when you were talking to her sometimes. I just chalked it up to her body still adjusting to the surgery.

"She'll be fine. It's just the trauma of what she went through . . . ask your mother," I said.

"I did," he responded. "She said that's not a usual side effect."

"Look, Mariah is fine, okay?!" I snapped.

Jamal knew he had hit a nerve so he just backed off.

The next day when I went back to work I must have called the house twenty times. It got to the point where my mother would just answer the phone, "Hello, Charisse, Mariah's fine," before hanging right up.

That Thursday night when I got home we were having dinner at the table. Mariah was in her high chair eating and we put a television in the dining room to keep her occupied because she *hated* that chair with a passion. We were sitting there talking when out of nowhere Mariah took her plastic dish and hurled it at my mother. She didn't scream or cry, she just had that glazed look in her eyes.

"What's wrong, baby?" I asked as I got up and walked over to her. "Let Mommy get you out of that seat."

As soon as I touched her she began to scream at the top

of her lungs. She wouldn't stop. I got so frustrated that I began to scream and cry.

"What's wrong with you! Stop it! Stop crying . . . no one is hurting you!" I yelled at her.

My mother grabbed me and pulled me away. She knew the stress and frustration of the past four years or so had reached its breaking point. I felt like I was having a nervous breakdown.

"Charisse, go upstairs and lie down, I'll take care of her. You won't be any good to her or anybody else if your ass ends up in a straitjacket," she said.

I went upstairs to take a warm bath and relax. For whatever reason, my mother was able to get Mariah to calm down immediately. She bought her upstairs and put her in the bed to watch television before knocking on the bathroom door and coming in.

"Charisse, why don't you go out after work with some of your friends and have some fun. You're a beautiful young woman—you need some kind of social life," she said.

"Maybe I will. We can go right to Uno's or BBQ's in the Village."

The next day when I got to work I found out that most people who have a life don't wait until Friday to make plans. Fuck it, there was always Blockbuster and the Chinese restaurant. About an hour before I was getting off I got a phone call from Jamal. He wanted to know if Mariah needed anything.

"No, but she had an episode last night . . . she got that distant look on her face and then she just started to wild out," I replied.

"See, I told you something is off. We have to take her to have that shit checked out," he said. "You going to be home tonight? I'll call you."

"Well, I was going out after work, but my friends all have places to go and people to see."

"Why don't I pick you up, we'll grab a bite, then I'll take you home and I can stop in and spend some time my daughter," he suggested.

My first thought was, *If he's free on a Friday night, then Niece must be either cut off or in the friend zone.* Either way I was glad he was picking me up. When I walked out of the bank, the car was parked right outside. I saw the girls I work with all watching. It felt good. It was like being picked up from school in the white 4Runner all over again.

"So what do you have a taste for," I asked.

Jamal looked at my breasts and thighs real suggestively before answering.

"I could eat whatever . . . feel me?" he replied. "What do you feel like having?"

We ended up driving into the city. I wanted to eat at Jezebel's soul food restaurant on Ninth Avenue, but Jamal insisted on the Motown Café on 57th Street. I had eaten there before and while the music and atmosphere were fly, the food sucked.

I loved NYC in the winter, especially Midtown. The rich bitches would be wearing the sick high boots and coats, *none* of which you could find on Fulton Street.

"There's parking on the street. You would have saved a grip if we looked for a spot," I told Jamal.

"This is Midtown, Charisse, a.k.a. Towaway and Ticket Central," he replied. "Turn your back for five minutes and your ass will be over on the West Side Highway about a yard and a half lighter in the pocket."

That night was the most fun I had ever had with Jamal. We laughed and drank, and he even got up on the stage with the fake-ass Temptations and sang "My Girl." Even the goddamn food tasted good. I wanted the evening to last forever. When we left I was feeling tipsy and for the first time in a long time, relaxed.

"You ready to go home?" he asked.

"That's up to you. . . . You're the one driving," I replied. "I'm down for whatever."

Before I knew what happened Jamal and I had checked into the Sheraton on 53rd and Seventh, and were in the bed fucking like there was no tomorrow. I hadn't had sex in quite a while, so it was on in that room. When we finished he got up to take a shower. I was lying there thinking all kinds of dumb shit, *Yeah, we can get an apartment, I'll transfer to a branch out in Queens.* And then it hit me, *No, I didn't just fuck my daughter's father with no protection . . . again.*

When Jamal came out of the bathroom he was fully dressed except for his socks and shoes.

"Get ready, Charisse. I have to work today . . . I wish I was off. I'm tired as hell," he said.

"You off tomorrow?" I asked.

"Yeah . . . thank God."

"You want to come by and spend the day with Mariah? I'll even try to cook dinner," I said.

"I can come by early afternoon, but I have to jet by three or four. Niece is taking me to the Beacon Theatre to see D'Angelo," he answered.

I sat there for a moment. I could have sworn he said Niece was taking him to a D'Angelo concert, but that couldn't be. He had just spent the night getting my brown sugar. I looked across the room at him putting his shoes on and realized he pulled some bullshit yet again, just to prove to himself he could get some ass. That's why he parked in the garage, that's why he insisted on the Motown Café, and that's why he *never* said he wasn't with Niece anymore, and he damn sure never said he was with me. I wanted to stab him in the eye with a pencil, but there was no way I was going to give him the satisfaction of acting like the wounded victim. I stood up and grabbed my clothes.

"A bitch needed last night, you earned that . . . but let's keep it between us, okay?" I said.

"Well, who the fuck shouldn't I be telling?"

"Nobody," I responded with a cryptic smile. "I'll be ready in a minute."

Jamal sat in that chair, pissed off. It was cool when he thought he was pulling a fast one on me and Niece, but he didn't like the thought that maybe he was some side dick, who had just paid for dinner and drinks.

When we got to Brooklyn I asked him to drop me off at the corner. I told him if he wanted to come see Mariah now to drive around for a few minutes and then call the house and say he was on his way and would be there soon.

"Fuck that. I ain't no trick-ass nigga off the street. I'll come see my daughter tomorrow," he said with an attitude.

When I stepped out the car I didn't say goodbye or even look in his direction.

"Thanks," I said nonchalantly. "Have a good day at work."

Jamal will never know how bad he hurt my feelings that day, but I'll be damned—this time I returned the favor.

Five Months later

It was Mariah's fourth birthday; we were having a big party at the house. All my aunts and cousins, as well as Jamal's mother and father, and some of my coworkers, were there; even Brenda, Dave, and her beautiful little daughter showed up.

"What time are we going to cut the cake?" Aunt Belle asked. "Where the hell is the cake now that I'm thinking about it."

"Jamal was supposed to pick it up at one o'clock."

"Well, it's three o'clock now . . . call him. The kids want cake and ice cream. I want cake and ice cream," she said with her teeth clinched.

"I just called him—he didn't answer. Relax, he'll be here," I assured her.

"Uh-huh, he better. He got his goofy-ass father and puny little dried-up mother sitting up here in hostile territory."

"You're the only hostile one here, Aunt Belle."

"Come here, Charisse," Aunt Della called from her folding chair a few feet away.

"Isn't that your friend Brenda over there with that old man?" she asked in a whisper.

"Yeah, that's her over there with her little man, feet just swinging under the chair. Go over there and give him a balloon or something to play with," Aunt Belle said as she leaned in from behind me.

"You might not want to worry about Brenda's man. It looks like yours is keeping himself occupied," I told her.

She looked around and there was Abadu, trying to get one of my coworkers to dance with him.

"Abadu!" she yelled. "Sit your monkey ass down!"

Abadu was so funny; he reacted just like an eight-year-old. He huffed over to the closest empty chair and pouted.

Mariah and the rest of the kids were playing and running all through the house. I hated that I had to monitor her playing, but she couldn't run hard for too long at one time without getting flushed and her little yellow face starting to turn beet red. I was happy to see her having such a good time. Physically she had recovered well, but the rate of her mental development and maturity definitely seemed slower since the surgery.

A few minutes later the doorbell rang. My seventeen-year-old cousin Emily answered the door. She came rushing back into the room and turned her chair to face the door before sitting down and crossing her legs.

"Who was at the door?" my mother asked as she brought in a few plates of food for the adults.

"It ain't a Jehovah's Witness!" my cousin replied. "Now excuse me while I get my ringside seat."

Jamal walked in the door, carrying a huge cake box. Niece walked in right behind him. He stood there for a moment, like he didn't want to take another step. Niece stepped out from behind him.

"Hello, everybody," she said.

Everything in the room stopped. Talking, dancing, eating, and I could have sworn even the CD player stopped all by itself. Niece was three or four months pregnant *and* had the nerve to have on a big fucking diamond engagement ring. I don't know why I was so embarrassed and pissed-off but I was. I didn't give a flying fuck that she was pregnant, but this was Mariah's day, and after all she had been through I just felt like it was fucked-up that you would you bring your pregnant bitch and unveil her in front of *my* family at *my* house, at *my* daughter's party. I looked at the ring and thought to myself, *Shit, all I got was some door-knocker earrings. I got the doorknockers, then we knocked boots, and then I was knocked up.*

I took the cake from Jamal and carried it into the kitchen. My mother casually strolled in behind me to prepare a few more plates of food.

"Can you believe that he brought his pregnant girl to my goddamn house!" I said.

My mother turned to me and smiled. It was that, *You never learn, do you?* smile.

"Jamal is who he is, Jamal is who he's been, and Jamal is who he's going to be," she said. "What part of that don't you understand, Charisse."

Aunt Belle walked through the door with a huge smile on her face. I thought for sure she was coming in to grab a butcher knife so she could, as I've heard her say on many an occasion, "Get to slicing a nigger . . . and I don't mean with 'ah' on the end."

"What the hell are you smiling about, Belle? You're not about to start no shit up in here on that baby's birthday," my mother said sternly.

"I'm not starting shit," she said with a silly grin. "We're going to have a good time, and on Monday morning I'll call my niece and tell her how the white women handle such behavior."

Two weeks later

When Aunt Belle and I got to court that morning, I wasn't sure if I was doing the right thing or not. Until I saw Niece pregnant, I wouldn't even have considered taking him to court for child support. He never really fronted on the dough when it came to Mariah. I tried to justify it by saying this was my guarantee, my insurance policy, but I was really there for the same reason that Aunt Belle had put me up to it, and why she came dressed in a blue business suit and pumps looking like a fake-ass Claire Huxtable: To see the look on his face when the paper went from "Optional" to "Mandatory."

"Now look, you're doing the right thing," she said as though she were a trainer talking to his fighter. "You've got to look out for you and that little girl. Now remember . . . take no prisoners. Momma said knock him out!"

The judge was a balding, middle-aged white man who wore horn-rimmed glasses, but whose mustache, beard, and sideburns were so tight that my aunt couldn't resist saying something.

"Excuse me, Your Honor," she said as she stood up. "Do people tell you that you look like Trapper John, M.D.?"

"Yes, yes they do," he said with a smile. "Now, please sit down, miss, and save the lookalikes for girls night out, thank you."

Aunt Belle nodded her head and sat back down. That was the first time I ever saw my aunt so docile, there was no neck rolling, teeth sucking, or attitude. After all this time, who knew that all Aunt Belle needed was a bald white man who doesn't take no shit to keep her in check.

The judge went on to explain exactly what child support was as defined by the court system, and that Jamal would have to pay 17 percent of his income to Mariah.

"Do you understand that, young man?" the judge asked Jamal.

"Yes, Your Honor. I am in total understanding and compliance with these terms. In fact, just before I got served I told my beautiful, supportive fiancée here that I personally planned to take the necessary steps to make the arrangement legal. I just haven't had time because I work two jobs and go to school," he replied.

"Well, young man, perhaps if you had stepped forward and accepted responsibility a little sooner we would not be here this morning," the judge responded.

"Excuse me, Your Honor, but I have been extremely responsible in my duties as a father. May I approach the bench?" he asked.

Jamal walked over to him carrying a folder. He handed it to the judge.

"I thought you were just taking him to court for child support. I didn't know this shit would turn into the goddamn OJ case," Aunt Belle whispered in my ear as she leaned over the wood banister.

The judge closed the folder and removed his glasses.

"Miss Hawkins, I'm a little confused. Maybe you can enlighten me. Now you are well within your rights to request child support, but according to these cancelled checks and receipts, Mr. Butler has not exhibited any reluctance to provide for his daughter. In fact, I would go so far as to say he's been quite generous."

Jamal had this smug look on his face that said, "Even when I lose, I win."

"Would you approach the bench, young lady?" the judge asked.

When I walked over, he leaned forward.

"I've been a judge longer than you've been alive, and I see what's going on here. Now, obviously I'm going to award you the maximum you can receive. I know you have a child at home who has special medical needs, but here's a little advice from an old timer: When two parents start playing emotional tag, you know the child ends up losing the game."

I went home having gained no more financially than I walked in with, and Jamal went home with that sense of satisfaction I kept vowing never to give him again.

Chapter 14

The more that time went by, the more I started to question if I had done the right thing by taking Jamal to court. The judge was right; it actually wasn't as good a deal as I had before. Jamal didn't slack up one bit on his time with Mariah, but all the little extra things he used to do ceased and desisted. I didn't realize how all those things added up. He was constantly picking up shoes, sneakers, and clothes in addition to the money he was giving me.

"Can you pick up a jacket for your Mariah?" I asked one day.

"Sure, no doubt," he complied with no hesitation.

That Sunday night when Jamal brought Mariah home, he gave me her child support check and the Macy's bag with the Tommy Hilfiger jacket he bought for her. I looked at the jacket; it was a really hot, but I wouldn't have paid the $80 for it that was on the price tag.

"You're a big spender, huh, daddy?" I said.

"So are you," he replied with a strange smile. "Come give Daddy a kiss, Mariah."

Jamal kissed Mariah goodbye and left. His smile left me feeling uneasy. When I got upstairs I opened the envelope and looked at the check. Enclosed was what appeared to be a receipt. I immediately noticed that the check was exactly $86.60 short, when I looked at the receipt it was for $86.60, which was the cost plus sales tax. When I turned the receipt over it read "Business, never personal," and he signed it "Nino Butler."

The next day at work I was standing at my window, staring at the ceiling. My mind was a million miles away on a tropical island. I envisioned myself lying on a beach in St. Bart's drinking a Caribbean Sunset, Sex on the Beach, a piña colada, and a Mimosa Hawaiian, all of them lined up on a table by my hammock as I'm gently swinging back and forth listening to Mary J. Blige's *Share My World* album in my headphones. I was so far gone that I didn't even realize someone was standing right in front of me, Nigel. I hadn't seen or spoken to him since that night at his house.

"Hey, you!" I said with a huge smile.

"What's up, Charisse?" he responded nonchalantly.

Nigel was looking really good; he was dressed in a blue suit and tie and had lost a few pounds (not that he was fat in the first place). He looked especially trim in that suit.

"I was just thinking about you. I was planning to give you a call," I said.

"Really," he responded cynically.

"Why is that such a big shock?" I asked.

"Well, considering that I haven't heard from you, yeah I guess it is."

"That was my bad. You know how it is when you're

busy: time flies. Anyway, I was thinking we could have a dinner . . . on me."

"I don't think so."

"I don't mean tonight. Maybe this weekend I'll *let* you take me out," I went on to say.

"Charisse, Charisse, Charisse," he said as he shook his head. "The world doesn't stop and go with some remote control in your hand. Oh, don't get me wrong. For about a month after that night I kept telling myself, she'll call, but you never did. What's the matter? You and your ex haven't gone shopping in a while?"

"That's over and done for good now," I replied. "Now, I'm not making any promises, but we can go out and see what happens."

"Charisse, I'm seeing someone now, no kids, no baby daddies, no hang-ups, no drama. Now, would you mind depositing my check or should I walk down to another teller."

I did the transaction for him and handed him his receipt.

"Thank you."

"Is there anything else I can help you with?" I asked.

"No, thank you," he said before walking out of the door.

My first thought was to blame Brenda for introducing me to Nigel, then I blamed Jamal for putting me in this position where I had to play these petty games. It was everybody's fault but mine. That night I took the train home. My car was in the shop and I didn't want to spend seventeen dollars on a cab, twenty dollars by the time I gave his almost certain-to-be-musty behind a tip. I sat on the train, looking around at all the people going home from jobs they probably hated, to an overpriced apartment they probably hated, in a neighborhood they probably hated. For whatever reason, I felt like I was above this. Me and my $11.50-an-hour, teenage-mother, high-school-diploma-having ass was too good to be sitting on this graffiti-written, noisy, beggar-filled tin can on wheels. No sooner did that unpleasant thought cross my mind than I looked up and saw this guy smiling at me. I rolled my eyes as hard as I could. But when I glanced over at his dumb-tight gray-tweed-suit-wearing ass he was grinning harder. I pulled a copy of *Source* out of my bag and started to read, which was my hint for his ass to stay right where he was. As I'm looking down at the magazine I can see a pair of black shoes out of my peripheral vision coming toward me.

"Do you mind if I sit down?" he asked.

I purposely looked past him in the direction from where he had come from, at the empty seats that he'd passed on his way. Then I looked back at my magazine, not acknowledging him or his question.

"Is that LL Cool J on the cover?" he asked as he sat down. "These young dudes ain't got nothing for L, know what I'm saying?"

This dude had to be in his early forties, dark-skinned, with touches of gray in his hair and mustache. He had really bad skin, and his breath smelled like he had eaten a shit sandwich.

"How you doing? I'm Kenny," he said as he extended his hand.

"Hello, Kenny, my name is not interested," I replied.

"I'm just trying to make a friend, baby girl."

"I've got all the friends I need, thank you," I snapped.

"Shit, you ain't got no friends like Kenny," he said. "I make three hundred thousand a year as a stockbroker, I got a condo on the Upper East side, a brand-new S class Mercedes . . ."

I turned my head to the side to look at him and immediately located the source of his horrendous breath: a mouth *full* of rotten-ass brown and green teeth.

"If you don't mind me asking, why are you on the train to Brooklyn then?"

"Why the fuck you black women always have to be questioning a righteous black man?" he asked angrily. "This is why when we get successful we run to the white man's women," he explained in animated fashion.

I didn't even hear what he was saying. I was too busy cursing myself out and promising myself that I would *never* ever catch myself on the subterranean psycho ward again.

"Why can't you just accept what I say?" he asked. "That's why I don't fuck with you raggedy bitches."

"Could you please just leave me alone, Kenny?" I asked nicely.

"Look, I really like you. I feel like I can talk to you," he said calmly. "I'm looking for a fine young thing like you to have some kids with, okay. I really don't care about the kids, and I just want you. I'll buy you a house, I'll buy you a nice car."

"What about the Benz?" I asked, as I couldn't help but snicker at him.

Crazy-ass Kenny jumped up again and started shouting.

"Didn't I ask you not to question me, bitch?"

At this point I was too scared to move, and the punk ass men in the car had me feeling like Patti LaBelle: "on my own . . ."

"Just give me your address and phone number. I'm about to get off," he demanded.

I was about to give him some fake shit when a police officer came in from the next car. I saw a Spanish woman make eye contact with him and direct him toward crazy Kenny, who was still standing in front of me. The cop walked over to us.

"Is everything all right over here, miss? he asked.

Before I could answer crazy Kenny jumped in.

"Yeah, me and my lady are just having a little disagreement, you know how it is," he said.

"I am *not* his lady. I don't know this damn man. He just came over here uninvited and started talking," I explained.

"All right, sir, when we get to the next stop I'm going to need you to step off the train," the cop said as he grabbed Kenny's arm.

"Get the fuck off me!" he shouted. "Boo, you just going to let him grab your man?!" he called out.

When the train pulled into the station the cop escorted Kenny off in handcuffs.

"Fuck you, bitch!" he yelled before trying to spit on me. "You ain't all that. That's why you ain't getting half of my money, cause you ain't right!"

It was the most embarrassing thing I had ever experienced, and the last time you heard "Charisse" and "subway" in the same sentence *unless* that sentence included the words "turkey and Swiss cheese with extra mayonnaise."

Fast forward to 1999

The next couple of years were really uneventful. I had totally lost touch with Brenda. She had another baby girl named Tamia, married Dave, moved into a townhouse in New Rochelle. And when you added in working, I guess she just didn't have time to call anymore, but at least I knew where she was. I hadn't seen or heard anything about Nitra since she popped up at my bank a couple of years ago looking like Pookie from *New Jack City*. It was hard to believe how drastically things had changed in seven short years. They say life passes by in the blink of an eye, and it sure did feel like just yesterday that the three of us were arguing about who's better, Black Moon or Black Sheep, Jodeci or Boyz II Men, and Aaron Hall or R. Kelly when he first came on the scene with Public Announcement.

According to every thing that I had ever envisioned for myself, I would have been in medical school, dating a fellow medical or law student, and planning to travel each summer to places like Italy, St. Croix, and Holland with my new rich friends from school, not that I was planning to cut off my old ones. I had always been a much bigger Prince fan than of Michael Jackson, but the Artist Formerly Known as Mr. "Why is your ass out?" had lied to me; it was 1999 and I wasn't partying like shit. I guess the whole concept of 2000

and the new millennium had some people looking forward
to the future, but I wasn't one of them. After two years
into my new position at the bank, the only real significant
increase I had seen was in the amount of work. I wasn't
dating and didn't have any decent prospects. Mariah had
fully recovered from her surgery physically, but she was
never quite herself again. And living with my mother was
getting played out. Every time I drove down my block I
would glance over at Jason's old house. He had moved his
family into a house in Tenafly, and a family of Puerto Ricans
had moved in. One day I ran into one of the guys from the
neighborhood named Curtis Summers who had gone to
school with us and played ball with Jason.

"Charisse, what's the deal? Where have you been
hiding?" he asked as he hugged me. "You still fine as all
hell," he added with a smile.

"I'm good, and you . . . you look great," I replied as I
noticed how nicely he was dressed, which was *not* his MO.

"Thanks. I can't front—my wife takes care of me. I'm
not allowed to go shopping without her," he said with a
laugh.

"I didn't know you got married," I said with surprise.
"Congratulations."

"Yeah, like eight months now."

"Anybody I know?" I asked.

"Nah, she's not from out here," he replied as if trying
to clarify that immediately. "What I mean is she's from
Georgia. We met in college," he explained, trying not to
insult me.

"You still live out here?" I asked.

"If you mean Brooklyn, yes. We bought a little condo in Park Slope," he answered. "Guess who was in my wedding? Jason."

"Really? How is he doing?"

"Chilling. Life is good. You have to see his duplex in Fort Lee. Damn! That spot is ridiculous. God bless him," he said. "I always thought you and Jay were going to get married, have a couple of pretty kids, and live happily ever after."

"Okay, Curtis, well, it was great seeing you," I said as I remembered the other thing about him nobody liked: He never knew when to shut the fuck up. "I'm running late."

"All right, well, it was good to see you. Tell your mother I said hello," he said.

The last thing I needed was Curtis standing there telling me how great Jason's life was and how we should have gotten together. I guess it wasn't meant for me to avoid thinking about Jason that day though. As soon as I escaped Curtis I looked up and there was a big Adidas billboard with him advertising his new JT3 basketball shoes.

That Saturday morning Jamal came by early to pick up Mariah. He had his other daughter, Essence, in the car seat in the back of his brand-new two-tone white and gold Infiniti QX4. I started suspecting that Jamal had some kind of side hustle. He had a good job working at Pfizer, Inc., one of the largest pharmaceutical companies around, but I knew how much he was paying in child support to me, and by this time he had pulled that same cheating, onto-the-next-pretty-face bullshit with Niece, so she had taken him to court as well. It was really none of my business, but

I was curious as to how he could afford child support for two kids, a brand-new forty-thousand-dollar automobile, an apartment in Middle Village, and still manage to stay a label-whore wearing Sean John, FUBU, Polo, Hilfiger, Timberland, and some kind of watch called a Breitling, that he told me cost $2,700 . . . must be nice.

"Hey, Daddy's big girl," he said as he stepped out and looked around, hoping someone was outside to acknowledge his new truck. "What's up, Charisse?"

"You tell me. Check's running a little late, huh?" I asked.

"My bad. It totally slipped my mind, and I don't have any checks on me. Why didn't you call to remind me?" He responded. "So, what do you think?" he asked, referring to his new toy.

"Nice." I said as I barely glanced at it. "So I'll be looking for that in the mail early next week, or better yet when you bring Mariah home just stick it in your pocket," I added with a smile. "Be good, baby. Mommy will see you soon, and give Essence a kiss for me when she gets up."

When I walked back in the house I could feel Jamal's eyes on me. He didn't like the fact that I wasn't sweating his new car or what he had on. Jamal got off on people making a fuss over what he had; everything about him, with the exception of his love for his daughters, was a front. It's amazing how you can go from *I think I'm in love,* to *What the fuck was I thinking?*

My mother came home a short while later looking extremely tired and worn out.

"Rough night?" I asked.

"Girl, all these years of working nights are finally

catching up with me," she replied. "I ain't as young as I used to be."

"Just admit it, you're old," I said jokingly.

"The hell I am," she snapped as she picked up the empty coffee pot. "You couldn't even put the water on for coffee?"

"I don't know how to work that thing."

"You put water in it and turn the stove on, water gets hot . . . ain't that amazing? The water actually gets hot when you put fire under it," she said sarcastically. "Where's Mariah? That child still upstairs sleeping?"

"Mariah left already. Jamal came and got her a little while ago," I told her.

"Damn! I've got a big surprise for you today, and I just knew my baby was going to be here," she said.

"Surprise? What surprise?" I asked.

"Well, you'll be here, right?" she asked.

"I'm going to get my nails and toes done, but I'll be back early. What surprise?" I asked again.

"None ya," she responded.

When I got to the nail salon I picked out my polish and sat down. The Asian women who owned the salon and worked there were always very professional. That shit always tripped me out, how we black women constantly spend money on our nails, and damn sure on our hair, but generally we don't own nail salons, or even the spots where you buy hair for weaves.

Nail salons were, by nature, supposed to be the exact opposite of hair salons. No gossip, no celebrity debates, no fights with your baby daddy, and absolutely no ghetto bitch exhibitions. They say you should never judge a book by its cover, but I looked over, and sitting down were two ladies who took ghetto fabulousness to a new level. One of them was tall and slim, with a long blond weave and a square shape to her jaw line, her light skin accentuated by her ocean blue contacts lenses and bad skin. She had to be in her late forties or early fifties. Her friend was medium height and dark-skinned, with a really nice figure, for which she found the tightest jeans and T-shirt to show it off. When the light-skinned one spoke her I saw a big-ass gold tooth in the front of her mouth, and I noticed a tattoo on her chest with her name inside a flower: it said BUTTER, but this old hooker was straight PARKAY. Her nails were the longest I had ever seen, and painted bright orange.

"Girl, your ass is bugging hard, it ain't even no competition," the woman with the six-inch orange talons said.

"Pssst, you're the one bugging, bitch," the fake-ass Faith Evans responded before turning to me. "Excuse me, would you please tell this chick that Foxy Brown is way better than Lil' Kim."

"You're smoking," Talons replied before breaking right, into a verse in the shop. "'I got no time for fake ones, just sip Cristal with these real ones,'" she recited. "That shit's fire!"

"Please," Fake Faith argued like it was a political debate. "What about when Fox boogie-ripped that shit with Jay-Z?"

I was praying this senior citizen didn't start rapping.

"'Aint no nigga like the one I got, no one can do me better, fools around but he gives me a lot,'" she rapped as she swayed back and forth before looking at me for approval.

"Actually, I like Salt and Pepa," I stated somewhat sarcastically.

Thelma and Louise practically jumped out of their seats with their toes still wet.

"'Now push it! Push it real good!'" they sang in unison.

The only thing they were pushing was sixty. I figured they were probably getting ready for some *Look at me, I'm still young* forty-plus party, or even more comical, a players' boat ride. My older cousin Renee took me to one a couple of years ago; it was better than *Def Comedy Jam*. I saw more cheap linen than in a motel laundry, and more Gators than in the Everglades.

Thank goodness my two new friends finished up before I did. The one with the nails opened her purse and handed me a flyer.

"You should come out tonight. The ballers will be popping champagne," she said.

"Word," the other chimed in.

"Thanks, I was just thinking about a boat ride," I replied.

"All right, well, it's free for the ladies until eleven, but if they try to front at the door tell them you're on Lady Fine's VIP list."

I saw the Asian ladies giggling and talking among themselves. I can only begin to imagine what they were saying about us.

When the two women left, all I kept thinking was that by the time I reached that age I hope I'm not chasing some dream of being taken care of by Mr. Right. It was hard being a black woman. I'm sure deep down they would rather have been taking a cruise, or even a bus trip to

Atlantic City with their husbands, but instead they were going to stuff their money makers into the tightest, most inappropriate short dresses they could find in the hope of going home with some cat who has a nice car, and some disposable income to spend to maintain their trips to the hair and nail salons. More than likely they would both end up going to a hotel with the cat who had the most Cristal on his table and being one-night stands for some middle-aged married men with two kids in college who had retired from either transit or corrections jobs.

I caught myself feeling sorry for them until it dawned on me that with all that said, they still had plans for Saturday night, which was more than I could say.

Chapter 15

When I returned home from the nail salon my mother was sitting in the living room in a pair of tight-fitting jeans, a tight blouse, pumps, her favorite long wig, and makeup. I thought maybe she had gotten one of the flyers for the party from the senior Salt-N-Pepa at the nail salon too.

"Who are you supposed to be, Patti LaBelle?" I asked.

I heard some rumbling coming from the kitchen.

"Who's in the kitchen?"

"That's my surprise!" she replied with excitement.

Just as she said that a tall, light-skinned man walked in from the kitchen. He was in his mid to late fifties, very handsome, with curly salt and pepper hair. He wore a small diamond stud in his left ear, and something in his face was very familiar to me. He stopped in his tracks and just stared at me with a big smile.

"Vivian, wait, don't tell me *this* is my little Charisse," he said. "You're not going to give your father a hug?" he asked.

"Daddy?"

I hadn't actually seen my father since I was three, and here he was standing in my living room. When I was a little girl I used to look at old pictures of him and imagine myself running into his arms, or him picking me up from school and taking me for ice cream. Now I was looking right at him and felt absolutely nothing.

"Doesn't your father look great?" my mother asked.

He walked over and placed his arm around my shoulder before bending down and kissing me on the cheek.

"My God, you a grown woman now," he said as though he was surprised.

"Yeah, people tend to do that when you don't see them for twenty years," I replied.

"So where is this beautiful granddaughter of mine your mother's showed me the photos of. She looks just like my side of the family."

"She's with her *father*," I replied, making sure to stress the word father.

"Speaking of which, I mean, what are your plans with this guy? Who is he? What does he do?" he asked with a serious face. "Obviously when I found out you had a baby at sixteen I was very disappointed, but . . ."

"But since you weren't around you really couldn't say shit, could you?" I stated with deep sarcasm.

"Charisse, you show some respect. You want your father to think I didn't teach you anything?" my mother said angrily as she stood up.

"Respect to who . . . him? Please, I don't care what he thinks you taught me, damn him and his opinions," I responded with venom.

"He's still your father!"

"No, he's *your* damn baby daddy," I replied. "But I guess I should thank him for not using a condom."

I could see the rage on my mother's face as she walked toward me; still, I wasn't expecting the slap across the face that I got. I placed my hand on my now stinging reddened cheek and smirked at my mother.

"Feel better now? You really want to slap yourself, don't you? Sitting up here all dressed up like Denzel Washington is coming over for dinner, talking about don't he look good. He should—he ain't been taking care of nobody but himself," I said.

"Charisse, I'm so sorry, but you just don't understand," he said. "Let me try to explain."

"Save your explanations." I replied as I tossed up the "talk to the hand" sign. "I understand enough. What . . . you thought I was going to run and jump into your arms, or maybe you were going to take me down to the corner for some ice cream so I can show everyone my big handsome daddy. . . . Hell no," I said to him before turning back to my mother.

"And you, always up in my ear about Jamal, make sure he's responsible for taking care of his daughter, don't let him do this, don't let him do that, and guess what, he *does* take care of Mariah. If this is what being old and lonely is like, fuck that . . . kill me now. I hope I'm never desperate for a man. Let me take my ass upstairs . . . no, on second thought I'll get out of here for a little while. I don't want your outfit to go to waste," I said cruelly before walking out the door and slamming it.

I had *never* spoke to Vivian McNeil like that before, but I was so heated I didn't know what else to say. Back in the day when my mother and I had a falling out I'd just go over to Brenda's house, but that was no longer an option; neither was going to get Nitra and taking the train downtown to wish shop and make out Christmas lists. It could be the Fourth of July, but when one of us was stressed, talking about the Triple F.A.T. Goose boots, jeans, and sweaters we were going to ask for always seemed like the thing to do.

The next morning I walked into the kitchen and found my mother sitting in her usual Sunday morning spot reading the *Daily News*. She didn't even acknowledge that I walked in the room. I grabbed a bowl from the cabinet and the box of frosted flakes off the top of the refrigerator.

"May I have the milk?" I asked.

She took one hand and slid the carton without removing the paper from in front of her face.

"Any good sales?" I asked in an attempt to break the ice.

My mother slid the circulars over to me. I quickly scanned through whatever was on top.

"Nobody Beats the Wiz is having a sale on cordless phones. Didn't you want to get a new one?" I asked.

My mother put down the paper, took a sip of her coffee, and a deep breath.

"He's dying, Charisse," she said.

"Who?" I asked.

"Your father. That's why he came here to see you, to meet his granddaughter and to ask your forgiveness," she said solemnly.

I didn't know what to feel, part of me felt like crying, and at the same time it was like hearing bad news about someone you didn't know.

"What's wrong with him?" I asked.

"Lung cancer," she replied. "I think you should go see him, and I think you should take Mariah. I wasn't telling you he looked good because I'm some kind of desperate middle-aged woman, I was saying it because it was something he needed to hear. I know how you feel about him, Charisse, but don't block your own blessings by having hate in your heart, give it all to the Lord; he'll give you peace and forgiveness," she said.

"That's all well and good," I argued. "But after everything he put you through, how can you . . ."

"Forgive him? Charisse, I forgave your father a long, long time ago. I don't need to walk around bitter. Every single one of us is going to have to answer for the things we've done on this earth, and it won't be to anyone of this earth," she said.

"I don't know if I can go see him."

"Well, you're a grown woman, and I can't tell you what to do or how to feel," she said as she handed me a piece of paper with his address and phone number.

I held on to that small piece of paper in my purse for more than a month, debating, changing my mind, feeling anger, sadness, emptiness, fear, and regret. I didn't know exactly how much time my father had left on this earth, but I was looking for a sign as to what I should do. I got a call out of the blue one day not long after that from my aunt

Ruby. Now, my aunts called my house on a regular basis for my mother. We talked whenever I answered the phone, but they never called specifically to speak with me.

"What are you and the baby doing Sunday, Reecie?" she asked.

"Nothing planned. You know Sunday is my Lifetime movie day," I responded.

"Well, instead of watching Lifetime, why don't you come to church with me and have the time of your life," she responded. "And don't say I don't know," she added right before I was about to say "I don't know."

"Aunt Ruby, you know how I am about church. I believe in God and all, but I do my praying at home."

"Girl, I'm not asking you to become a pastor," she joked. "But there's something there for you Sunday, Reecie. You need to make it if you can."

Aunt Ruby wasn't the pushy type; she said what she had to say and left it at that. I still wasn't planning on going Sunday.

That week was one headache after another. Every customer who came in the bank had an attitude or some type of monumental problem with their account. Every night at least one teller would have a big difference in their cash drawer. I lost my cell phone. I broke the heel on my expensive Fendi pumps. And the engine light on my car came on so it had to go in the shop.

"The devil is a busy man, ain't he?" my mother remarked on Friday night when I collapsed on my bed.

"Thank God it's Friday," I said.

"You need to thank him in person," she responded.

"My car is still in the shop, and Aunt Ruby's church is way out in Far Rockaway," I argued. "I'll go next week when I have my car back," I added as my new cell phone rang.

I wanted to die when the mechanic on the other end told me that my $200 sensor problem was actually going to be a $900 overhaul.

I got up bright and early Sunday morning and took the A train out to Far Rockaway; I left Mariah home because she didn't like being underground on the subway. Aunt Ruby picked me up from the train station so I didn't have to take a cab once I got off at Mott Avenue. The church service was all about forgiveness, as if the pastor was talking to me directly. Every word seemed to touch an aspect of my life that I had been thinking about. I felt good after church, like I had taken a spiritual shower and it had washed away all the insignificant things I had been worrying about. I prayed for Mariah and my mother. I prayed for Brenda, and that Nitra was safe wherever she was. I even prayed for Jamal and his mother, and I even prayed for my father.

That Thursday when I got off from work I went home and picked up Mariah. My mother had her all dressed up like she was going to a cotillion. She had on a white dress with ruffles, patent leather Mary Jane shoes, tights, and some Jamaican bows in her hair. She was so excited to be going to meet her "new Grandpa" as she described him.

My stomach had been unsettled all day. I was so nervous, partly because I didn't know what to say to him, especially after the exhibition I had put on when he came over. I took a deep breath and told myself I wasn't the only damn person who ever went through something like this. All my life, or at least until I got old enough to know better, I used to fantasize about all the things my father would take me to do, like amusement parks, museums, school plays, and even open school night. I remember being with my mother at the shoe store one time, and there was another little girl about my age there with her father. He sat there patiently when she tried on different sneakers. I watched as he told her each pair looked a little better than the last, even the ones that looked terrible. At one point she sat down right next to him and placed her head on his shoulder. I couldn't stop staring at them; the look on her face was so peaceful, so happy, and so secure. My mother was peeping the whole time. She felt so guilty that she bought me two pairs of shoes and a pair of sneakers that weren't in her budget. That night I cried all over those shoe boxes.

When I pulled up to my father's building on Ocean Parkway I found myself wishing that I wouldn't find a parking space right away, but of course I found one immediately right in front of the building. My father's apartment number wasn't written on the piece of paper I had, so when we walked through the outside door I had to look on the list of tenants. I saw M. HAWKINS—4B. I was just about to ring the intercom when someone came out of the building and held the door for Mariah and I. As I stepped on the elevator I couldn't believe that I had found the courage to pay a surprise visit to my father; not even my mother knew that I hadn't called him in advance. I hated lying to her about where I was taking Mariah, but I didn't want her to know until after I came home.

I walked slowly down the hallway when I stepped off the elevator; Mariah squeezed my hand as if she sensed my hesitation. I adjusted my clothes and knocked on the door, and after a few moments he opened the door. He was dressed casually in a polo shirt and slacks, and he had an expensive looking wood pipe in his mouth.

"Charisse," he said in utter surprise.

"Hey, uh, Daddy . . . this is Mariah," I said nervously.

"Please come in . . . come in," he replied, almost equally as nervous. "I wasn't expecting you. I would have prepared a little something, but I can order some food if you're hungry."

"No, we're fine," I assured him.

"So you're Miss Mariah," he said as he bent over and shook her hand. "I've heard so many wonderful things about you."

Mariah was never the overly friendly type, but when he picked her up, she did not resist.

"She never wants to go to anybody," I said.

"So what's your name?" Mariah asked him.

"My name is Mr. Mario, almost like Mariah, huh? But since you're such a beautiful little girl you can call me Mar . . ."

"You can call him Grandpa," I intervened.

My father's eyes welled up with tears.

"Grandpa . . . now I have two grandpas . . . I'm the bomb," Mariah said.

My father hugged Mariah tight. That was the hug I always wanted from him, and this was my chance to get it. I walked over and he opened his arms and held us both.

"Why are you crying?" Mariah asked him.

"'Cause Grandpa is very happy right now," he replied through the tears.

After a little while I actually began to feel a little comfortable. I began looking around the tastefully decorated living room, which included a black piano, a thirty-six-inch television set, and a suede sofa. I came to a large glass wall unit with several rows of pictures. The bottom row was him with a bunch of different politicians and dignitaries. A few of the photos were in what looked like foreign countries. I thought he was a building superintendent, I said to myself, or at least that's what my mother had told me. A few rows up there was a school picture of myself; in fact, there was a whole row of school pics ranging from me with pigtails and missing teeth to the extension braids to my Halle Berry haircut. My mother had been sending him pictures every year, which I never knew. I looked around for any pictures of the other eighteen or nineteen brothers and sisters I supposedly had, but there was no sign of anything, and I couldn't just come out and ask him, "So Mario, where is the rest of your tribe?" I did notice that there was a man next to my father in several of the photographs. He seemed a little older than my dad, maybe a shade darker, but certainly not dark-skinned. He was quite a bit shorter than my dad and quite handsome in his own right. In each picture he had a huge smile on his face. I didn't know if he was my uncle, or maybe a business partner of his. I was just so curious about everything, because I knew very little about this man who was 50 percent responsible for my life.

"So do you play, or is this just for show?" I asked as I walked over to the piano.

He stood up and carried Mariah over and placed her on the stool before sitting down.

"Let me see if I can remember a few chords," he said.

My father began to play "Ribbon in the Sky" by Stevie Wonder. His hands seemed to glide effortlessly across the keys as we watched and were mesmerized. He then began to sing the lyrics in a voice that reminded me of Jeffrey Osborne, my mother's favorite singer. I remember thinking that between his pretty boy good looks and that voice, I understood how Vivian McNeil got "caught up in the rapture" on some Anita Baker shit.

We sat there and talked for hours. Mariah had long since fallen asleep on the sofa between us. He told me all about my grandmother and grandfather, and how they were a biracial couple from the Midwest who had moved to NYC because his father got a job working for the Domino Sugar Company in Brooklyn. *Nothing* he told me about himself matched up with the stories I had been told over the years, until finally I couldn't hold my tongue anymore.

"Do you have eighteen other kids?" I asked out of the blue.

"Do I have what?" he asked with a mortified look.

"Do I have eighteen other brothers and sisters on this earth somewhere?" I asked directly.

He burst out laughing so hard that it frightened Mariah in her sleep.

"I don't *know* eighteen damn kids, much less *have*

eighteen children," he said while still laughing. "Where did you get a ridiculous idea like that from?"

"Mom told me that. She also told me you were a building super," I explained.

"Damn, she couldn't even make me a building manager or a landlord . . . I had to be a super," he responded jokingly.

I didn't think it was funny. I was now becoming as angry as I was confused. Why had she lied to me all these years? And if my father didn't have all those other kids, why wasn't he a part of my life?

I had so many more things I wanted to ask, but it was getting late. I needed to get Mariah home and I had to be at work 7:30 the next morning to open the bank. My father carried Mariah downstairs and placed her in her booster seat before strapping her in.

"This was the best surprise I ever got . . . well, except for the bike I got when I was ten," he said, trying to hide his emotions.

"So what happens now?" I asked as tears welled up in my eyes. "Do I come back another eighteen years from now?" I asked half jokingly.

My father smiled at me through whatever fear and pain he was feeling.

"I'm sure you know I don't have another eighteen years, so maybe we should plan on doing it sooner than later," he said comfortingly.

"Do you know how long you have?" I asked.

"Not nearly long enough," he responded as he touched my face. "You're amazing. I can't believe I missed out on someone so amazing . . . my daughter," he added.

I hugged him as tight as I could and got into the car. I think we both wanted to tell the other "I love you," but the words didn't come out.

"So I'll see you guys Sunday for dinner . . . I'll make my specialty," he said.

"Why don't I bring your girl Vivian?" I suggested.

"I don't think that would be such a great idea," he replied with a cryptic smile. "Besides, there's someone I want you to meet," he added.

I understood perfectly. It would be a little awkward for the three of us to show up there to have dinner with him and his lady friend, especially when no matter what she said, my mother was *still* in love with him.

"I went to see my dad with Mariah yesterday," I told my mother the next morning over breakfast.

"You went where?" she asked while almost choking on her Raisin Bran. "Why didn't you tell me? What did he say? Did he ask about me?"

"Because I didn't want you talking about it 24/7. He said a lot of things. And he asked about you. Does that answer your questions?" I replied.

"I hope you plan on keeping in touch with him," she said.

"He invited me back over on Sunday for dinner, and I said yes."

Sunday afternoon I got dressed and ready for dinner at my father's apartment. Mariah was spending the weekend with Jamal so I was going alone, which in a way made me happy. I had never had my father all to myself, and without Mariah there I didn't have to be anyone's mommy—I could just be someone's daughter.

When I got to my father's house I could smell the food when I stepped off the elevator. The scent of Spanish cooking filled the beige-and-brown trimmed hallway. I knocked on the door and heard my father yell out.

"I'm coming . . . just a second."

He opened the door with a spoon in his hand and wearing a light blue apron. I couldn't put my finger on it, but there was definitely something different about him.

The apartment was immaculately organized and clean just as it had been a few days before. I noticed that not one Ebony magazine was even slightly out of line in the stack on the coffee table and every photo on the wall unit was spaced equally, as though he had used a ruler.

"I hope you like Mexican food. I made shrimp in damiana and tequila sauce, and crab cakes with chipotle sauce," he said. "Where's my baby girl?"

"With her father," I replied. "She's been talking about her grandpa Mario though."

Just then someone came out from the back of the apartment. He was about my father's age, nice-looking, with a mocha brown complexion, clean-shaven, and nicely built with a tight T-shirt. He looked very familiar.

"Charisse, this is Benjamin. Benjamin, this is my daughter, Charisse," my father said.

"Charisse, you are all this man has been talking about for the past few days," he said.

"Nice to meet you, Mr. Benjamin," I responded as it dawned on me that he was the man in all the pictures with my father.

"Don't be so formal—everybody calls me Benji," he stated with a touch of Little Richard in his voice.

"Dinner's ready . . . I hope you guys are hungry. I think I outdid myself," my father said.

"Mario, hush," Benji said before turning to me, "He's always bragging about his damn cooking . . . he can burn though."

We sat down at the glass table and my father brought out the food and served it. He then fixed his own plate and sat down.

"Charisse, bless the food," he said.

"Dear Lord, thank you for the food we are about to receive to nourish and strengthen out bodies for Christ's sake, Amen."

"Amen," they both repeated.

"So how do you two know each other?" I asked naïvely.

They looked at each other before my father answered.

"We're partners," he replied.

"Business partners?" I asked.

"Not exactly," Benji replied coyly.

"Partners in crime?" I asked jokingly as I took a forkful of food into my mouth.

"We're life partners, Charisse," my father came out and said as he placed his hand on top of Benji's.

I almost choked to death as my food flew right back out of my mouth.

"You two are faggots?" I blurted out. "I mean . . . you're gay!"

"Yes, does that surprise you?" he asked.

"Does my mother know?"

"Yes. I don't know why she never told you instead of making up all those stories."

"To protect her daughter," Benji said. "What we have might feel natural to us, but the majority of the world still doesn't approve," he added.

"Lies don't protect people, they disillusion them," my father stated.

I wasn't sure what I was feeling at that point, but it was definitely uncomfortable. I just kept thinking that after I leave and the dishes were washed, these two good-looking middle-aged men were going to crawl into bed and rub their hairy ass legs against each other's.

I gobbled down my dinner so fast that I couldn't remember if it was good or not. All I wanted to do was not be rude and just take my behind home.

"God knows I love weekends, but Sunday evenings get me depressed because I know it's back to work tomorrow," I said in an attempt to make it known that I couldn't stay long.

"Amen to that," Benji agreed.

"I better check to see what time Jamal is bringing Mariah home," I said before pretending to dial a number and hitting the volume button on my phone in case someone really tried to call me.

"Hey, where is my baby?" I said to no one. "What time are you taking her to the house? Oh, okay, well, I'll make sure I'm home," I went on to say.

"Let me say hello to my granddaughter," my father said as he reached for the phone.

"Oh, she's sleeping in the backseat," I lied before looking at my father. I ended the pretend call.

"I know it's a cliché, but I hate to eat and run. Jamal's bringing Mariah home in a little while," I said as I stood up.

"Well, let me pack you up some food," Benji said. "Mario made so much."

"No, I'm so full I can't even think about food, and I'm sure Mariah and Mommy have already eaten," I replied.

Benji was a sweet man, and you could tell he had a good heart. I could see my father looking at me suspiciously out of the corner of his eye. He knew I was full of shit and just wanted to leave. And he knew there was no one on the phone. That's why he asked to speak to Mariah. I knew from my two visits that Mario Hawkins was a gentlemen and extremely proper in his behavior. Not the type to reach for a cell phone when someone is talking.

"So, Charisse, when will we see you again?" my father asked.

"Soon," I replied.

I gave him a hug and kiss on his cheek and then hugged Benji before hurrying out the door.

I never considered myself homophobic or prejudiced toward gay people in any way. In fact my limited exposure to them was generally positive and pleasant, but this was my father, the *man* my mother had sex with to conceive me . . . that shit was nasty. I couldn't wait to get home so I could ask her what was up with her and Aunt Ruby getting married or having children with these black Liberace cats. I mean, I'm no relationship expert, but I don't think when they tell a woman she and her mate should have something in common it should be an affection for penises.

When I pulled up in front of my house, Jamal drove up right behind me with Mariah, who was asleep in the backseat. When I told Jamal about my evening, he just shook his head and chuckled.

"So let me get this straight, no pun intended. Your father is a sweet super?" he asked, recalling what I had originally told him.

"You're half right. He's not a building super at all," I replied.

"So what does he do?" He asked.

"He has some type of government job I think. He's very secretive."

"Maybe he's a top-secret salami smuggler," he said.

"Oh, you got jokes."

"No, I'm just concerned about my poor father. I mean if our parents ever go on *Family Feud* and it's grandmothers against grandfathers, he'll be outnumbered three to one, and that shit ain't fair," he said with a serious face.

I picked up Mariah and took her into the house and put her to bed. My mother came home about thirty minutes later.

"So how was your big dinner? You've been so damn secretive lately," she said as she barged in my bedroom.

"Interesting, enlightening, surprising—is that enough *ing*'s for you?" I asked sarcastically.

"What happened?" she asked as she sat down on the edge of the bed.

I knew that she didn't think my father would be so

honest with me about his lifestyle. My mother was a Southern woman, and that shit was taboo where she's from. I remember there was a family across the street with a son who, even as little girls jumping rope, we knew was what the adults called a sissy. But the family all tried to act like he was a normal heterosexual boy. They'd talk about all the women that wanted him. Which I'm sure was true because he was a nice-looking guy. They just didn't know that he didn't want women.

"Daddy had company. Actually I think maybe Daddy has a roommate," I responded with a peculiar look on my face.

"You mean like he's living in sin?" she asked.

"More like he's living in men," I replied.

My mother's eyes got as wide as two golf balls. Her mouth flew open with a fake yawn.

"I am so tired—let me take this weary soul to bed," she said as she stood up and began walking out of the room.

"You could have told me the truth," I said just before she reached the door. "I could have handled it."

"But I couldn't . . ." she said with her back to me as she walked out.

For the next month or so I pretty much avoided my father without doing so overtly. I mean, I took his phone calls most of the time, but whenever he tried to make plans for us to get together my schedule was full. One day I got a call from Benji; he was crying. He told me that my father's health was deteriorating and it would mean so much to him if he knew that I loved him, no matter what had happened in the past or what his lifestyle choice was.

"Love is unconditional," he said. "Whether it's your

father, your daughter, or the bum on the corner, if you love somebody it comes with no strings or stipulations," he added.

I decided I was going to take Mariah to see him that weekend. The urge to see him, hug him, and tell him that I loved him became stronger and stronger until Saturday couldn't come fast enough.

Mario Antonio Hawkins passed away in his sleep on Saturday morning at six a.m. from cardiac arrest.

"Charisse, your father went home to rest," Benji said in a very calm, peaceful voice when he called.

I knew immediately what he meant. I wanted to cry but I didn't. I felt empty and sad.

"We're not going to see Grandpa, are we?" Mariah asked.

"No," I replied.

"Don't worry. God is going to take care of him," she said as she hugged my waist.

"Yes baby, he sure is," I replied.

Chapter 16

*I*mmediately after my father died I found myself more focused and dedicated at work, and as a mother. I even enrolled in some college courses at New York Technical College on Jay Street, right near the job. The only area of my life that was still totally empty was my romantic life. I would date once in a blue moon, but never with a man I was totally attracted to. If a guy who I thought was attractive or simply seemed interesting asked me out, I turned his ass right down. But a guy who didn't do shit for me had a shot. This way there was no pressure, because I knew from the jump he wasn't getting no ass. Usually they were very agreeable and acted like gentlemen, in hopes of getting some ass, but it didn't matter to me if I ever saw them again after the date.

My mother also changed after Mario Hawkins passed away. Even though they hadn't been together in *years*, I think that a small part of her died with him. I never really understood why she wouldn't date. Men found her attractive, and even with a few extra middle-aged pounds on her she was still shapely. But she loved my father, and I'm sure that when she discovered he was gay her heart never fully healed. I was afraid the future held the same fate for me.

About three months after my father died I got a call from Benji.

"How have you been?" I asked.

"Hanging in there. After nineteen years of seeing someone every day it's an adjustment, but God is good," he replied. "How have you been?"

"I'm good, Mariah's good . . . no need to complain," I said.

"I know that's right," I sensed a smile in his voice. "Besides, no one, including God, wants to hear it," he added.

"My father didn't strike me as the type of person who complained much either," I said.

"Child, he *never* complained. Sick, well, good days, bad days, whether the sun was shining or it was a blizzard and he had to go out in it, he kept it moving with a smile," he told me. "Charisse, I have something for you, something Mario wanted you to have. Can you come by tonight?" he asked.

"Yes."

"Okay, take down the address," he said.

"I know where you live."

"Please, I moved out of that apartment three weeks after he died. Too many memories for me to be walking up in there every night."

After work that evening I went straight over to Benji's apartment. It was in Brooklyn Heights, not too far from where I worked. When I got there Benji was so happy to see me, we hugged at the door and I could see the tears welling up in his eyes. At first I thought, *We only met that one time,* but then I realized that when he looked at me, he saw a living, breathing part of Mario Hawkins. Benji had put on some weight. He also had bags around his eyes and his hair was uncut with patches of gray that he no longer cared to dye. The apartment was inside a brownstone that reminded me of the house on *The Cosby Show*. Once inside I saw unpacked boxes everywhere, Chinese food cartons were all over the place, and clothing was scattered on the furniture. This was nothing like the pristine apartment that he lived in with my father.

"Sit down," he said as he looked around the cluttered room. "If you can find someplace to sit."

I sat down on a large box marked TOWELS AND LINENS. Benji walked over and picked up a large black, leatherbound Bible. He opened it and handed me the long white envelope that was inside it.

"Mario wanted you to have this, and so do I."

I took the envelope; I fully expected to find a letter from my father inside. When I opened it I found a photograph of my father holding a small baby.

"He told me you were two days old," Benji said.

I looked inside the envelope again and there was a check from Benjamin C. Miles made out to Charisse Hawkins in the amount of $83,000. I couldn't believe it.

"What's this?" I asked in total shock.

"Mario left me *very* well taken care of and he wanted to make sure you and Mariah were okay."

"I don't know what to say. . . . Thank you, thank you very much."

Benji hugged me again, this time tighter than the first.

"Goodbye," he said with tears flowing down his cheeks.

"Benji, are you all right?" I asked. "Maybe you should go visit some family for a while," I suggested.

"I don't have any," he replied. "Mario was all I had in this world."

"I'll come and check on you—we're practically family, you know," I said.

Benji didn't say a word; he just smiled and walked me to the door.

I went and sat in my car and stared at the check. I finally understood what it meant for something to be bittersweet. I thought of all the things I was going to do with the money, all the things I could buy, and I thought about the look on Benji's face when I walked out the door.

Just as I turned the key I heard a loud pop, it sounded like a firecracker. It startled me, but I really didn't pay it any attention, Brooklyn Heights wasn't the type of area where you heard random gunshots in the evening, and it wasn't the Fourth of July.

The next morning I was getting dressed and watching the Channel 11 news when I heard the reporter say something that made my heart stop.

"And the body of fifty-six-year-old Benjamin Miles was discovered in his Brooklyn Heights apartment after a neighbor thought she heard a gunshot and called 911. When police arrived Mr. Miles was found on the floor by his front door, suffering from a self-inflicted gunshot wound to the head. He was pronounced dead on arrival at Long Island College Hospital."

"Oh my God!" I shouted.

My mother came running into the room, and I woke Mariah out of a sound sleep.

"What's wrong?" she asked as the burst through the door.

"I just saw on the news a man shot himself. It was Daddy's friend," I said.

"Daddy's friend who?" she asked. "What are you talking about?"

"Benji, Benjamin I mean, the man who lived with my father," I explained.

My mother had never met nor seen Benji, but still they were connected in a strange way; there was a sadness that came over her, almost like she had lost a friend. I cried on my way to work, I know that suicide is a sin, but I hope God saw fit to allow Benji to see his friend again in Heaven, that's all he really wanted.

When I got to work my mind was so preoccupied with things that I actually forgot about the check in my purse. I didn't want anyone in my branch to know that I had come into that much money, so I went to another branch on my lunch hour to deposit the check.

It took the check seven days to clear. I remember the morning I checked my account on the phone and the electronic voice said, "Your account balance is eighty three thousand forty six dollars and seventeen cents, and your available balance is eighty three thousand forty six dollars and seventeen cents."

I hung up the phone and my mind started racing a million miles a minute. As much as I had always condemned ghetto fabulous people, and talked shit about Jamal for fronting, I made up my mind right then and there that I was calling in sick the next day and going out to the Roosevelt Field Mall on Long Island to do some *serious* shopping. I hadn't even told my own mother about the money yet. I tried to convince myself that it was because I didn't want her spreading my business through the family, but I was on some real selfish shit. Subconsciously I guess I felt like that money was severance pay for all those years he wasn't around and didn't pay child support.

"You're not working today?" My mother asked when I came downstairs at seven forty-five still in my nightgown.

"Nope," I said with a big smile. "I'm calling in sick today."

"You don't look sick."

"Well I am . . . sick of working," I replied. "I'm not trying to set some perfect attendance record; the bank won't shut down 'cause I'm not there."

"So what are you going to do all day, lie around the house?" she asked. "We could clean out these closets finally."

"I know you don't think I'm staying home from *work* . . . to *work*," I responded. "Besides, I have plans already. I'm going to the mall to do a little shopping."

"Shopping. . . . You don't get paid again until the first, and wasn't you just complaining last week about being broke?"

"What's with the interrogation?" I snapped. "Damn, can't I take a freaking day off and go shopping without you turning into Columbo."

I stormed out of the kitchen and went back upstairs to get Mariah ready for school. After I dropped her off I went to IHOP on Hillside Avenue for breakfast. I sat by the window, looking out at the bright, sunny sky and reading the newspaper as I waited for my food. This was the first time I had ever gone to an IHOP and there wasn't a waiting list; instead there were a few older people scattered throughout the restaurant. *Being rich is the shit,* I thought to myself.

After I ate I headed out to Roosevelt Field and treated myself to a new Dolce & Gabbana bag from Nordstrom, a stainless steel Movado watch, two pair of Ferragamo pumps, and four new outfits. I spent $2,700 and felt like I was still caked the fuck out. On the way to the parking garage I accidentally bumped into this white chick; she may have a few years older than I was, but no older than twenty-six. She looked like money. She was slightly tanned with blond hair and blue eyes. Her faded ripped jeans, black boots, and butter-soft lambskin jacket were casually fly, and the glistening diamonds from the bezel on her yellow gold Rolex President really let muthafuckas know what time it is.

"Excuse me, I'm sorry," she said in a friendly manner.

"No, it was my fault . . . I apologize," I responded.

I guess she looked at all the shopping bags and assumed I was some rich black chick from Great Neck or Manhasset.

"I so hate this mall," she said. "I can never find shit here. This place is like fucking Green Acres with a few bells and whistles."

I wasn't sure if she was trying to diss me or was just making conversation. I mean, obviously I did find some shit out here that I thought was worth buying. I don't know why I felt the need to go along with her, instead of being honest and saying, "Well, bitch, this place is a big deal to me."

"I know, but sometimes I just don't feel like dealing with that traffic in Manhattan," I said.

"And who feels like taking the LIRR and all that shit. I usually drive up to the Westchester Mall, but that's a nice little drive too," she said.

I didn't know a damn thing about the Westchester Mall; I didn't even know Westchester had a mall.

"Yeah, the Westchester Mall is where I usually go too," I lied.

When we reached the parking area she handed the valet her ticket.

"Well, it was nice to meet you. I'm parked over in the garage," I said.

"You too. Have a good one," she responded as her cell phone rang.

I kept looking back to see what she was driving. I was impressed by how fly this chick was. Her whole body language was like, *Yeah, I'm that bitch, I know it, you know it, they know it . . . we all know it.* But she didn't come off like she was trying to be fly.

Just as I reached my car I saw the valet pull up in a silver Mercedes truck. She got in and pulled off after handing him a tip. Looking at my car and realized I needed to step my game up. Dolce & Gabbana + Ferragamo do not = Ford. Right across from me in the garage a white guy was getting into what looked like a newer model BMW sedan. It said

740iL on the back, but it looked a little sleeker than the one Brenda had driven to my house a few years ago.

"Excuse me," I called out.

The man, who was in his late sixties or early seventies, all of five-two, looked scared as hell.

"May I ask you a question, sir?" I asked as I began to walk toward him.

He cautiously started to meet me halfway, looking around as though he were expecting my carjacking partner to leap out and pounce on his little bald-headed ass.

"Yes?" he asked as his fears and racial insecurities seemed to ease by staring at my breasts. "How can I help you, young lady?" he asked with a big smile and never making eye contact.

"I was just wondering where you got your BMW," I said.

"Oh, that old thing," he bragged. "That's a ninety-eight. I also have a brand-new Corvette, and a Range Rover HSE with a Harmon Kardon system," he added.

"Those are nice cars," I said. "But which dealer did you get that one from?" I repeated.

"BMW of Bayside, on Northern Boulevard. Wait a minute, I think I have one of my salesman's business cards in the glove compartment."

He jogged over to his car, I guess to show me he was still youthful, and went into his car. He jogged back with the card in his hand.

"Here you go. His name is Sergio. He Spanish, but I don't think he's like Puerto Rican or Mexican. He's probably from Argentina or Spain or something. He's very smart and honest," he said as only a true closet racist could.

"Thank you."

"Now just in case he gives you a hard time, I'll put my name and number on the back of the card. You just call me and I'll make sure your well taken care of," he said. "Hell, I had him and his wife out to my beach house in Southampton, so he better give you a good deal," he made sure to tell me. "My name is Sol."

"Thanks so much, Sol. My name is Charisse."

"Charisse—what a beautiful name," he replied. "Let me know how it goes either way," he added.

Sol strutted back over to his BMW and actually tried to put a little bebop in his walk. I remember once hearing that old white men liked busty black girls. But all this shit proved to me was that nine times out of ten when a man of *any* race, creed, color, age, or religion was talking to you, he was thinking about fucking you. The one out of ten was the man who refers to you as "girlfriend" when he spoke.

I stopped at a gas station to get directions to Bayside BMW with the intention of just looking and sitting in my dream car, the 325 convertible. As soon as I walked in the showroom door a tall man, mid-forties, with a mustache and an olive complexion, walked up to me.

"Hello, you must be Charisse," he said as he shook my hand.

"Yes, but how did you . . . ?" I began to ask.

"Sol called," he said as he chuckled and glanced down at my tits. "He described you to a tee. So what I can put you in today?"

"Nothing today. I'm just looking, but the 325 drop-top is my dream car," I said.

"New or preowned?" He asked.

"Preowned."

"Well, come on. Let me give you an idea of what's available, and maybe we can make those dreams come true."

Sergio walked me to the outdoor lot in the back where there were rows and rows of cars.

"Any particular color?" he asked.

"Black."

Sergio smiled at me and let me right over to a black 1997 328i convertible. The shit had black leather interior, wood grain console, six-cylinder engine, and a multidisc CD player.

"I'll be right back," he said. "Go ahead and sit in it."

I opened the door, and the smell of that leather hit me like fresh biscuits in the morning. I sat down and felt that steering wheel and touched the wood gearshift knob. This car had me open. *A bitch would kill the streets with this muthafucka,* I thought. I must have completely zoned out, because when Sergio walked back over and handed me the keys through the window he scared the shit out of me.

"Start it up," he said.

I placed the key in the ignition and turned it. The engine started so smoothly that you barely felt it or heard it. Sergio walked around to the passenger side and got in; he hit a button, and the top started to come down. He didn't have to say another word to get a bitch strung out.

"What's the mileage?" I asked, trying to sound knowledgeable.

"Only thirty-one thousand. It comes with another three years or thirty-six thousand miles on the dealer warranty," he said. "Do you have a trade-in?"

"I have a 1995 Ford Taurus. I still owe, like, two thousand dollars on it," I said.

I don't what the fuck happened after that. All I remember is sitting in his office watching him enter all kinds of different numbers on his calculator.

"How is your credit?" He asked.

"Not bad," I replied. "But I'm not trying to finance shit. When I make the move it's going to be cash," I stated confidently.

"Well, I'm not trying to get into your business, but you sound like you're pretty sure you're coming into that kind of money," he said.

"I already have that kind of money," I bragged.

Sergio's eyes lit up and he sat up perfectly straight.

"Charisse, what can I do to help you get into your dream car today?" he asked passionately.

The next thing I knew I was driving on Grand Central Parkway in my black 1997 BMW 328i with the stereo blasting 98.7 Kiss FM and with my bank account $26,000 lighter than it had been two hours ago. Fuck it. I *loved* the way people were clocking me on the road when they pulled up alongside my car, and I still wasn't done yet. I remembered passing this place on Atlantic Avenue that sold rims when Jamal and I had gone to White Castle. I stopped there and dropped another $1,700 on a set of chrome racing dynamic wheels. All I could think about at that moment was when I saw Jamal, I was going to throw on some black

Star Trek shades and a leather Golden Child hat and say, "How you like me now?"

Later that evening I finally told my mother about the money Benji had given me. I really wanted to keep it a secret. I mean, I could buy clothes and shoes all day and basically go under the radar. But how the fuck do you hide a BMW? My conscience was also starting to fuck with me; I had spent more than thirty grand and hadn't bought shit for Mariah or given my mother one red cent.

I gave her a check for $5,000.

"A BMW, Charisse. A BMW convertible to park on the street in Brooklyn?"

"Oh, Ma, you only live once, and tomorrow isn't promised."

"No, it's not," she agreed. "How much did that BMW cost?"

"Thirty thousand," I said proudly.

She gulped. "Thirty thousand dollars?! Have you lost your ever-loving muthafucking mind, Charisse? That's a down payment on a house!"

"I didn't have to give them thirty. I gave them my old car as a trade and twenty-six thousand," I explained. "I think I'm going to take Mariah out to Queens so we can pick up the clothes she left at Jamal's house."

"This evening? There's nothing over there that can't wait until he comes to get her this weekend," she said. "And there's nothing over here that can't wait until he comes over to get her this weekend either," she added.

"Don't you want to take a ride in Mommy's new car?" I asked Mariah.

"Can we stop at McDonald's?" she asked.

"Yes," I replied.

I was so excited and anxious for Jamal to see my new car that I didn't even bother to call him and say we were coming over. I wanted to see the look on his face when he came outside and saw my shit sitting there like, "*BAM . . . What Negro what!*"

"I thought you got past all that," my mother said. "You still care what he thinks. Still trying to prove he didn't break you. You should have taken that twenty-six thousand and bought yourself a life," she added before shaking her head and going upstairs.

I put Mariah's jacket on and headed out the door. When I got on the Jackie Robinson Parkway it was bumper-to-bumper traffic and moving at a snail's pace. It took twenty minutes just to get to the first exit at Highland Park. A voice inside my head told me to get off, turn around, and take Mariah to McDonald's before going back home. But I tuned that voice out. It took another thirty minutes to get to the Metropolitan Avenue exit.

"Mommy, can we just go home? I'm tired," Mariah said.

"We're almost there," I said.

"Almost where?" she asked.

"Daddy's house," I answered.

"Why are we going there?" she asked.

I didn't even respond. I was getting frustrated with the traffic, and frustrated with myself because I knew the answer to her question.

We finally got to the 188th Street exit ninety minutes

later. It turns out all the traffic was caused by an accident. Mariah was fast asleep by the time I pulled up in front of Jamal's house. I didn't see his car in the driveway but I rang the bell anyway. I guess I would have to settle for his mother telling him, "Charisse came by here. You should see her BMW. She must be doing great."

When I rang the bell his father answered.

"Charisse. Hey, how have you been? Good to see you," he said as he came outside and gave me a hug. "Is everything okay? Where's Mariah?" he asked.

"Everything is fine. She's in the backseat sleeping," I said as I pointed to my car.

"Nice car. Look at you," he said enthusiastically.

Jamal's mother came to the door with her usual scowl. She had softened a bit over the years, but deep down she still didn't care for me, and vice versa.

"Oh hello, Charisse. Where's my granddaughter?" she asked.

"She's in the car knocked out," I replied.

"Look at Charisse's car, honey. Isn't that beautiful?" his father said.

"Who bought you that?" she asked sarcastically.

"It was a gift to me, from me," I answered. "I was hoping Jamal was home, Mariah has a few things here I need to pick up."

Jamal's parents looked at each other and then looked at me.

"Jamal doesn't live here anymore," his mother said with a devious smile. "Jamal has a condo in Forest Hills where him and Niece live. Two bedrooms, two baths, doorman building, beautiful little girl, and he just bought her a *Five* series BMW. What's that, a little Three? Aw, how cute."

His parents went over and each kissed Mariah as she slept. I wanted to drive right back to Northern Boulevard and get my $26,000 back. I didn't buy it specifically to impress Jamal, but that damn sure was something I was looking forward to. But this sneaky-ass nigga had a new condo *and* bought his woman a 5 series. There was no traffic on the way back and my ass was flying on the Jackie Robinson. I didn't even see the pothole until I was dead up on it . . . and in it. It jarred the car so much that it woke Mariah up.

"Are we at Daddy's new house yet?" she asked.

"You didn't tell me Daddy had a new house," I said.

"You didn't ask me," she replied innocently.

I didn't say another word. I just took her to McDonald's and bought her a Happy Meal. When I got back to my block there were no parking spaces anywhere on the block, and I was not parking my car around any corners or on the next block with the crackheads. I parked right in front of my house, in front of a hydrant. There was no way I could get a ticket at ten o'clock at night, and I'd get up and move it early the next morning when a few spaces opened up.

When I came outside the next morning I had a fucking parking ticket and a flat on my front tire. It looked like the rim had gotten bent when I hit that pothole. I could see my mother peeking out the window as I nearly broke down out of frustration. I called in sick to work again to wait for a tow truck to come. When I took the rim back to the place where I bought it they told me it was going to be another $200 to fix.

"What's up, Charisse? I heard you were looking for me."

"I wasn't looking for you," I made clear to him. "I wanted to pick up a few of Mariah's things."

"No doubt. Well, what did you need and I'll have Niece drop it off with your mother."

"In her new Five series?" I asked.

"What?"

"Nothing, Jamal. Oh, and by the way, congratulations on the new place."

"Thanks."

"Why didn't you say something? I mean, I can afford to get you a housewarming gift: a fucking plant, a toaster, some shit," I said.

"We're good. I don't think we need anything," he said, "So just give me a call and let me know what you need," he added before hanging up.

Jamal didn't even mention anything about my new car. Maybe his parents didn't bother to even mention it, or maybe he just didn't give a fuck. I didn't think I did anymore, but obviously I did.

One day a few weeks after that I was at the car wash. I met this guy named Brad, he was the thug type, but seemed like a nice guy. He was about six-one, dark-skinned with a short haircut and 360 waves. He drove a gold Lexus coupe that said GETOKID on the license plate. We exchanged phone numbers and went out to eat a few times in the city. Brad had a girlfriend whom he lived with, but he said shit was really bad between them and they didn't even sleep in the same bed anymore; ordinarily that would have sounded like some real bullshit, but Brad didn't strike me as a liar. He was even honest about what he did for a living.

"I hustle." He replied straight out when I asked him. "I dropped out of school in the tenth grade. I tried that nine-to-five thing, but that shit wasn't cutting it. I was making just enough paper to buy tokens to get back to work. That whole working shit is the biggest hustle they got going," he explained.

"But you don't want to do that for the rest of your life. That's not a career," I reasoned. "You seem like you could go back to school and do anything you wanted."

"Are you serious?" he laughed. "That's that movie bullshit. You want to know when muthafuckas like me get their degrees?" He rhetorically asked. "When the only other options are studying the Quran or lifting weights in the yard," he went on to say.

Brad told me he had five kids by four different women, and none by the chick he was living with. I don't know what it was about him that had men so intrigued. I felt like I could turn his life around, make him into a legit businessman. It was obvious that he had the intelligence, if not the education, to be successful at anything he put his mind to.

Physically I was attracted to him, but I hadn't been with anyone since Jamal. In fact Jamal was the only man I had ever been with.

"I don't know who you're saving that dried-up coochie for," my friend Carol from work used to ask. "You act like that shit is laced with gold . . . use it or lose it."

"I'm not just fucking anybody to be fucking," I would reply defensively.

"Bitch, please. You're so scared somebody is going to hit it and bounce that you're afraid to open up . . . literally and figuratively," she would add. "That fine shit ain't going to last forever. You're like a pretty-ass car that won't start on purpose 'cause it doesn't want to get a scratch. You better let somebody drive that shit."

Brad wasn't really stressing the whole sex thing, which made me wonder if he was still either getting it at home or had a bunch of chicks on the side. I knew he wasn't gay, and I knew he wanted to smash by the way he always looked at me. But he was too cool about it. One time I even brought it up and his response was a little too nonchalant.

"I really want to go down to Atlantic City for the weekend," I said.

"Word, let's do it . . . I'll get us a room at the Sands, play a little blackjack. I'll see if there's any fights coming up," he responded.

"I don't know if I'm ready for that yet," I said.

"Ready for what . . . we're going to AC to chill, not to Vegas to get married," he said while laughing.

"No, I mean ready to sleep together."

"Oh shit," he said as he laughed a little harder. "You sure Mariah is your daughter?"

"Yeah . . . why?"

" 'Cause you be acting like a virgin or some shit. That's why I don't even talk about sex. That time I hugged you from behind when we was at that club, I felt you tense up like a nigga was about to handcuff your ass. I was like fuck this, you too uptight for me. I'll just lay in the cut until you give a nigga a sign or bend over in front of me and say get to work or something."

I couldn't help but laugh. He had that way of being serious, but saying it in a way that made you laugh.

"So are you still fucking your girl?" I asked fully expecting a denial.

"Sometimes." he said without hesitation.

"Excuse me?" I said.

"Sometimes." He repeated clearly. "Look, that muthafucka is a pain in my ass for real-real, and she got to go, but right now I don't have time to be out here messing with these hookers, and tricking and frontin' like I'm really interested in that bullshit they be talking about, so when she walks through the house with that fat Dominican ass bubbling out the bottom of them panties, sometimes a nigga got to put his differences aside."

I knew Brad liked to keep it real, but I didn't expect him to be so blunt. I just sat there with my mouth wide open.

"You asked . . . don't knock on the door if you don't really want to see what's inside," he added.

"Well, I'm glad your honest, but this is one of those times when honesty may not be the best policy."

"What's that supposed to mean?" he asked.

"Well, let me sing you a little medley that basically describes me and you from this point on.

"'Friends / How many of us have them?'" (Whodini) "'That's what friends are for.'" (Dionne Warwick) "'But you say he's just a friend / But you say he's just a friend.'" (Biz Markie) I sang to each melody.

"Wow, it's like that," he responded.

"Muthafuckin' right. You might be cool and shit, but I already know how you get down."

I was expecting a little resistance, or an argument, or even a little disappointment, but Brad looked more relieved than anything.

"Damn girl, that's what's up. I felt like we should just be friends since that night at the club. You've got too much emotional baggage for me to go on that trip. I mean, it's hard because you're good people and you look so fucking good, but you're not looking for Mr. Right, you're looking for Mr. Perfect, and to the best of my knowledge that nigga don't exist," he said.

Brad and I ended up being mad tight. There was always that attraction and sexual energy in the air between us, but after his live-in ex-girlfriend got pregnant with child number six, there was zero chance that anything would ever jump off. He tried introducing me to a few of his friends, but I wasn't feeling any of them. The ones who had it going on had drama galore, and the ones he said were drama free looked like a combination of Craig Mack and Smoking Joe Frazier after the Ali fight. I had reached the point where I wanted to be in a relationship. I wanted a man to spoil me, make a fuss over me, be jealous, and tap this ass right on a regular basis.

The money in my account was dwindling as fast as

my patience for finding a man. I bought Mariah a $2,000 dog that she didn't give a flying fuck about. Working in downtown Brooklyn didn't help matters either. I shopped damn near everyday for myself, Mariah, or my mother. I treated myself to a $6,000 full-length short hair mink coat, a pair of $2,000 1 karat diamond studs, and I dropped $3,800 on a stainless steel Rolex with a diamond bezel. Within six months I had less than $15,000 left. I told Brad, who by now was my closest friend and confidant, about how I fucked up all that money.

"Yo, Reece, don't be so hard on yourself," he said. "You did what every muthafucka who gets some real paper for the first time does . . . you lost your muthafuckin mind."

"I work at a bank, I should know better," I responded.

"Fuck that. It don't matter where you work. That shit is all socioeconomic," he explained. "That's why rappers take their advances and go straight to the diamond district, and athletes borrow money from their agents to get a muthafuckin' six hundred before they even get drafted. You never hear about a nigga asking his agent to advance him $100,000 because he got a hot tip on a stock or he wants to invest in a real estate deal, do you. When you ain't never had shit, and you don't feel good about yourself, you think you can buy your self-esteem and put that shit around your neck like a chain . . . that's just real talk . . . that slave mentality is embedded in us to this day."

"I hear you, but I still should have been smarter than that. If my mother knew how much money I had left, I don't even want to think about living in the house and hearing her mouth every day," I said.

"You know what I'm going to do you for you? I'm going to flip that triple nickel for you a few times. Build your stash back up, and then you can do what you need to do . . . cool?"

Because I had so much confidence in Brad I didn't even hesitate to withdraw the $14,680 I had left in my account and give it to him. Besides, I had seen him with five times that much on more than one occasion.

"You sure your conscience is cool with this, right?" he asked. "I mean you know I'm not taking this money to buy oranges to sell on the highway."

"Yeah, I'm sure," I responded without hesitation. "I'm not out here dealing the shit myself."

About three weeks later Brad called me from North Carolina.

"Reece, you already doubled your cheddar. You want me to just put your shit aside and hit you off when I get back up north?" he asked.

"Let it ride!" I said excitedly. "Let that shit ride!"

It's amazing how quickly humility and remorse are forgotten when the forecast changes and things look up. When I hung up with Brad I was like, "Yeah, I'll let him keep flipping it until I get like $100,000 and then I'll trade in my Beemer and get that drop-top Jaguar." Two weeks after Brad got back to New York, Federal agents ran up on him at the Galaxy Diner on Linden Boulevard and arrested him. Turns out they had been watching Brad for more than a year. They confiscated his Lexus, Ford Expedition, Mercedes E320, two motorcycles, a condo in Mill Basin, a house in Charlotte, three kilos of cocaine, and $420,000 in cash, $29,360 of which belonged to me. I should have taken my money when he asked me. Now I was flat broke and Brad was about to spend the next ten years behind bars in Illinois.

If Vanessa Del Rio and Midori were *porn* stars, then I was a *pawn* star, because all the shit I bought with the exception of the car, and the full-length mink ended up at Gem pawnbrokers on the corner of Flatbush and Atlantic Avenues at some point over the next three or four months. Brad wrote me a letter from prison, saying that he apologized for what happened. He didn't specify anything about the money, I guess in case they read his mail; he didn't want them to think I was associated with his business in any way. I respected the fact that even though his ass was a lot worse off than me, he still had the decency to apologize, but that shit didn't help me get my money back or all my stuff out of hock. I figured I would use my tax return to at least get my things from Gem, but I ended up owing the government $800 dollars because I claimed two dependants who didn't exist. The Notorious BIG hit the nail right on the head when he said, "Mo' money, Mo' problems."

Chapter 17

2008

*T*ime had flown so fast that I could hardly believe it. It was already 2008, seven years since the 9/11 attacks and the passing of Aaliyah. Jay-Z and Beyoncé were a couple, and it seemed like every city in the country had their own set of Real Housewives.

"Does Jason Tucker still play for the Nets?" I asked one teller who was in his early twenties.

"Who?" he responded.

"She's talking about that light-skinned cat that used to play for them back in the day," another guy said. "Nah, Charisse, JT been on like six different teams since then. He messed up his knees. He's had a decent career, but teams keep trading him like a baseball card," he added.

"Who does he play for now?" I asked.

"The LA Clippers, I think. At least that's where he was last season," he replied. "He's from right here in Brooklyn, you know?"

"Yeah, I know. We grew up together," I said.

"Word. Can you get him to sign my basketball? Shit, he's still an NBA player and he made the All-Star team two or three times," he said.

"I haven't talked to him in *years*, we kind of lost touch," I explained.

"He's one of those pretty boys," he said. "My girl used to be in love with that cat until she found out she wasn't his type. His wife is white."

"Wife! He's married?" I asked in shock.

"Yeah, I saw him on *NBA Inside Stuff*. They met when he was in school in LA. She's from New York too, I think."

I don't why that ruined my day, but it did. I hadn't even thought about Jason for years, and I sure wasn't expecting him not to be with anybody after all this time. But married . . . and to a white chick? No, I wasn't expecting to hear that.

At almost thirty-two years old I thought I was over everything from my past. No one could believe I was as old as I was. There's no greater compliment to a woman than another woman telling you with all sincerity that they thought you were twenty-five or twenty-six when you're on the other side of thirty. I was still working at the same Chase branch on Fulton Street. Friends and acquaintances whom I had made at the bank had come and gone. Some I certainly kept in touch with, some just disappeared out of my life just as quickly as they entered. This wasn't what

I had planned for the rest of my life, but I had worked my way up to assistant branch manager, making almost fifty thousand a year. And since I hadn't gone back to school like I planned, where else was I going to make that much money, other than sliding my ass down an unsanitary silver pole that smelled like others women's asses.

I still lived at home with my mother, something else I hadn't planned, but the arrangement still worked for both of us. I handled most of the bills and she did the cooking and the cleaning as always.

"Hey, old lady," I said as I walked in the door from work.

"I got your old lady," she replied. "How was work today?"

I gave her that *don't even ask* look.

"Excuse my language, but shitty," I answered finally.

"Well, excuse my language, but its about to get shittier," she said. "Mariah's school called today."

"What was it about? Is somebody picking on her again? She didn't feel well and needed to come home? She forgot her homework at home?" I asked sarcastically.

"She got caught with a boy . . . in the boys' bathroom," she answered.

I heard her say it clear as day. I was looking right in her mouth when she said it, but I asked her to repeat herself because there was no way I had heard her correctly.

"She got caught doing what?"

"She got caught in the boys bathroom, and she wasn't in there smoking. The principal said they were kissing."

"Mariah!" I yelled.

"Now, before you go up and kill the poor child, you

might want to ask her why she was doing it, and why she felt like she needed to do it," my mother said.

"She fucking knows better!" I said angrily. "I'm not raising any little tramps around here," I replied before I went upstairs.

Mariah was fourteen now, but she was still very small for her age; she could easily pass for eleven or twelve. Mariah had the bedroom door closed, and when I opened it she was lying across the bed and watching television like nothing had happened.

"Turn that television off! We need to have a talk," I said.

"Can we wait until my show goes off?" she replied casually, without moving a muscle.

"Mariah, turn that fucking TV off now!"

She sucked her teeth and picked up the remote. After she turned the television set off she picked up her Sony PSP and turned it on. I walked over and snatched it so hard it flew all the way across the room and hit the wall.

"See, you're going to break it," she yelled.

I was now three times angrier than when I entered. I grabbed her by the collar and lifted her ass off the bed.

"You think I'm fucking playing with you! I'll kill your ass in here! You want to be kissing boys in a bathroom? What the hell is wrong with you!"

"Nothing's wrong with me. It's my mouth. If I want to kiss somebody I will," she said defiantly.

I let her collar go. I had to catch myself because I felt a rage in me that would have me ending up on the news.

"You know what? I'm not dealing with this. Let me call your father, you tell him it's your lips and your mouth and see what he says. . . . You think you're bad."

Mariah's eyes welled up with tears. She was afraid of Jamal, and he had never hit her once in her life. I busted her ass on a regular basis, and ever since she turned thirteen she would test me every chance she got. I called Jamal and told him what happened. He immediately blamed me.

"What the fuck are you teaching her over there!" he yelled. "And I told you about letting her watch all that stupid shit you watch on TV. You don't even need to watch all that mindless reality bullshit," he ranted.

"Look, Jamal, you're Mariah's father, not mine, all right. Save your speeches and just talk to your damn daughter. I deal with her shit everyday and I'm tired," I responded.

"Put her on the phone, dumbass," he said, trying to pick a fight.

"Your momma," I responded, before handing her the phone.

"Hi, Daddy," Mariah said meekly before bursting into tears. "I'm sorry, Daddy. He's the only boy who ever liked me, and I just kissed him."

I was like, *Where the hell did all the attitude go? How come I get all the grief?*

Mariah and I had a strange relationship. It was like she was my biggest antagonist. And in all fairness I was hers. I had never met a teenage girl who didn't like shopping, clothes, shoes, or getting their hair done. All she wanted to do was play video games, watch *Hanna* Damn *Montana* and live in some television fantasy world. She was also perpetually unhappy. I mean, I understood that she didn't have the freedom of your average fourteen-year-old, because her maturity and appearance wasn't that of an average fourteen-year-old. And the reason she didn't have many friends was because the NYC school system didn't know what to do with her. She couldn't keep up with the regular students' work and wasn't as socially mature, and she certainly wasn't special education material. But that's exactly where they placed her. There was nothing she hated more than being picked up every morning by the yellow bus. It made her frustrated and angry, and I, not Jamal or anyone else, was to blame for everything. By the time I was fourteen I was a full C cup, had the onion in the back, and grown-ass men were watching me. Mariah had yet to even break into a training bra, and I was still shopping for her clothes in the kids' section.

After she hung up with her father she shot me a look. An antagonistic one. I just rolled my eyes and went back downstairs.

"I love my daughter, but God forgive me for saying this, I don't like her," I said to my mother.

"You don't know her well enough not to like her," she replied.

"She's my child. I know her better than anybody."

"No, what you know is that your child isn't the way you want her to be. She's not like you, so getting to know her takes a little more work than you're willing to do," she said.

"Wait a minute . . . don't—"

"No, you wait a minute, Charisse. You are *the* most selfish person I've met in my entire life. You think coming in here with bags and bags of clothes, clothes that she don't give a rat's ass about, that you're doing something. That *stuff* doesn't make up for time. You know, Jamal might not be much of a boyfriend, but you could take a few parenting lessons from him."

"Mariah and I just don't vibe, our personalities clash," I said.

"Are you taking about your daughter, or somebody you work with at the bank? You don't have a choice in this," she said emphatically. "You made a decision, a choice, that you were going to have a baby, and guess what, nobody could tell you shit. But if things didn't work out the way you had pictured in your fantasy, and Mariah's not the second coming of Charisse, she's still *your* daughter. You don't get to pick how she came out, like you ordered a fucking Cadillac," she added before storming off.

Her words cut through to my soul. I wanted to just break down and cry. My mother had pulled my card like a blackjack dealer in Atlantic City.

Over the next couple of months things were extra tense between Mariah and I. If we were in a room together for more than ten minutes there was either complete silence or an argument. No matter what I said she found it necessary to disagree. If I said, "Jennifer Hudson has a beautiful voice and her song is hot," she would immediately say "She ain't better than Beyoncé," with an attitude, and if I tried to be agreeable by saying, "I'm not comparing because Beyoncé is great too," she would roll her eyes and say, "So now everybody on the radio is all that, huh?" I was constantly asking God to forgive me for thinking, *Why this little pompous B.I.T.C.H.?* My mother kept telling me I needed to talk *to* her, not *at* her, all the time. That she was, in her own way, asking for me to reach out. But I just couldn't communicate with her the way a mother should be able to. My mother said she noticed that Mariah was coming in a little later everyday, and when she did come in she would lock herself in the bathroom and talk on the phone until it was almost time for me to come home. I didn't think much of it. This sounded like typical behavior for a teenager. Mariah had always been little less mature than kids her age. I just figured maybe this new social, more outgoing Mariah would be happier and more apt to do the things teenage girls do.

"So, who's your new friend?" I asked one night, trying to make small talk. "I used to live on the phone with Brenda and Nitra when I was in school."

"What, now you got Grandma spying on me?" she snapped. "Damn."

"Watch your mouth. You're really getting beside yourself these days," I said.

"And," she said defiantly, "what are you going to do . . . hit me? I don't care if you do. I'm not afraid of you!" she added before storming out of the house.

I was like, *What the fuck! I don't need this shit!* I'm calling Jamal; she can go live with him. I called Jamal again and told him what was going on, and again he spoke to her for ten minutes and she hustled him the same way she did her grandmother with all that crying and fake-ass innocent, confused, *I can't do anything right* bullshit.

Two days later I get a call at work from Mariah's school, telling me that I needed to come right away. It was an *emergency*. I immediately thought she had gotten sick or jumped by some girls, so I hauled ass over to the school ready to fight and fuck somebody's kids up. When I got to the principal's office Mariah was slumped down in a chair, biting her nails. Across from her was a young Spanish boy who had the look of pure fear on his face. He was a very handsome young kid with dark hair and olive skin, but when he stood up to throw something into the trash can, he looked to be about the same height as Gary Coleman.

"Have a seat, Ms. Hawkins," the principal said.

I sat down right next to Mariah.

"What happened?" I asked her as I leaned into her ear.

"Ask him. He's the one that called you, right?" she replied out loud to embarrass me.

I just closed my eyes and said a quick prayer. It was obvious my daughter had a death wish, and I needed all the restraint that the good Lord could provide me with to avoid granting that wish.

"Mariah, would you and Luis step into Vice Principal Zimmer's office for a moment?" the principal said.

The vice principal escorted the two of them into his office.

"Ms. Hawkins, you're aware of the recent incident involving Mariah kissing a boy in school, aren't you?"

"Yes. . . . Please don't tell me they did it again. I spoke to her, her father spoke to her, and her grandmother spoke to her."

"Ms. Hawkins, I wish it was that simple. Mariah was caught having sex with Luis in an empty shop class."

"Sex as in touchy-touchy feely-feely? Or sex as in . . ."

"Sex as in . . ." he responded.

I was sick to my stomach; I couldn't believe that Mariah would let some boy talk her into having sex.

"I don't know what to say. I mean, she's knows right from wrong, so I'm not putting all the blame on the boy," I said.

"Well, I'm glad to hear that, because according to both of them, it was Mariah who initiated the encounter. Luis actually didn't want to go, but she tricked him into the room. He's in one of our special ed classes as well," he said. "Obviously this is a very serious situation, and unfortunately we're going to have to put Mariah out of school."

I was so hurt that I couldn't even get angry with her when she came back into the room. When we left we got into my car and I took her directly to the clinic for a checkup to make sure she didn't have any sexually transmitted diseases, and to get her some birth control pills.

"Are you going to tell my father?" she asked as we sat in the waiting room.

"I don't know," I answered.

I was really debating what to say to Jamal. I had to tell him something when he asked why she was changing schools, and, "because our daughter is a little tramp," doesn't really roll off the tongue too smoothly.

"Mariah, how many times have you had sex?" I finally asked.

"With Luis?" she asked calmly. "Today was the first time."

"Well, how may other people have you had sex with?" I asked with a mortified look on my face.

"Three or four," she answered.

I just began to cry as I put my arm around her and held her. She began to cry as well.

"I'm sorry, I'm sorry, Mommy. . . . I just wanted to get your attention," she said.

She may as well have reached into my chest and ripped my heart out.

"No, baby . . . Mommy is sorry."

All the tests on Mariah were negative except for one. Mariah Butler, fifteen, was pregnant by some other Spanish boy the kids called Cheeseburger. That was the bad news, but in true representation of the term "every cloud has a silver lining." The good news was that she didn't think she was in love with Cheeseburger, and she damn sure didn't want any part of having a baby. I never told Jamal or her grandmother that she had an abortion. I told her that if she ever wanted to tell them it would be her choice.

Niece and I had somehow become really cool over the years. After she and Jamal broke up and we had the whole ex-girlfriend/baby momma shit in common, it became like a little support group, a Jamal-bashing free-for-all, or in my case a chance to hear all the gossip about the shit he put her through. Niece was actually good people. We were out having drinks one night with some of the girls from my job when she told me that she and Jamal initially met at the Green Acres shopping mall about the same time I had Mariah.

"Did you work at the mall?" I asked

"No, I was there shopping with my cousin," she explained. "I tried on this little two-tone gold hugs and kisses bracelet in a jewelry store, and he walked up to us and started complimenting me and talking shit. I was like, *Get lost, weirdo,* and we stepped, 'cause you know the world is full of crazy asses."

I thought to myself, *Damn, that sounds a little familiar.*

"Anyway, we kept it moving and finished shopping. I didn't think no more about him, until he ran up to us when we were leaving and put something into my shopping bag that he said was a card with his number on the back. I got in my cousin's car, looked in the bag, and found a bracelet. At the time I had a man, but we was going through shit, and one day I came across Jamal's number and called him . . . I knew I should have used that card to light the oven."

I wanted to laugh so badly. I couldn't believe that Jamal had used the same exact cheap gold jewelry routine on both of us with the same exact result. My girlfriend from work later asked me why I didn't tell Niece about meeting Jamal at the Albee Square Mall and the bamboo earrings.

"I'm over Jamal, been over him, but I think Niece still has feelings for that dude. Matter of fact, I think they still knock boots every now and then." I said.

"Knock boots . . . you are dumb old," she laughed.

Summer 2008

It was a bright and sunny 85 degree Saturday and Niece was throwing Essence a big birthday barbecue at her house in St. Albans. After fighting all morning about her having to go, Mariah and I arrived around three p.m. The large backyard was beautifully decorated with streamers and balloons, and there were at least thirty guests who had already arrived. Niece was setting up the food table.

"Hey, girl," I said as I walked over to give her a hug.

"Hey, Charisse. Hey, Mariah," she replied with a huge smile. "I'm so glad you came. Essence is going to be thrilled. Charisse, you know she thinks you're as fly as Rihanna," Niece said.

"I can't believe she's eleven already," I said.

"I know, especially since I'm still only twenty-one," she replied jokingly.

Essence came running over all dressed up in her birthday outfit.

"Look at you! Your outfit is bananas. Happy birthday, princess," I said as she ran over to give me a hug.

"Happy birthday, Essence," Mariah said. "Wait until you see what I got you!" she said with surprising and unusual enthusiasm.

"Mom, I'm taking my sister upstairs to see my room." Essence said as they walked off.

"So where is . . . ?" I attempted to ask.

"Stupid ass is not here yet, but the cake's in the house. I picked it up my damn self," she responded, with a disgust I could relate to.

"So how do you feel about being home again?" I asked.

"Embarrassed, frustrated, angry," she replied.

"Well, at least you left and then came back. I still haven't left."

"Please, I came home with the same things I left with, plus an eleven-year-old. I'm more upset with myself. I was living in a dorm at Hofstra, driving my little Nissan Sentra, and yeah, I was dating an asshole on the football team, but that's what you're supposed to do in college. Jamal came into my life on some real I'm-going-to-take-care-of-you-forever bullshit, and it's been a roller coaster ride ever since. I love my daughter, wouldn't trade her for all the tea in China, but if I had it to do all over again . . . well, you know."

"Yeah, I do know," I replied. "But at least you got a bracelet, a diamond ring, and a BMW out of the deal," I said jokingly.

"The bracelet, which I actually still have, cost a hundred dollars, the ring which I had appraised at four hundred dollars because the gold was real but the stone, which was a high-quality cubic zirconium, got lost when I threw it at Sir Front-a-lot after I found that out. And that BMW 5 series he so-called *bought* me back in the day, well, that got repossessed when he couldn't keep up the payments on it. And the shit was in *my* name, so it went on *my* credit," she explained.

Niece and I walked to the front of the house. I wanted to get Essence's gift from the trunk of my now eleven-year-old BMW 328i with 130,000 miles and worn leather seats. That car was all that remained of what my father had left for me, and I vowed that I would keep it forever. As we reached the front of the driveway a shiny black Range

Rover with tinted windows pulled up. All we could see was the silhouette of two people, a man and a woman. The truck parked, but no one got out.

"Aw shit, this feels like a drive-by," I said jokingly.

"I don't think people parallel park during a drive-by," she replied.

I got Essence's gift from my car and we went into the backyard.

"I'm about to sing 'Happy Birthday,' but Jamal's going to miss it. He'd be late for his own damn funeral. Frontin' like he's always so busy," Niece said.

At that moment I saw something that damn near made me choke. Jamal came walking into the backyard, carrying two shopping bags full of gifts.

"Niece, for once he wasn't fronting. He's been getting real busy."

Niece turned around and looked at Jamal. She took the knife in her hand that we were about to use to cut the cake and flipped it over into the position to stab someone. I took the knife out of her hand before anyone noticed and walked her into the house.

"Come on. Let's go get the cake from inside," I said.

By this time everyone had noticed Jamal, including Niece's mother and granny, who were looking out the back window. When we got in the house Niece was visibly upset. Her mother was standing there shaking her head, and her eighty-five-year old grandmother was sitting at the table, eating the icing off the birthday cake.

"So what are you going to do, go out there and start a fight?" I asked.

"Charisse, I know right now you're like *this bitch has got a lot of nerve,*" she said. "Excuse my language, granny."

"This ain't about me. I'm just telling you don't feed into what he does. You know him already. Don't tell me you're shocked?"

"The boy doesn't like his momma," Granny said.

We both stopped and turned to the elderly woman who looked great for her age, and whose face didn't reflect a fraction of the stress that was visible on Niece's and mine.

"When a colored man don't like his momma, they take it out on the women in their lives," she said before eating a little more frosting. "When a white man don't like his momma they go on a killing spree."

Charisse and I went back outside with Essence's birthday cake. Jamal was standing there with his newest conquest, a beautiful half black/half Asian–looking woman in her mid- to late thirties . . . and she was about five months' pregnant.

"Charisse, Niece, this is Yvonne," Jamal said with pride.

I smiled and looked her up and down, looking for the gold trinket that she got from Sir Tricks-a-lot. She had on a diamond anklet . . . bingo.

Niece tried her best to have a good time at the party, but she still had feelings for Jamal. I believe she was still holding on to a strand of hope that he would change. Seeing his new girlfriend pregnant, a girlfriend she didn't even know existed, was a dose of reality she hadn't planned on swallowing. There was an air about Yvonne. She was attractive and she knew it. Her long silky hair and hazel eyes made her what black men considered a trophy chick. Her features were hard though, like she had been through some real shit in her life. I was willing to bet she had dated drug dealers since she was a teenager. I kept catching her watching Niece and I. Women are by nature competitive and insecure creatures. So when she met not one but two of her man's exes/baby mommas, and they looked good, it must have been a little unsettling, because common sense tells your ass, *I guess my looks are no guarantee that this is going to last.*

"Damn, Charisse, you're looking good. That five or six pounds you put on went to all the right spots," Jamal said to me when we were standing there alone for a second, "Maybe I made a mistake."

"Jamal, you *are* a mistake. Now take your tired, fronting, damn-near-forty-year-old, still-don't-know-who-you-are, Jay-Z-wannabe-ass away from me . . . please."

Mariah and Essence had just recently gotten used to the fact that they were sisters and had to share his attention, but neither of them was too pleased to hear about Daddy's surprise news. I don't think Jamal ever took a moment to look at how his actions affected anyone but himself. I guess he felt like as long as he spent time with them, the checks cleared, and the shopping bags were full, it was no harm, no foul. That he was in some twisted way punishing Niece and I for not putting up with his bullshit. The only question now was how long before Jackass started up some new foolishness, if he hadn't already.

Chapter 18

A few weeks later I was pulling out of the parking lot after work one day. I was listening to Jay-Z's "Reasonable Doubt" (that shit is a classic), and I had Mary J Blige's "Share My World" next up in the CD changer, with Anita Baker after that. That was the vibe I was on that evening. I had to drive up to Harlem to pick up a cake from this spot called Bake My Cake on Seventh and 137th, and I already knew what traffic was going to be like during rush hour, so I just wanted to zone out into my music and chill. I forgot to call my mother to tell her I was going to be coming home a little late. So I reached into my purse and pulled out my new BlackBerry Curve. I didn't bother to put my earpiece in because this was going to be a ten-second call at best. No sooner did I go into my contacts, hit MOM, and lift the phone to my ear than I heard a police siren. I pulled over so they could pass, because they couldn't be fucking with me. I hadn't even said "Hello" yet. When I pulled over on Flatbush Avenue in front of LIU, the flashing red, white, and blue lights pulled over behind me.

"Aint this a bitch. These fake ass *Law & Order: SVU* muthafuckas don't have a crime to solve or something," I blurted out.

"License, registration, and insurance card please," the female officer said.

I was nervous as shit. This was the first time I had ever been pulled over. *It would have to be a black woman,* I thought as I saw her hand reach for my information.

"Officer, I was just checking my cell phone for the time," I said meekly.

"Please step out of the vehicle," she said firmly.

I didn't want to get out. Thankfully the traffic was thick, so I had a million witnesses in case she tried to Rodney King my ass. As a joke I was going to say, "Can't we all just get along?" but she might not have found that shit funny.

I stepped out of my car and still didn't make eye contact with her.

"This license must be a fake," she said seriously. "The Charisse Hawkins I know thinks she's way too cute to drive herself around."

I turned around and looked at her like "What the . . . ?" I couldn't believe my eyes.

"Oh my God!" I screamed before embracing Nitra. "When did this happen?"

The last time I had seen Nitra she was high as a kite and staggering down Fulton Street. That was more than ten years ago.

"I've been on the force about five years now. I never quite made it to law school, but by the grace of God, maybe one day," she said.

"But the last time I saw you . . ." I responded before catching myself.

"You can say it," she said with a smile. "I was on some shit, and I was *on* some shit."

"And your son?"

"He was in foster care back then. He's been back home with me for years now. He graduating from high school next year and they already offered him a scholarship to the University of Bridgeport," she said, beaming with pride.

"I hear that, but if he's playing ball on that level he must have taken his height from somebody in your family, 'cause you and Nice don't reach six feet if you stood on top of each other," I said jokingly.

"No, sweetie, it's an academic scholarship . . . premed," she clarified. "But he is five-ten, thank goodness."

"So you've been a cop for all that time and you couldn't stop by and see a bitch?"

"I just transferred to Brooklyn a few weeks ago, and I kept saying I was going to stop by the bank and see if you still worked there," she said.

"And where else would I be?" I responded. "Where am I going?"

"To medical school, where you always belonged," she answered.

"Please, you know how old I am, because you're the same age. The medical school train left the station a long time ago."

"If that's what's still in your heart, put it in God's hands. He'll lead you right down the path that's intended for you, whether you're thirty-one or seventy-one."

Nitra was as crazy as ever. I'd heard of the Flying Nun, but now here was the Preaching Cop. I always used to have a fear that I was going to get a call or run into an old acquaintance who would tell me something bad had happened to her, but here she was, doing well. Life had taken its best shots and she had gotten up a little stronger each time.

"Whatever happened to Nice?" I asked.

"He got his diploma, believe it or not," she said. "And maybe he can use it to get a job when he gets out of prison."

"I used to keep in touch with Brenda every once in a while, but I haven't spoken to her since the day after the World Trade Center attacks, and that's going on nine years already," I said.

"I spoke to Brenda. She and the kids are fine. She has three now. Her and Dave finally got that son . . . Mark."

"I can't believe her and Dave are still together. That's like sixteen years," I said. "I guess it's your turn next," I said playfully.

"This October," she replied before flashing a beautiful engagement ring. "Can you believe it?"

No, I really can't, I thought to myself. Nitra looked good in the sense that she was doing well, but she still looked like Alf. How the fuck did she have an engagement ring and I didn't. *She bought that ring for herself. She probably got some cat that don't work and she takes care of him.*

"So what does your fiancé do? Tell me about him," I asked.

"His name is Aaron. He's an electrician for NBC, he's a Christian and just a good guy. I am so blessed."

That means he either looks like the bottom of my shoes, or he's old enough to retire. Nitra pulled out a picture of herself and a handsome man in his late thirties, who, judging from the photo, was about six-feet-tall, slender, medium brown complexion, with a goatee and a bald head. He reminded me of a darker version of Common.

"Oh, you guys make a nice couple," I said with mixed feelings. "Does he have kids too?" I asked.

"No, he can't have kids, but he coaches the church basketball team, and he and my son are really close, so it's all good," she said. "What are your weekends like? We should get together and have lunch one Saturday, all three of us."

"I work every other Saturday, so just let me know when and it's on," I said. "Damn, girl, it's good to see you."

"You too."

We exchanged numbers and embraced before getting into our respective cars and pulling away. I was so excited that I couldn't wait to tell my mother whom I had just ran into, so I called her.

"Mom, guess who I was just with for the last ten minutes?" I asked excitedly.

"Who?" she asked.

Just as I was about to answer I heard the sirens and saw the flashing lights again in my rearview mirror. This time it wasn't Nitra through. I got a $200 cell phone ticket and another $55 ticket because I forget to put my seatbelt on.

"Play 255 straight and box," my mother said when I told her what happened. "Call your aunt and ask her what the number is for getting a traffic ticket too," she said, dead serious.

I'm out $255 dollars and she wants me to go the bodega and stand behind some person on public assistance who has a list of numbers two feet long so I can be pissed because that's my muthafucking tax dollars they're using. At this point all I wanted to do was go to bed.

Later that night

I was in bed sleeping. I mean that knocked out-with-slobber-running-out-of-my-mouth, White-Castle-hamburger-farts-won't-even-wake-you-up, you-mean-there-was-an-earthquake last-night? kind of sleep. I thought I was dreaming because I kept hearing a phone ring. The ring tone was Jay-Z's "Show Me What You Got." So after a few minutes I came to the real-ization that I wasn't dreaming. I knocked over an $80 bottle of Yves St. Laurent perfume as I reached for the phone. I glanced at the clock, and it was 1 a.m.

"Hello," I said angrily. "Who is this? It's one o'clock in the morning."

I could hardly understand what the person was saying through all the damn crying.

An hour later I was standing in my kitchen in my robe and slippers, pouring a glass of juice for Jamal's girlfriend Yvonne. . . . What the fuck, man!

"I didn't know who else to call. I found your number in one of his cell phones," she said.

"Yvonne, I'm more than happy to listen, preferably not at two a.m., but I don't know what to tell you. Sounds like you need to talk to Jamal," I responded.

"I haven't seen Jamal in three days. He hasn't come home," she said. "He calls the house with this nonchalant attitude like nothing's wrong, and if I say anything he tries that reverse-anger bullshit, and we haven't had sex since I told him I was pregnant. He must be getting it from somewhere else."

"Pump your brakes, sister . . . I *hope* you don't think we . . ."

"No, not you," she replied quickly.

A second later my mother came bursting in the kitchen with a large pair of scissors and her wig on crooked.

"I thought somebody broke into the house!" she said.

"And what were you going to do, hem his pants?" I asked sarcastically. "Ma, this is Yvonne, Jamal's girlfriend."

She didn't say a word. She just smiled at Yvonne and shook her head at me. I could almost hear her laughing at me in her mind and saying to herself, *Damn, you're stupid for no reason at all—just because.* Then she went right back to bed.

"I think he's still creeping with Niece," she said.

"Why?"

"'Cause she asked him for a car. Shit, she been taking Ebony on the bus," she stated.

"Essence," I said, correcting her.

"And I told him that shit straight out. I said she been taking Jet on the bus, she ain't no baby no more."

"Maybe she really needs the car?" I said, trying to be diplomatic.

"Yeah, well, he damn sure went out and bought her an X5 . . . cash money. And a bitch knows when your baby's mother asks for a whip, *if* she gets one, it's a damn minivan unless they're still smashing."

I couldn't have cared less about Yvonne's problem. *He bought Niece an X5,* I thought to myself.

Yvonne and I sat there and talked until four a.m.; even after I put my head down and went to sleep, though, she kept going. *This might just be the reason he hasn't been home in three or four days. He took his eardrums on vacation,* I thought. When Yvonne finally did go home I felt bad for her.

About a week later Nitra called me. She had caught up with Brenda and we set a date to meet in the city on my next Saturday off, at T.G.I. Friday's on 49th Street and Seventh Avenue. I was so excited. It was going to be like Patti LaBelle reuniting with Sarah Dash and Nona Hendryx, or Diana Ross with the Supremes, or even SWV, as long as they recognized that I would be Coko.

I was the first one to arrive, so I got a table on the upper level and waited anxiously for the Brooklyn Bitches reunion tour to start. Nitra arrived about five minutes later.

"Brenda got stuck in a little traffic, she'll be here in a few," she said as she sat down.

"So, Charisse, I can't wait until Brenda gets here to start. What happened with you and your daughter's father? You still deal with him? You got a restraining order against him? He got a restraining order against you . . . what?"

"No, shit just didn't work out. You know how it is," I replied.

"I never liked that cat . . . *never.* I mean, I don't pass judgment on people anymore because I am not God, and I also know that Nice was a piece of doo-doo, but at least he wore his doo-doo outfit with pride and right out front where you could see it *and* smell it. That cat was so busy

frontin' and faking moves that I can only imagine the drama
you went through with him. When he ran up to us in the
jewelry store and started talking that fake Billy Dee Williams
crap I was like, *Is this fool for real?*"

After all these years it still hit a nerve when she said that.
It wasn't that I gave a damn about Jamal, but she was right
about him then, and she was right about him now, and that's
what bothered me. Brenda came staggering up the steps
right at that moment. My eyes damn near popped out of my
head when I saw her. Brenda was always a big girl, but she
was more shapely and voluptuous back then. Brenda—the
2008 version with three kids and a house—was 270 plus,
and that plus could have been anywhere between 10 and 30
easy.

"You bitches couldn't get a table downstairs?" she asked
while huffing and puffing. "I have a bad knee."

*It's not the knee that's bad, it's the pressure that knee is under
that's bad,* I thought to myself.

"All right, all right, my knee is fine. I'm fat, okay? Let's
say what you're thinking and get it over with," she said.

We all looked at one another and burst out laughing so
loud everyone turned around with that, *Oh no, the rowdy
black women are here,* look. It was just like the old days.

"Damn Charisse, you still look like a teenager. You really
haven't changed a bit. I'm jealous, bitch," Brenda said with
a sincere-looking smile. "And don't feel no pressure to say
you too. I got nine or ten mirrors in my house and two
scales, so I know the deal," she added.

We talked, ate, and drank all afternoon. We shared
stories about what had happened over the years in each of

our lives. We cried when I told them the story of my brief reconciliation with my father, and when Brenda told us that her mother Gail died alone on a park bench high on heroin. We laughed at all the silly things we did as teenagers and reflected on how, at the time, we had no idea we were living the best times of our lives. Three twelve-year-old girls making up dances to Chubb Rock's "Ya Bad Chubb," and later to De La Soul's "Me, Myself and I." We sat there making plans about all the family trips we were going to take together, who was going to have the first barbecue, and how we were going to make it our business to stay in touch. But as we paid the check and prepared to leave, it dawned on me that it wasn't just like old times. We weren't all going to get on the same subway to hang out on my stoop or spend the night at Brenda's. We were each going back into our own little world, one that didn't really include one another. It made me sad as we hugged and separated to go to our cars. There's a reason that memories are so precious, because at the end of the day they're all you really have. It was great to see my friends and know they were doing well, but I figured the next time we got together would probably be at Nitra's wedding.

Chapter 19

Six months after giving birth to Jamal's third daughter, Brianna Jamela Butler, Yvonne ended up just like Niece and I, in court for child support. He had put her out but told her the baby could stay. Now, he knew damn well no mother in her right mind is leaving a newborn behind. She eventually moved back in with her mother. I found that out during one of Jamal and Yvonne's arguments, Yvonne's mouth went into overdrive, and she mentioned that she and Niece had confided in me about their situations with him. Jamal knew that Niece and I were cool, but I guess he figured there's no way in hell all three of these women are going to form a triangle against his black ass.

"Damn, Reece, I thought we were cool. I thought we let bygones be bygones," Jamal said when he called my cell phone.

"What are you talking about?" I asked.

"You put Yvonne up to taking me to court," he replied. "Don't deny that shit. I know you. I can hear you now:

"'Uh huh, get his ass, don't let his ass breathe, suffocate him and his wallet.'"

"Jamal, you are bugging. You think I don't have nothing better to do than give legal counsel to your damn woman?"

"Did Yvonne come to your house late one night a while back?" he asked.

"Yeah."

"And did she or did she not divulge personal information about things in our relationship?"

"Yeah, but . . ."

"And did you, Charisse Hawkins, listen to said personal information for more than three hours and offer her advice on said personal information?"

"Yeah, but . . ."

"I rest my case," he stated.

"You are a damn fake-ass Johnnie Cochran. I did not tell her to take you to court," I said, defending myself.

"Yeah all right, Charisse. I thought you was better than that, but if that's how you want to play it, cool," he said before hanging up.

I just chalked the call up to Jamal's usual foolishness. This cat had *zero* accountability, no matter what he did to people; he didn't expect any reactions for his actions. Repercussions were for other people, not Jamal "Mr. Bullshit" Butler.

Two weeks later at work I was sitting at my desk, looking at clothes online as usual, when one of my tellers came up to me.

"Excuse me—there's someone here to see you," he said.

I got up and went out front. There was an older African-

American man standing by the front desk. He looked very kind and grandfatherly.

"Hello, may I help you?" I asked.

"Are you Charisse Hawkins?"

"Yes."

He then handed me a document.

"Miss Hawkins, you've been served. Thank you."

This old Grady-looking, muthafuckin' dusty old man had served me with court papers from Jamal. I had no idea what this was about, but when I saw Jamal's name I could almost smell the shit in the air.

After that sneaky bastard managed to get his child support payments lowered, he had the audacity to roll up on me in the parking lot in his Range Rover.

"Nothing personal, Reece. It's just business. I'll pick Mariah up on Saturday," he said.

I wanted to pick up a big-ass rock and smash his windshield. But just then something in my heart changed. I looked up at the sun and I wasn't upset anymore. I stood there and let it all go, everything Jamal had ever done to me, every single lie he had ever told, all the cheating and bullshitting . . . gone. I literally laughed right in his face.

"You're out your damn mind, girl. I didn't mean to drive you crazy," he said.

"You couldn't drive me to the corner, not even in your big, pretty Range Rover. I'm laughing because you're funny, like a joke."

"Please, I ain't no joke," he replied defensively.

"You know what, you're right. You're pathetic. I don't

begrudge you—I feel sorry for you. You'll be fifty years old still popping up at shopping malls, lurking around to see whom you can run your little pathetic pussy hustle on, and then running them out of your life before they figure out you're not who you pretend to be. That's what it's all about, Jamal. You're not a fucked-up person, you're just fucked-up. You don't even know who Jamal Butler is. He's Jay-Z, he's P. Diddy, he's the hustler on the corner, he's everybody, because in reality, he's nobody."

"Fuck you!" he shouted before driving off like a maniac.

I could see in his face that I had hit a nerve; he was about to cry like a little bitch. I had stripped him of all his designer labels, his watch, and his Rover and exposed him in broad daylight. That was the worst thing you can do to someone like him: Transform into a mirror and show them their reflection.

I couldn't wait to get home to tell my mother about my day in court. I knew she had been worrying about me, and at least now I could set her mind at ease.

"Ma . . . wait until I tell you what your boy did now," I said out loud as soon as I walked through the door. "Ma."

I stuck my head in the kitchen and saw a cigarette burning in the ashtray, so I knew she had to be home. As I walked upstairs I could hear her television.

"You need to stop leaving cigarettes burning all over the house. You need to stop smoking period," I said as I walked up the stairs.

I looked in her bedroom and the television was playing, but the room was empty. I started to get a feeling in the pit of my stomach that something wasn't right. I walked down hall to the bathroom and opened the door. She was lying in the floor, unconscious.

"Ma! Oh my God!" I screamed.

I ran to the phone and dialed 911. I don't know how I managed to give them the address accurately, because I was screaming and couldn't tell my head from my behind. The ambulance arrived in what seemed like an hour, but turned out to be five to seven minutes. I was in the waiting room of the emergency room when Aunt Belle and Abadu arrived. Niece bought Mariah a few minutes later.

"Is Grandma going to be okay?" Mariah asked.

"Yes, baby, she'll be fine," I replied.

"So what happened?" Aunt Belle asked.

"When I got home from court I found her lying on the bathroom floor."

"What did the doctor say?"

"Nothing yet. They've been in there with her since we got here."

The doctor came out and told me she had had a stroke. I never felt so helpless in all my life. She was in a coma, and nothing in the world made sense at that moment. I couldn't even imagine what life would be like without Vivian McNeil. My mother was the most perfect person God ever created, and I begged him not to take her, even though I had often taken her for granted. The doctor let me go in to see her. She looked like she was resting, and she was probably was. She had spent the majority of her life taking care of me, and then taking care of Mariah and me. I knew she wouldn't want me to feel guilty, but I did. I was thirty-two years old and *still* leaning on her, instead of the other way around.

My mother had been in the hospital for about a week. Nothing had changed. I had taken a leave from work so that I could be both at the hospital and at home to make sure Mariah was okay. Her grandmother had always been the one constant in her life, the one person who never wanted her to be anything but Mariah. Niece and Yvonne were both a great help. Nitra called everyday to see how was she doing, or if there was anything she could do. Brenda was all the way up in Westchester, but she even drove down with the kids twice that week to bring food. These were my friends, and they were there when I needed them.

The next morning after I got Mariah off to school, I decided to do a little house cleaning before going to the hospital; this way if she woke up and asked me. "Is my house clean?" I wouldn't have to tell a bold-faced lie. I was mopping the kitchen floor when the doorbell rang. I opened the door, and the first the thing I saw was a beautiful bouquet of flowers. I looked up and damn near fell out.

"Jason . . . Jason Tucker!"

"How are you, Charisse?" he asked with a big smile.

I opened the door and he came in. He was even better looking at thirty-two than he had been as a teenager. He had grown a nice little beard and mustache and had filled out so he wasn't as lanky and thin.

"I was just cleaning up the kitchen," I said.

"You . . . cleaning the kitchen," he said jokingly. "I must be in the wrong house. My Charisse wouldn't even clean up our little play area in the classroom in kindergarten. If I remember correctly you told her you were going to have a maid."

"You still remember that?"

"Hey, I heard about your mother. I just wanted to drop by and give her my best."

"How did you hear?" I asked.

"Well, you know Miss Frazier who lives down the block?"

"Old Miss Frazier. The one that's like a hundred and ten?"

"Yeah, well, she's discovered e-mail, so my mother checks up on her, and she e-mails my mother the neighborhood news," he said. "How is your mother doing anyway?"

"The same," I answered. "It's rough—it doesn't even seem real. I always thought my mother was Superwoman."

"How is your daughter?" he asked as he noticed a photo of her on the mantle.

"She's okay, hanging in like the rest of us," I said. "And what about you, Mr. Big-Time Basketball Star. I hear you're married now."

"I was . . . didn't really work out," he replied. "You always hear about how NBA players cheat on their wives, but I found out the hard way that it goes both ways."

I didn't know what to say, so I just gave him that wide-eyed "Yikes" look.

"Well, I'm going to let you finish up. I'm sure you'll be heading over to the hospital soon," he said as he handed me the flowers.

"Thank you. This is so thoughtful. I'll take them to the hospital later," I said.

"The flowers are for you. I hope your boyfriend doesn't mind."

"If I had one I'm sure he wouldn't appreciate it, but I think you're safe."

Jason kissed me on my cheek and gave me a hug.

"You take care of yourself and your mom okay," he said, as he looked me in the eye. "And if you need me, just tell Miss Frazier to e-mail me."

Jason left and I watched him through the window as he got into his navy blue Cadillac Escalade and drove away. Something in my heart told me that this wouldn't be the last time I saw him.

When I got to the hospital Aunt Belle, Aunt Della, and Aunt Ruby were all there. They were praying around my mother's bed.

"What happened?" I asked in a panic.

"Nothing, child," Aunt Belle said. "We're praying—that's what people do at the hospital around sick people."

"Jesus, just give us strength and guidance. We know that you are a perfect God and you don't make mistakes, and we pray that you help us to make the right decision, Lord," Aunt Ruby said.

"What decision?"

"Charisse, we have a decision to make. Does your mother want to live like this?" Aunt Della asked.

My mother had always said that if she ever went in a coma and didn't come out to let her go in peace. "I didn't come in the world with no machine and I don't need one on my way out," she would say. I guess I was in denial. I kept telling myself she was just taking a little break, a vacation from everyday life and the past thirty-two years. When the administrator from the hospital came in to talk to us. I sent her away.

"That won't be necessary," I said calmly, "She just needs a little more rest."

My aunts all gave me that "She's about to go coo coo for Cocoa Puffs look, so let's not press the issue today look."

That next Monday I went back to the bank. I had a dream that my mother told me to *Take your ass back to work. This is my vacation, not yours.* There was nothing I could do anyway. I had put it in the Lord's hands, and even Aunt Belle, who ordinarily would have put up a fight, didn't offer any resistance.

I was sitting at my desk and looking at all the work I had to catch up on, when one of my tellers walked over and placed a small box and a card on my desk with my name on the envelope.

"Who's this from?" I asked.

She just shrugged her shoulders with a cryptic smile and walked away.

I opened the card first and it said, "Some people are unforgettable . . . Love, Jason." When I opened the box there were five pieces of penny bubble gum inside, the same kind he used to buy for me in kindergarten. I couldn't help but to cry.

"Charisse you have a call on 4042," another teller shouted over to me.

"Hello."

"You didn't go to my senior prom with me, so I figured I'd bribe you *before* I asked you out this time," Jason said.

"With bubble gum?" I asked jokingly.

"Hey, there's a recession, and besides, you know my brother Archie is a dentist, so worst case, I'll bring the family a little business," he replied.

"I meant to ask you, shouldn't you be in Los Angeles? I thought that's where you played now."

"I'm retired. I wanted to keep playing, I'm only thirty-two, you know."

"So why didn't you?"

"My knees are seventy five," he answered. "L-A wasn't really my kind of place to live, so I never bought any property out there. I just rented, so when I decided to hang up my sneakers, I still had my house in New Jersey," he explained.

That night for the first time since she went into hospital, I didn't go to see my mother. Jason took Mariah and I to dinner. He kept insisting that he didn't mind if we went by there first, but I felt like my mother would've just wanted us to go out and have a good time. I couldn't believe how Mariah opened up to Jason; I honestly hadn't seen her smile that much in the past two years combined. We had a great evening and while I certainly didn't forget my problems, it felt good to laugh and smile for a few hours.

That Saturday morning Jason came by to take Mariah and me to breakfast. I had forgotten that Jamal was coming by to pick up Mariah as well. When he showed up we were just getting into Jason's truck. Jamal had his new girlfriend with him in the car; she couldn't have been older than nineteen or twenty. I wanted to say something to him like, *Nice, you bought somebody for Mariah to play with*? or, *Which store at the mall did you meet this one, Build-a-Bear*? But I kept my thoughts to myself; besides, the look on his face when Jason stepped back out of the truck was priceless.

"Mariah, did you forget I was coming to get you?" Jamal asked.

"I'm sorry, Daddy. I forget all about it. Is it okay if Mommy drops me off at your house later? We're going to breakfast right now," she replied.

"Jamal, this is my fault. I forgot too. I should have called you and told you to come this afternoon," I said.

Jamal was pissed now, and it didn't have anything to do with the fact we forgot he was coming.

"So, are you going with them, or you coming with me?" he asked Mariah with a slight attitude.

"Excuse me, I don't mean to butt in, but I really don't mind dropping her off wherever this afternoon," Jason said as he walked over.

"Yo, I didn't even notice you over there," Jamal said, lying through his teeth. "Sorry to hear about your career. Too bad you never got that championship ring."

"That would have been nice, but it just wasn't in the cards," Jason replied. "No complaints though. It's all good."

I guess Jamal's little girlfriend caught a glimpse of Jason because she jumped out of his truck.

"Oh shit! You're that basketball player! My older brother is a senior in college and he used to love you. He had your sneakers and all that," she said, sounding very much like someone who still had posters of Chris Brown and Bow Wow on her bedroom wall.

"He's retired," Jamal said.

"I don't care. Can I have your autograph?" she asked.

"Damn, you are so fine!" she added like a star-struck teenager.

Jason signed a twenty-dollar bill for her as Jamal seethed off to the side.

"Mariah, I'm not going to be home later, so either come with me now or I'll see you next week," he snapped.

"Mariah, go ahead with Daddy," I whispered in her ear. "He hasn't spent any time with you in a while and we don't want him to feel bad. I'll give Grandma a big kiss for you."

Mariah displayed a maturity that I hadn't seen in her before. She didn't pout, and she didn't complain.

"I'm going with you, Daddy. I need to run in and throw some things in a bag," she said.

"Don't worry about that. We're going to the outlets in Riverhead. We'll get you some things. You know Daddy's paper is long," he said boastfully.

Jason wouldn't even look at him. He was embarrassed for him, and I was embarrassed for me, and Hanna Montana over there with him. She was too young to even realize that she should have been embarrassed at all.

"I just want to apologize," I said.

"For what?" he asked.

"Jamal can be an asshole sometimes," I said.

"He didn't do anything . . . and FYI, never apologize for someone else's actions," he said. "I played in the league for ten years, Charisse. Cats like Jamal are pretty common."

"What do you mean?"

"Oh, I'm not judging homeboy, but I meant people who put up things in front of themselves so you can't see who they are, or who they aren't. Now, whether those things are flashy cars, pretty girls, or money, it's all the same thing."

"So you think that girl was pretty, huh?" I asked.

"She's a little young for my taste, but let's call a spade a spade. Ladies and gentlemen, we have a winner."

About forty-five minutes we were in the middle of breakfast at the IHOP when my cell phone rang. I didn't recognize the number, but it was from a 718 area code, not an 800 number, so I knew it probably wasn't a bill collector. When I answered Aunt Belle was on the other end, screaming hysterically. My heart dropped and I felt faint. She was yelling for me to get to the hospital.

"We have to go. That was my aunt at the hospital!" I said as the tears began to stream down my face.

Jason called the waitress over and handed her a fifty-dollar bill. The check couldn't have been any more that twenty dollars, but we hurried out and didn't even wait for his change. I couldn't stop trembling. I closed my eyes and prayed and tried to prepare myself for the worst as Jason placed his hand on top of mine and rubbed it gently.

When we got to the hospital I ran right past security to get upstairs. They didn't even bother to try and stop us. My heart began to race faster and faster as I got closer to her room, and I was incredibly thirsty.

I burst into her hospital room to find all my aunts surrounding her bed, but there was no crying, just laughter.

As I approached the bed I swear everything seemed to slow down. I could hear a voice in my head telling me that I was being given a gift, and to cherish it, for it could be taken away at any time. I saw all my mother's sisters turn around and look at me in slow motion with smiles on their faces as they cleared a space for me to step in. Vivian McNeil was sitting up in bed and drinking apple juice out of a small plastic cup.

"Oh, Ma!" I cried as I gently kissed her on the forehead. "I missed you so much."

"I missed you, too," she said calmly. "But I needed to get some rest and pray in peace."

"That ain't nothing but Jesus!" my aunt Ruby shouted as she held her Bible in the air.

At that moment Jason walked into the room. He stood back for a moment and looked on in disbelief. My mother looked over at him standing there and smiled. Their eyes met and he began to cry.

"Come over here for a minute," she said.

Jason came and stood by me. My mother took his hand.

"Life always comes full circle. What is meant to be will be. You have *always* loved my daughter, and nothing happens before its time," she said to him. "And as for you, Charisse, don't let him go away again."

Jason and I had reopened the lines of communication because a 110-year-old woman named Miss Frazier e-mailed his mother about my mother being sick. I had a very good idea what Vivian McNeil had been praying for.

Chapter 20

2009

*T*he next twelve months were the best in my life. My mother retired from work and became even more involved in her church. I basically took care of everything, including all the bills, and while I was no chef, I was becoming a better and better cook. It was my turn to take care of her, and she had no reservations about letting me do just that.

"It's about time," she would say jokingly. "Now, if you could learn how to make some decent collard greens you'd be saying something!"

Mariah and I also took our relationship to an entirely different place as mother and daughter . . . we became friends. We were still as different as night and day when it came to the things we were passionate about, but we finally started to take the time to get to know each other. Now, I know it sounds strange that a mother would say she needed to "get to know" her own daughter, but when you're so caught up in being selfish, and getting the things you want, and the way you want people to be, sometimes you never really get to know the people closest to you.

I also kept in contact with Nitra and Brenda. We didn't see each other as often as we would have liked, but we damn sure were on the phone every chance we got.

"You and Jason play too many games. When is the damn wedding already?" Nitra asked during one of our three-way calls.

"For real. I need an excuse to fit into a nice dress, so that will be my motivation to lose some weight," Brenda added.

"I have no idea," I replied. "Look, he was married before and it didn't work out. Maybe he likes things the way they are," I replied.

"Yeah, but you guys been together for over a year now. Do I have to call him? You know I'll call him," Brenda threatened.

"No . . . please don't," I pleaded with a chuckle. "I forgot who I was talking to, the damn enforcer."

"You better ask somebody," she said. "Like my husband. Every now and then he sticks his little bird chest out and tries to put his foot down about something . . . and then it's chin check time."

Nitra and I burst out laughing because we knew it was true.

"Well, don't feel bad, Reecie. I was supposed to be married in October, and I'm still waiting," Nitra said.

"Well, that's your fault." Brenda said. "You took your wedding savings and bought a house. Damn, what you want everything at once?"

"Your big ass got a house, right?" Nitra snapped.

"Damn right, but my big ass also got married at city hall. You're the one who wants this big Princess Diana–Prince Charles shindig."

This is what I missed most about my crew. We had been talking shit to one another for twenty years and nothing had changed—well, almost nothing. When we were young I used to think I was doing them a favor by being their friend, but in hindsight, they were doing me the favor by being mine.

Niece, Yvonne, and I had also grown extremely close. Niece got promoted to director of operations at her job, and bought a condo in Long Island City. She was dating a really nice guy named Freddie who was half black and half German. Jamal couldn't stand him. He was the VP of a publishing company and Niece met him at an event she attended with Jason and me, so he couldn't stand me anymore either. Yvonne turned out to be smarter than any of us thought. She may have been a little ghetto, but she was a lot enterprising. Yvonne had been stacking her chips for a few years and began saving the money Jamal gave her for travel and clothes.

"I loved him, but I never trusted him," she declared. "One time when we first got together he gave me like five thousand dollars to take my two girlfriends to Vegas for a weekend. I knew he just wanted me out of town so he could smash this white broad who was coming into town from Miami. I took that dough and stayed right in the Bronx with my cousin and saved that paper. I went to the store and played the lotto for five dollars so if he asked me did I do any gambling I could say yes with a clear conscience."

Jamal had opened up a few barbershops and hair salons in Queens and Brooklyn; he also had one in Miami and one in Atlanta. I always suspected that his shops were a front for something else he was into—not drugs, he didn't have the heart for that—but definitely something crooked.

Yvonne took her stash and opened a little boutique on Austin Street in Forest Hills called UNITY. She carried all the top labels for women and men in casual wear, and for the grand opening she had a champagne reception to which Jason invited some players from the Knicks and Nets to attend. Jamal heard about it and showed up with another one of his *My Super Sweet Sixteen* rejects. He was turned away by security at the door.

"My muthafucking money, which you stole by the way, made this shit possible and I can't get in . . . that's some bullshit!" he ranted when she came to the door.

"Thank you for being a silent . . . silent partner, and no, you can't get in. Take your little friend to Romper Room or wherever it is you hang out with your lollipops and cotton candy. Now poof, be gone," she said.

A month later I was taking Mariah over to Jamal's for his birthday. She had called him the day before and asked him if he would be home to sign for the gift she sent him, but she just wanted to make sure he would be there when she got there. Mariah asked me to buy him a shirt and a cake from Mrs. Maxwell's bakery so she could surprise him. Niece and Yvonne were also going to drop off Essence and Brianna as well. As I pulled up I saw Jamal and his dog standing outside the house. There were men in black IRS windbreakers removing boxes and furniture while another group was putting his Range Rover on a flatbed truck. Jamal pulled out his cell phone to make a call when one of the agents literally took it out of his hand while walking past him. I looked over at Mariah. My biggest concern was how she would react, but once again I underestimated her maturity.

"Looks like my father is in deep shit," she said calmly. "Excuse my language, Mommy."

I immediately called Niece and Yvonne and told them what was happening. Niece was shocked and said she still wanted to come by and be nosy; Yvonne's response was more like she was expecting to hear something like this at some point, or she had something to do with it.

"Damn, the IRS got him hemmed up like that," she said.

I never mentioned that it was the IRS; all I had said was "the authorities" were at Jamal's house taking his things out. I think Niece and I had learned to forgive, if not forget all the bullshit Jamal Butler had put us through. But Yvonne was the wrong bitch to mess with, and at the end of the day she was going to exact her revenge. Getting all his shit taken turned out to be the least of Jamal's problems. A few days after that, he was arrested for money laundering and tax evasion. Yvonne, who seemed to know every little detail about what was going on, told us that he had accepted a plea bargain with the Feds to do thirty months. My suspicions about Yvonne's involvement were all but confirmed when I went by her shop and asked her if she had an address to where Mariah could write her father. The store had a quite a few customers, and she told me if I went to the back I would actually find an envelope with his information on it. I copied the information and put the envelope back down, which felt like some type of greeting card. Like most women, my (let's call it) curiosity got the best of me and I picked it back up. I looked over my shoulder like the sneaky bitch that I was being and looked at the card. It had a picture of an old hound dog on it and inside was blank except for what Yvonne had written, *It's business, never personal.*

I was beginning to get a little concerned about my relationship with Jason. For the past two weeks he seemed to be preoccupied whenever we spoke or saw each other.

"What's up with you?" I asked at dinner one night. "Your body is here, but I think your mind is back in Los Angeles."

"Nah, I just got a lot on my mind. It's funny because when you're still a ballplayer you don't even really think about money or finances, because that dough is guaranteed and it's coming from everywhere, the team, shoe deals, video games, endorsements, but when you retire and you realize that you're in unknown territory, it makes you a little insecure about your future," he explained.

"You invested your money well though, didn't you?"

"Yeah, but it's not the same security as when somebody is paying you eight or nine million dollars a year. And I'm not into that coaching thing. That's a bigger sacrifice timewise than being a player," he said. "My agent called me about becoming an analyst."

"Well . . . you're articulate, well-spoken, nice to look at."

"Thanks, but it's hard for me to sit there and critique other ballplayers, because I've been there."

"I would think that makes it easier," I said.

"Just the opposite. I know how hard it is to score on a seven footer, or shoot forty percent from a three-point range, or to *try* and stop Kobe Bryant. So for me to sit there and say this player should have done this, or he's not doing that . . . just doesn't suit my personality. I used to laugh with them guys whenever I visited ESPN and say, you've just spent two hours with a panel of experts dissecting every nuance of the game and why this particular basketball team or football team is going to win the game, and then they lose. I prefer to just watch the game and be a spectator as opposed to a speculator."

"I understand. I'm sure you'll work it all out," I said.

"I was thinking about going back to school . . . law school," he said.

"Really . . . why don't you?" I asked excitedly. "I would love to go to college and then medical school," I said.

"Really, why don't you?" he asked.

"It's not that easy for me. I have a job. I have Mariah. I have my mother," I said.

"Yeah, I agree. It's not easy when you have a family," he said.

"But you don't have that problem. It's just you," I said.

Jason looked at me and reached into his pocket. He pulled out a black velvet ring box and opened it. Inside was the most beautiful princess-cut diamond engagement ring I had ever seen. It was set in white gold and had to be at least two karats. I looked up at Jason and tears were welling up in his eyes. He took a deep breath.

"Charisse Hawkins, I've known you since I was four-years-old, and I have loved you since I was four-years-old.

When I retired from basketball I thought to myself I'll never win a championship, I'll never reach the mountain top or the pinnacle, but then something brought us together and I realized I still had a shot to reach the top. Will you marry me and make that possible?"

I started to cry and I couldn't even get my voice together to say a word, so I nodded my head yes.

When we got back to my house I was so excited that I ran in screaming and yelling like a maniac. I almost scared my poor mother to death.

"Ma! Ma!" I said as I began to cry again.

"What's wrong?" she yelled as she came down the stairs.

"Look! Look!" I yelled as I flashed my hand in front of her. "Isn't it beautiful."

My mother was so happy that she just smiled and hugged me, and then she went over and hugged Jason.

"I knew it. . . . I knew it before you two knew it. I'm just so happy," she said. "Now I'll have a place to visit on the weekends until you get tired of me," she added.

"We'll never get tired of you," I said.

"I don't know, we just might," Jason said with a serious face. "I mean, seeing someone everyday, you know, that can be tiresome," he said.

"Oh no . . . I can't live with you kids. This is your life."

"Have you seen the size of my house? All that space going to waste, empty rooms. No, you'd be helping us," he said.

"Yeah, Ma, his house is huge, and it's close to New York."

"No, I'll be fine right here," she insisted.

"Look, you're going with us," Jason said firmly. "And I won't hear another word about it. Now you ladies have a wedding to plan. Just make sure you remember to invite the groom."

Jason and I decided to get married in Prospect Park that September. Most people usually take at least a year to plan their wedding, but we put things together in record time. And it doesn't hurt when money isn't a really a concern. Jason told me not to worry about how much I was spending, but I was already thinking like a wife and watching every dollar. My dream wedding didn't include 500 guests and a honeymoon in Hawaii. I just wanted to be surrounded by family and friends and I was hoping for great weather. My bridesmaids were Brenda, Nitra, Niece, Yvonne, and Mariah, and they were all going to look beautiful in their turquoise-blue dresses. I picked out a white Vera Wang dress that all my girls agreed was stunning.

The night before my wedding I had gone out by myself and drove around. I was scared to death; Brooklyn was all I had ever known. The house I lived in, the block I grew up on, these were the foundation of all my memories, good and bad. I drove to my old high school, and the visions I had of coming out of the front door with Nitra and Brenda were as vivid as if they had happened the day before. I drove by Nitra's old house, as well as Brenda's, and reminisced about sitting on the now crumbling cement steps, where we jumped Double Dutch or ran from the boys we liked when they chased us. I went into the corner bodega, the same one I had been going to for twenty-five years. The owners had changed quite a few times as they each made their small fortune before returning to Puerto Rico or the Dominican Republic, but the feeling was still the same.

"Congratulations, *mamí,*" the owner said in her deep Spanish accent. "I heard you getting married to a football player."

"Thank you, but he played basketball," I said.

"Football, basketball, baseball, fuck that, he's got money, so now you got money," she said.

For some reason her words touched me, they resonated within me. I can't count how many women I know, outside of my four close *friends,* who were saying that very thing, or something similar. They didn't ask me what kind of man he was, how he got along with my daughter, or whether we loved each other, all they knew was he played sports and he was rich. I kept hearing things like, "Shit, if he cheats, who cares, you got the ring and you'll get the house." Or, "If he does fool around, just get you a little friend on the side." I never really even thought about how much money Jason had or all the things I was going to be able to do. One thing I learned, if nothing else from my experience with Jamal, and even from my mismanagement of the money my father left me, was that material things don't mean shit. A woman's lust for material items, which in most cases is just to impress other women, or a desire to be taken care of, or obsessing over finding that male love many of us didn't have growing up, can be a black woman's Achilles' heel.

The morning of my wedding day was pure chaos. I ran around my house like a chicken with its head cut off, looking for things that were already in my hand, crying one minute and mad the next. At one point I was putting a little makeup on Mariah's face, while yelling at the top of my lungs, "Mariah! Would you come on so I can put this makeup on you!" All I kept thinking was, *God, just let me get through this day. . . . Please, Lord calm my nerves.*

My mother walked into the room a few seconds later. She was getting a kick out of my hysteria.

"You act like you're the first person who ever got married. Like all mankind is watching you to see if this union of man and woman thing is a good idea. Calm down and relax, please," she said as she handed me an envelope.

"Whatever, nobody can tell me what to feel," I argued.

I look inside the envelope and it was a letter from Jamal. Whenever he wrote to Mariah, he always addressed it directly to her, so I was confused as to why this particular envelope was addressed to me. I placed it on the dresser so that I could finish applying Mariah's makeup. I looked at the envelope and thought to myself, *I'm not reading any of his negative bullshit on my wedding day. If he doesn't have anything better to do than sit around and blame everyone else for his situation, that's his problem.*

In the midst of all the things on my mind that morning, I kept thinking about the envelope. Finally I went back and picked it up and took it into the bathroom to read. The letter was dated about two weeks earlier, but I guess mail from prison has to go through a process before it leaves there, or maybe he wrote it and had been hesitant at first to send it.

Dear Charisse,

I hope this letter finds you well and feeling great. I always ask Mariah how you are doing, but when she writes to me she never says anything, almost like she's telling me I don't even have the right to ask, without coming out and saying it. My father told me that you're getting married to Jason . . . good luck, to Jason that is (lol) . . . just kidding. You might wonder why I'm writing you for the first time in sixteen years, but I felt compelled to do it. I am very sorry for all the things I did to you and put you through. I am sorry that when I saw you in the parking lot at the diner I didn't just admire you and not think twice about it, and I really regret buying you those earrings and taking advantage of a young woman who had big dreams and plans. I once heard a rapper named Dana Dane use the term "full circle," and that's what life is. I thought I did something when I came between you and Jason and ended up having you, but look, shit has come "full circle" and you guys are getting married, and I can honestly say I'm happy for you . . . you deserve it. I am going to write letters to Niece and Yvonne as well, but I felt it necessary to write to you first. I never said anything, but your mother called me and told me she found some documents about Mariah's having had an abortion. I also felt the effects of "full circle," but I still didn't get it, I guess sometimes you have to hit the bottom before you can look up. Anyway, thank you for taking care of our daughter, and good luck.

> *God bless*
> *Jamal Butler*
> *P.S. That's right, I said GOD . . . ☺*

Something about Jamal's letter made me feel better. It gave me a sense of comfort that he actually cared enough to feel bad after all these years, that my life meant something to him.

I had the most beautiful wedding ever. After a year of marriage I finally went back to school at NYU, but not for medicine. Jason convinced me that being a film producer and director was my true calling. My mother actually moved out of her house and into a nice little one-bedroom apartment on Grand Avenue in Englewood. She got her driver's license and we bought her a white Nissan Sentra that she called "Betsy." She also met a nice *friend* at church named Willie whom we all liked. Just seeing her happy and enjoying life bought me joy. Mariah was a senior in high school and worked as an intern at the New Jersey Nets office in East Rutherford after school. Jason decided to go into broadcasting. He became the play-by-play analyst for the Nets, which kept him close to the game *and* close to home. As for his concerns about not making the kind of money he made as a player, well, one of his investments in Phoenix, Arizona, which had been just a large piece of land he bought with dreams of one day building an apartment complex on it, became the location for the next super Walmart. He turned out to be a better businessman than a ballplayer. Jamal Butler got out of prison and married one of his baby mommas. Denise "Niece" Carter became Denise Butler. He got a job at the hospital where his mother still worked, and they moved out to Hempstead, Long Island. I don't know if that's the life he envisioned for himself, but hey, *You get what you play for.*

Acknowledgments

Thank you God, first and foremost, for keeping your merciful hand upon me. You are worthy of all praise.

Thank you to my family and friends for being my inspiration and support system.

My wife, Monique; son, Mark; daughter Ryan; goddaughter, Jacquanda; stepdaughter, Asia; and the rest of those I love. Thank you.

Malaika Adero, Todd Hunter, and Atria Books. Thank you for your belief and support.